BEWARE
THE
WOMAN

ALSO BY MEGAN ABBOTT

The Turnout

Give Me Your Hand

You Will Know Me

The Fever

Dare Me

The End of Everything

Bury Me Deep

Queenpin

The Song Is You

Die a Little

The Street Was Mine

BEWARE
THE
WOMAN

A NOVEL

—◆—

MEGAN ABBOTT

G. P. PUTNAM'S SONS
NEW YORK

PUTNAM
—EST. 1838—

G. P. Putnam's Sons
Publishers Since 1838
An imprint of Penguin Random House LLC
penguinrandomhouse.com

Copyright © 2023 by Megan Abbott
Penguin Random House supports copyright. Copyright fuels creativity, encourages diverse
voices, promotes free speech, and creates a vibrant culture. Thank you for buying an
authorized edition of this book and for complying with copyright laws by not reproducing,
scanning, or distributing any part of it in any form without permission. You are supporting
writers and allowing Penguin Random House to continue to publish books for every reader.

LCCN: 2023933987
Hardcover ISBN: 9780593084939
Ebook ISBN: 9780593084946

Printed in the United States of America
1 3 5 7 9 10 8 6 4 2

Book design by Nancy Resnick
Title page photograph by Camille Hyytinen/Shutterstock.com

For Dan, who plucked me from the sea

Beware of the man who wants to protect you;
he will protect you from everything but himself.

—Erica Jong

BEWARE
THE
WOMAN

W e should go back," he said suddenly, shaking me out of sleep.
"What?" I whispered, huddled under the thin bedspread
at the motor inn, the air conditioner stuck on HI. "What did
you say?"

"We could turn around and go back."

"Go back?" I was trying to see his face in the narrow band of
light through the stiff crackling curtains, the gap between every
motel curtain ever. "We're only a few hours away."

"We could go back and just explain it wasn't a good time. Not
with the baby coming."

His voice was funny, strained from the AC, the detergent haze
of the room.

I propped myself up on my elbows, shaking off the bleary
weirdness.

We had driven all day. In my head, in my chest, we were still
driving, the road buzzing beneath us, my feet shaking, cramped,
over the gas.

"But you wanted this," I said, reaching for him. "You said we
should go *before* the baby comes."

He didn't say anything, his back to me, the great expanse of his
back, my hand on his shoulder blade.

"Jed," I said. "What is it?"

"You're dreaming," he said, his voice lighter, changed. It was like a switch went off.

"What?" I said again, looking at the back of his head, lost in shadow.

"You were dreaming," he said. "Go back to sleep."

A strange feeling came over me. It hadn't been Jed at all. It had been some boogeyman shaking me awake, warning me to go back, go back.

Some boogeyman.

Like Captain Murderer, the smeary white man I used to dream about when I was little.

Captain Murderer.

Who? my mother used to ask me. *Someone from one of your comic books, or a grown-up movie you snuck over to the Carnahans to see?*

The Carnahans, with six kids from ages four to twenty-four, lived next door in a rambling house, and two of the Carnahan boys fed me warm beer in the basement once when I was ten, and another time I split my lip when one of the girls slammed a screen door on my face, and they loved to set off firecrackers in the driveway all summer long, once burning down the old sycamore everyone loved and it changed the light in our house forever.

But no, Captain Murderer didn't come from the Carnahans' big console TV, videogame cords dangling like spider legs. He didn't come from my comic books or the slumber party stories swapped in our sleeping bags.

He didn't come from anywhere at all. He was always already there.

But who is he? my mother kept asking, unease creeping into her voice.

Captain Murderer, I kept repeating because I assumed she knew him, too, deep down. Like the tooth fairy, the devil with his pitchfork and his flaming tail, like on the can label in the cupboard. *Captain Murderer!*

My mother, face drawn together in worry, would stop what she was doing, folding laundry or wiping glasses in the drying rack, and make me start at the beginning.

And I'd tell her how he was all white, white as milk, head to toe, with white nails and white lashes, teeth like little bones, and one red spot in the middle of his back, between his shoulder blades.

How he moved like bedsheets snapping. How he bit you and his teeth popped out, leaving you with little bones under your skin that everyone would say was a mosquito bite, a fire ant, chiggers.

But where did he come from? my mother would plead. *Was it a story someone told you at camp? Where did he come from?*

Later those nights, after she thought I'd fallen back to sleep, I would hear her moving from room to room, checking all the locks on every window and door.

Click-click, click-click, bolt.

I would hear her breathing all through our little house.

Captain Murderer came from nowhere. But you couldn't tell your mother that.

He came at night, for me.

Captain Murderer came for me!

Later, the hint of blue dawn, I felt for Jed's wrist. Half lost in sleep, I clambered for him, the crazy, dream-thick thought: *What if Captain Murderer got him?*

But he was in the bathroom, the light under the door, the drone of the automatic fan.

When he came out, a blue shadow in that blue dawn, he stood at the foot of the bed looking at me, his face too dark to see. Only the flicker of the whites of his eyes, wide and wary. Somewhere, a snarl of mosquitoes buzzed, a light sizzling.

Jed, I said, my voice gluey with sleep.

His hands clenching at his sides, looking at me as if I were this strange thing, landed in his bed, come to do him harm or wonder, an alien, a ghost, a succubus.

Jed, sweet Jed, so nervous. My fingertips tingling.

Lifting the sheet, I told him to come inside and he put the heels of his hands on my legs and dragged me to the bottom of the bed, and it was like never before.

All our times, romantic and sticky whispers, but this time something else. Something blue and strange and piercing and I shuddered all through, my breaths catching against his ear.

DAY ONE

We'd been driving forever, the Midwest finally sneaking up on us, the hard smack of road-salt as I-75 widened and widened again.

I'd never seen Jed so nervous. Excited. Both. It was hard to tell.

It was our first road trip together and everything felt impossibly fun: the oversized rental car—a toothpaste-white Chevy—lurching across the lanes, the burr of the air conditioner, the rest stops with the beef jerky and neon flip-flops, the toaster muffins in plastic wrap and the hot dogs slinking on an endless roller grill.

On the crinkly map we traced our route up the great paw of Michigan, I-75 snaking up the state like a wriggly vein.

Sometimes we sang along to indifferent radio. Lite FM and classic rock, the occasional Christian devotional show.

Sometimes we clasped hands clammy from shivering Big Gulps in the cupholders.

Sometimes we made long lists of baby names. We'd already decided we didn't want to know the sex. We didn't care, and just naming names made it feel glorious and impossible all over again, my hand on my belly.

I never even thought I'd have a baby, he was saying, *and now here I am and it's the rightest thing I've ever done*, and we're rattling off names, Jed rejecting my favorite, "Molly," swiftly and without mercy, confessing finally that he was once *sick with love* over a girl named Molly Kee at summer camp when he was fifteen.

That can't be true, I teased. *You told me you'd never been in love before.*

He had said it—I never forgot it—one muggy Sunday morning, both of us too tired to make coffee, our arms and legs entwined.

Well, you know, he said now, shrugging, smiling a little, caught.

Sick with love, the phrase so unlikely from his solid, square-jawed Midwestern mouth, the words made me inexplicably sad. Before I knew it, I was crying. My sunglasses sticky from it. It makes me feel silly and sad to think of it now. To feel so close, so encircled and encircling with love and yet . . .

Is it the hormones? That's what he kept saying, hearing the hitch in my voice, sneaking anxious looks at me, wondering if he should pull over.

I'm fine, I sputtered, and then laughed even as the tears slathered me, and somehow he thought that meant keep going, because he kept going, talking about this Molly girl, how she had a chipped tooth that drove him crazy, and how she could land bullseye after bullseye at archery with a longbow she made herself, and how she sang "Coat of Many Colors" at the talent show, and what he would have done, back then, for one glancing touch of the back of her left knee.

Behind my sunglasses, I was crying and couldn't stop and he kept going because he couldn't see. Crying behind one's sunglasses—is there anything lonelier than that?

Finally, my voice became a sob and then he looked at me and stopped the car, skittering up the shoulder.

Jacy, Jacy . . . what's wrong? What did I do?

I wanted to say, *Aren't you sick with love for me?*

What woman doesn't want that, especially with her belly slowly swelling with their first child?

Why did I tell you that? he said at last, shaking his head, grabbing my hand, gripping it until all our fingers went white. *I don't know why I told you that.*

And I felt silly. I was silly. *The hormones, yes. The hormones are killing, killing.*

It's just the hormones, I swear.

Thirty-two years old, too old to be in love like this, with such teen ferocity and force, but that was how it was and there was no fighting it. Why would I?

I've had men in love with me before—high school Paul, the poet who used to bake me cookies, and Benjy, who broke both my heart and five front windows of the dorm I lived in. I've had men in love with me before, but it never felt like this. Never both of us in the same way at the same time, like two spiders sewing a silken web together.

After our city hall wedding, four months to the day we met, I remember walking into that impromptu party at that random Irish bar (the Bucket of Blood!) near the courthouse, walking as if I were floating, as if I were a queen entering a palace, a goddess entering heaven. It was all so haphazard and lovely, a clutch of friends hauling a Party City bag bursting with tissue streamers, birdseed confetti, plastic champagne flutes, hanging a curling JUST MARRIED sign above the steam tables, corned beef and cabbage for the day drinkers.

And after everyone had left and we were kicking up streamers under our feet as we dragged ourselves along the carpet, florid and undulating, I remember nearly tripping—an errant champagne stem snapped under my foot—and reaching for him, clutching the front of his shirt.

And I could feel his heart beating like a rabbit's under my hand. Fast and frightened, pounding and alive and terrified.

It charmed me, moved me.

Here he was, a man so strong, so upright, a good man, a man born with certain advantages: middle-class comforts, a college fund, no dependents, a thirty-year-old white man, a craftsman who works with his hands, a solid and kind man with an artistic eye and artistic yearnings. You might think a man like that has never been acquainted with doubt, with fear, with desperation.

And yet. And yet.

I looked up at his face, a narrow slick of frosting on his collar from the cake-cutting—

I looked up at his face, my hand over his thundering heart—

And his eyes were shining with such love, I tell you.

I tell you, it was love. It was love, even if it scared him. The love scared him.

But the truth was Jed ran into the fire. That's how he'd put it: with the proposal, the wedding, the look on his face when the pregnancy stick was still shivering in my hand. He ran into it, the fire, the fear. He said it made him feel alive.

He was looking at me, eyes blinking as if shaking off the sandman's grit from them. Like my grandma when I was little, putting her cool hand over my crusted eyes.

He was looking at me, his face full of wonder—*Could this be true? Could it? Could we be married? Could you be my wife?*

He was looking at me like I'd saved his life. Which, he whispered to me in the blue-dark of our honeymoon suite hours later, I had.

✻

I never thought this would happen to me, Jed told me that night, our wedding night. *I'd given up on it happening.*

When he said it, I thought, how strange for a man to feel that. To feel like a girl, waiting, waiting, like when all her friends at school got their first period, one by one, the tampons in their purse zipper pocket, the whispers about the ruby slick on their underpants and now they were women . . .

I was afraid I wasn't made for it, he told me.

For marriage? I asked, smiling gently, nudging him, teasing. *Or love?*

For anything, he said. And that's when I saw it in his eyes. How deep this went and how impenetrable it felt. How had I never known this. How—

For anything but being alone.

Most men are that way, sweetie, my mom always said. *And it doesn't change when they get married. They think if they get married, it'll change it. You think that too. But they're lone wolves, these kinds of men. Most men.*

But that was my mother's generation, the world they lived in, the world of women huddled in kitchens and over playpens, with their husbands at the grill, a ring of khakis, fingers clipping beer necks and busting chops over a bad trade, never able to connect, to relate, unless on the football field, on the ice, feelings forever unspoken, unspoiled.

Jacy went and married a signmaker! my mother shouted to Aunt Laraine when I called her, the two of them forever sitting at my mother's kitchen table, sneaking cigarettes and beating their breasts over the news.

I had to explain, yet again, that Jed was not merely a signmaker. That neon is both an art and a science, and yes, while commissions—for the occasional casino, for food trucks, trendy hotels—and restorations were his primary income, he also worked on his own pieces (*like the picture I sent you!*) and on restoring grand old signs from back before jumbotrons and LED and plastic, back in the day when neon was king.

If you could see him in his studio, I wanted to say. Heating the glass tubes with torches, bending them into these glorious glowing creations. Manipulating voltage and gas, heat and pressure. The red of neon, the cool blue of argon. The inside of each tube coated with colored powder, the blending of colors. The scorching pinks and sizzling purples.

I remember when he first showed me. *No gloves,* he said, laying his hand on the radiant tube, its center flamed, his face glowing. *Gloves get in the way.*

How I gasped when he placed his hand on the searing glass. The hiss of the constant flame.

He had burned his hands countless times, patches on his palm, a knuckle, his thumb joint, like his hand had been put back together hastily. There were hard flaps on his skin where he could barely feel and I loved when they brushed against my cheek, between my thighs.

We made promises that night, our wedding night. We drained the bottle of Mumm's—the one that appeared at our apartment in a misted bucket courtesy of my new father-in-law, whom I'd yet to meet. We drained the whole thing while Jed washed my hair over the sink to get all the confetti out, the birdseed.

His hands on my hair, the strength of those hands, their delicacy—a sculptor's hands, a sculpture of heat and light—and I had to have him all over again, sinking to my knees on the soft pill of the bath rug.

The sweetness of him, the amniotic salt, the shudder that went through him.

It's real and it's forever, I had told my mom over the phone the next morning.

Good, honey, she said, a choke in her voice. *If you don't think that now, you're really in trouble.*

Yes, it had happened fast. Too fast for our families to come to the wedding.

I had had to make amends to my mom, my cousins, my aunt and uncle.

But Jed only had his dad and his dad was traveling. I had the feeling they weren't close, though it was hard to know.

The following week, we had dinner with him on our way out west for our honeymoon. And Jed was nervous, so nervous, but it had gone so well. Perfect, really.

He's here, Jed said, his eyes bright, head bobbing, as we stood in the hotel lobby.

Under the garish chandelier, a silver-haired man smiled at us, his teeth gleaming.

Doctor Ash, I said, so tentative.

I'd had this idea of him—from Jed's stories, from the blurry father-and-son-at-graduation photo, radiator-curled, on Jed's bookshelf—that he was an old-school dad, a Midwestern white dude, the kind all those fish-tackle and golf-club Father's Day cards are for.

So I was surprised how dapper he was, handsome like Jed, but

Jed in nice clothing, a fine wool suit and stylish Italian loafers alongside Jed's flannel and jeans.

His voice so low and gentle, a little burr in it, I felt instantly at ease. He started by teasing me gently about the sort of woman who'd take on an Ash man. Then he said he was sorry we hadn't met before, but not to blame Jed. After all, he lived way up in the tippy top of Michigan, the vacation home of Jed's childhood, and didn't travel much in his early retirement. *After a lifetime of travel for work*, he laughed, *all I want to do is stay home, in my study, with my books and my bourbon.*

I said that sounded pretty wonderful to me.

But mostly, he said, he wanted to make sure Jed was taking good care of me and whether he washed the dishes and to make sure I don't, not once, pick up after him, not even a stray sock.

As if Jed ever left socks around, or anything.

What matters most to me is that whenever you're talking he's listening.

What matters most to me is that you feel loved. Jed is, in some ways, still learning to love.

And he explained that Jed's mom, dying as she did, when he was so young—well, that had to leave its marks.

I tried to give him everything, he said. *But there are limits to what a father can offer a son. Maybe that makes me sound old-fashioned.*

I told him it did but only in the best way.

He took us to the finest restaurant in town, cracked crab and French wine, and he gave me all his attention. He wanted to know all about me, starting at the beginning. The warm feeling when he smiled at Jed a mere ten minutes into dinner, telling him, *My boy, you did good.*

After two glasses, my own head slightly wobbly, he started regaling us with stories of his own blessed wedding to Jed's late mother, gone since Jed was a baby. They'd exchanged vows overlooking Bridalveil Falls in Michigan's Upper Peninsula and he really, truly had forgotten the ring and they'd had to improvise with a gumball-machine ring from a nearby IGA, even though everyone warned them it was bad luck.

How delightful and surprising it had been to watch Jed watching his father. Doctor Ash had raised his glass to toast us and as he did, his voice warbled a little, a sneaky choke in his throat. What a thing from a man so barrel-chested and robust, six feet two—two inches taller than his son, he told me—and the rolling shoulders of a youthful swimmer. A man so dignified and assured.

Jed, the look on his face seeing that.

And I realized in an instant they were much closer than I'd guessed.

That's what marriage is, I thought. *Discovering something new about your spouse every day.*

Young love, pure and true, Doctor Ash said as we all raised our glasses on the swollen terrace of the restaurant. *Let it last, trap it in amber. Do what you can while you can.*

How Jed had swallowed hard, turning his face away.

So moved he was, I was.

When we arrived in Honolulu for our honeymoon, a message awaited us:

Now the work of love begins! Love, Dad

"When I was a kid, he still sent telegrams," Jed said with a funny smile.

"I thought telegrams were only in movies," I said, charmed by it. "Like ascots and bonbons."

"Yeah, well," Jed said, "he's old-fashioned, I guess."

❧

My mom told me once that I had "terminally bad" taste in men. It was after Benjy, because it took me a dozen calls with all three credit bureaus and two cycles of antibiotics to clean up after him.

Honey, if anyone should know about bad men, she said, *it's me.* How it can happen, a vulnerable moment, the way they can come on so strong, burrowing into your bed, your life. Everything was so exciting at the start with Benjy. I read about it later in a book someone gave me—the "love bomb," they call it, which is what it feels like, an explosion in the heart. It's only later, after—after the open-handed smack, after he pockets the rent money, after you find his nineteen-year-old drawing student in your bed, her thong wrapped around the bedpost—that you learn the warning signs. Which were warning sirens, warning explosions.

I had bad taste in men, but then came Jed.

Sometimes you don't know for a long time, sometimes you know right away.

With Jed, it was our second date, and I'd dragged him along to a colleague's birthday dinner and then I'd eaten that bad mussel and gotten so sick in the cramped restroom of the loud restaurant, the maître d' pounding on the door.

How Jed interceded, helping me to my feet. How he quietly remonstrated the maître d' and put his arm around me, guiding me past the crowded tables, the newly sickening stench of brine and drawn butter. How small and safe I felt under the shield of him, of Jed, of Jed the rescuer, the gallant knight.

My jacket and purse draped over his arm looked like doll clothes.

How he'd taken me home in that sweaty cab and didn't blink when the fare over the county line jumped into three digits and when we idled in front of my building, the front door lock taped open so the neighbors could smoke out front.

How he walked me past the trio of sullen teenagers and the wrinkly lady who read fortunes out her front window. How, in the lobby, the lights hurting my eyes, making my feet feel rubbery and my knees, too, he asked if he could come inside and help me and we could leave the door open if I wanted but four floors was a long way up.

On the stairwell, I thought I might be sick again, and we stood on the second-floor landing, me bent over at the waist, afraid to move or even breathe.

How embarrassed I was, sure I smelled of vomit, a slick of something on my throat.

And yet Jed persevered, delivering me, wobble-kneed, to my door.

Come in, I said, my clammy hand on my keys.

Jed made me ginger tea and draped my ratty throw over me. He took my temperature with the back of his hand. He told me his father was a doctor and then got embarrassed, adding he knew that didn't mean anything and did I want him to go, did I want some privacy?

And how I didn't, not at all.

All I wanted was him to rest that hand on me again.

When you throw up in front of someone, you jump three stages, he'd said the next morning, laughing.

So you see, everything was different from the start.

And that's what I told Doctor Ash.

Everything was so different, like no other boy or man. And I was different with him, different than with Benjy, the rest. Letting him make me dinner, giving him a key to my apartment, ordering him that special pillow he needed for his back.

We take care of each other, I said.

Everything was different, right from the start.

Everything was different, like love is.

It's not like I'm marrying a stranger, I'd told my mom over the phone the day we went to city hall.

Honey, she said, *we all marry strangers.*

That's what she said.

DAY TWO

IRON MOUNTAIN, 127 MILES

We were nearly there, nearly there!
Jed, I kept saying, *it's gonna go great.*
It is, he kept replying. *I just haven't been home in so long.*

The morning mist made everything ghostlike. Neither of us had talked for an hour or more, still in an exquisite sex trance, the night before still efflorescing in our heads.

Wakening at the motor inn to his hands on my thighs, remembering how quick and heavy it had been, catching shuddery glimpses of us in the mirror behind the TV and how my teeth had sunk into him, thinking *what's wrong with me,* but nothing was. It had to be done somehow, like he had to do what he did, my forehead pressed against the headboard so hard, my knees burning against the sheets.

Checking out of the motel like lovers on the run, Jed wearing dark sunglasses, that skittish, antic energy he'd had ever since we left home.

I hoped we'd burned it all away in the night.

Did I hurt you, he'd asked after, in the blue dark of the motel room. *The baby?*

I told him no, I told him of course not. I didn't dare tell him the truth: I wouldn't have stopped him if he had, the wanting so bad. And needing him to want to too.

It was the first time like that since the day we got the news.

It was as though, after we knew I was pregnant, he'd instantly decided that I was a blown-glass figurine, a dainty thing to be hidden on a high shelf. It was as if he had to protect me from the world, everything, but most of all himself.

IRON MOUNTAIN, 34 MILES

We were going north until it seemed like we couldn't go north any more, the radio off, only the *thud-thud-thud* of the car bouncing on the empty highway.

We drove over a sweeping bridge that never seemed to end.

THE LONGEST SUSPENSION BRIDGE IN THE WESTERN HEMISPHERE! the road signs boasted.

Then, suddenly, after humming mindlessly along I-75, flat and pocked for what seemed a hundred years, we entered another place, verdant green and air so clear and not another soul for miles to see.

Jed was driving, my hand on my stomach, an acrid taste like a tongue stroking the inside of my mouth. I hadn't had morning sickness, not really, but something felt off, tilted. That morning, back at the motel, Jed had shown such extra care, even dropping to his knees to put on my shoes. The sight of him, bent there, his strong back and nicked arms, ringed with the two burn welts I loved to touch, to dapple my fingers over. Feeling his hot hands on my cool feet, the air conditioner under the window chugging mercilessly, as it had all night, leaking a spreading puddle on the old carpet beneath.

Feeling those hands gently sliding my feet into my sandals, the delicacy of his fingers, my hand now stroking his hair as he kneeled before me.

IRON MOUNTAIN, 13 MILES

The closer we got, it was as if the air pressure in the car had shifted, Jed's head keening to the right slightly, as if lost in that cruise control hypnosis I remembered from elementary school, those long weekend drives with my mom to visit Mr. Panarites on one of his business trips, and Mrs. Panarites none the wiser. My mom was in love with him my whole childhood and he never left his wife, who had an unnamed immune disorder and sometimes slurred her speech in public and everyone thought she was a drunk but she was really just sick, so sick. He was never going to leave her, it never changed. Finally, he retired and moved to Scottsdale, his wife dying two months later. My mother saw the death notice in the paper, and we never heard from him again.

They don't make 'em like that anymore, my mother sighed wryly whenever his name came up.

Once, years ago, I heard her talking on the back porch with my aunt Laraine, her voice so urgent and ragged, like I'd never heard it before or since.

I can't help it, Laraine. He's got my number. He always has.

He sure does, Aunt Laraine replied. *But, honey, your number is up.*

"This is us," Jed said, his first words in two hours as the sign ahead promised, IRON MOUNTAIN AWAITS YOU!

He looked at me and smiled, his chipped tooth showing. He smiled and it was like I was looking at Jed the little boy, *Are we there yet? Are we there?* And we nearly were.

. . .

It turned out Jed's dad didn't live in Iron Mountain, with its bustling seven thousand residents, but two dozen miles farther, deep into a dense, mossy forest that eventually stretched into Wisconsin. A town of three hundred or less, a town with no town at all and a name that my mouth couldn't make work.

"Barripper," Jed said. "It's Cornish. All the old mining families up here are Cornish."

I asked him what it meant, but he couldn't remember or wasn't listening, giddy with excitement, pulling the car into the long, muddy drive, his pupils wide from the ride, his right arm tugging his left sleeve down over his fading Ghost Rider tattoo.

Just as we were turning one last bend on the road, I saw something, someone in the corner of my eye. A dark figure moving through the trees—gliding really, as if pulled on poles.

"Who's that?" I asked, pointing.

But the figure was gone, the tree leaves shuddering in its place.

"Probably an animal," Jed said, distracted. "They're everywhere up here."

The road dipped, a spray of mud half-blinding us, and there he was.
    Doctor Ash.

Through the green haze, Jed's father emerged, silver-haired and beaming, a pair of hedge shears in one hand, waving with the other, cap brim shielding his face.

"Dad!" Jed called out, waving so hard his arm might have fallen off as Doctor Ash opened the creaking property gate, the road rising again, the steeple of the house piercing the sky, the air startlingly clear, the smell suddenly of fresh earth.

So eager to leap from the car, Jed nearly forgot to turn off the engine, his fingers fumbling with the rental key fob.

"There he is," Doctor Ash called out.

"It's . . . it's so great to see you," Jed said, striding over, words fumbling in his throat. "We're so glad to see you."

Father and son ghost-hugged in that way men do, coming close without ever embracing, slapping backs instead and patting arms and making jokes, Doctor Ash spotting Jed's arm tattoo in an instant, with the X-ray vision of parents. *How many is that now, Sailor Jerry?*

"And there she is, our Jacy," Doctor Ash said, reaching for my hand, his eyes taking in my growing belly. "Here at last."

Doctor Ash bent in for a gentle little hug, like Jed did, as if I were a fragile bauble that might tumble from one's hands.

"I'm so happy," I said, "to be here at last."

The few times Jed had talked about it, he'd described the house in which he'd spent his childhood summers as *the cottage*, a place in the sticks. *Boys' Life* stuff, he'd said with a slight roll of the eyes, calling to mind a rustic cabin, tangle of fishing poles by the door, worn beach towels, a hallway full of flip-flops, hot dogs charred on a rusty kettle grill and slapped on garage sale plates.

But it was no cottage. Low and large and filled with light, sun flooding the windows, streaking the maple beams and brass, it was grander than I could have ever guessed. Inside was forest-green everything: curtains and sofas and lampshades and trim. Like a hunting lodge in an old movie, I thought, like we should all be wearing jodhpurs and high boots.

While Doctor Ash cleaned up, Jed showed me the cozy kitchen with knotty pine cabinets, the brass-fixtured powder room with guest soaps shaped like pine cones resting on fingertip towels, and Doctor Ash's study, all the greens giving way to an astonishing crimson, the walls covered in crimson damask, the mahogany shelves bulging with crimson leather-bound books. A big fish mounted on crimson baize.

"Walleye," Jed said, laughing. "Used to spook me as a kid."

The longer we looked, the more stunned Jed seemed by it all, moving through the space with such puzzlement, like a tunnel back in time, stopping at the immense bay window that faced an endless expanse of piney woods so scenic you could almost mistake it all for a painting, or a mirage.

He hadn't been back in more than a decade. He barely remembered it, he said.

"After all these years," I said, watching Jed stand, rapt, at the window, his fingers running down the stiff pleated curtains, "it must look so different."

Jed turned and looked at me, surprised. Almost as if he'd forgotten I was there.

"It looks," he said, "exactly the same."

It was only when we settled into the living room—with its outsized plaid wing chairs, the plaid ottoman—that I could see nothing was new at all but meticulously maintained, the smooth maple finishes heavy with lacquer, the cushion covers starched stiff, the dull maroon pillows faintly bleached from the sun.

Jed gently opened the door to the breakfront, shaking loose a dusty veil on the decorative plates inside.

"It's still here," he said, reaching inside for a brass-framed photograph, one of those portrait studio shots with the luster finish. It was a just-prepubescent Jed standing on a dock, pale and long-necked, dwarfed by his handsome father, in pale linen and a deep summer tan. Both held up prize catches, slippery dead-eyed things, in their raised-high hands. Matching in cutoffs and bare chests, Jed sweetly puffing his puny chest to match his father's broad physique.

"What a time," Jed whispered with a reverence I'd only heard in him once before, when Doctor Anwar told us I was five weeks pregnant. I had to repeat it three times because he seemed to be in shock and wasn't saying anything at all. *You're going to be a dad, Jed. A dad.*

Looking at him now, there was a feeling I couldn't trace. Something that seemed like that little boy in the portrait, that ten-year-old with the skinned knees and ribs poking, his chin raised high and desperate. And it made me want to promise him things, buoy him and also, strangely, to step away. To step back and touch my own belly, and feel the weight of things to come.

"There she is." A brawny voice hummed deeply through the air like a proclamation. "We haven't scared you off yet."

It was Doctor Ash, tidied up from his outdoor work, just as handsome in his worn madras and boat shoes as he'd been in his fine suit at the fine restaurant, but this time his skin golden from the sun that must appear sometime, amid what seemed to be the Upper Peninsula's boundless white sky.

"I should have guilted you two up here ages ago," he said. "It's been more than a year since the wedding."

"Nearly two," Jed reminded him, slipping his arm around my shoulders.

"Guess we know who's counting," his father laughed, then looking toward me, lifting my hands lightly in his, his eyes taking in my belly. "Let me get a look at this one. This sainted thing."

He stepped back, and I thought he might spin me around like a showroom model, or a Cinderella princess. But he only smiled warmly.

"How was the drive? I told Jed you should fly. Better for you in the first trimester. Michigan is just one big pothole these days. I'm sorry for that. How was the suspension in the car? Are you peaked? What can we do?"

His eyes dancing merrily from my face and again to my belly, my hands instinctively moving over it. I wondered if he wanted to touch it. People didn't seem to do that anymore, but I was already used to it from my students—seven- and eight-year-olds full of open-mouthed wonder, poking at me and insisting there was no way there could be a baby in there.

But never adults, of course, and most pregnant women I knew hated it. But for a fleeting moment, I found myself not minding if he wanted to take those golden hands of his—former physician's hands, after all—and rest them on me.

Because he felt familiar, like Jed, but a Jed turned outward, forward-facing, comfortable in his skin, that emollient ease to him.

"Ten weeks, right?" he asked, sweeping me back up in his hospitality, offering me an iced tea (*with wild mint from the backyard, can't beat it*), or a cool glass of water from the local spring (*the best, the absolute best*).

"Actually, thirteen," I said, smiling.

"Really? Jed never could get the math right," he joked, winking at Jed, who didn't seem to be listening, returning to the breakfront, meandering slightly as if light-headed, as if sunsick.

"My boy, come sit with your beautiful wife," Doctor Ash said, a teasing scold in his voice.

"He's just a little tired," I said. "He did most of the driving."

"I'm not tired," Jed said, sitting down beside me now, setting his hand on my left leg with surprising intimacy. "I'm just glad we're here."

Doctor Ash paused and smiled. "Me too, Jed. Me too."

It was going well, so well, and it was so cozy and easy after the endless interstate and Jed's leg-shaking and skittishness, his anticipatory nerves.

There was something so classic and patrician about Doctor Ash, the way he insisted I sit and rest myself, moving pillows, making sure the sun wasn't hitting my eyes. (*I've sat where you're sitting. It's like getting the third degree!*)

I felt so cared for, tended to. In that same way as Jed that first night, guiding me, wobbly-kneed, up the stairs. Like he was so glad he was there to help me when I was feeling so weak.

We'd been chatting easily, amiably, for a quarter of an hour when, suddenly, a woman appeared in the doorway with a tray, a tall aluminum pitcher, and three cool glasses veiled silver with condensation.

"Oh," Jed said, jumping to his feet, reaching for the tray. "Mrs. Brandt."

"It's good to see you, Jed," she said, moving toward us while removing the glasses and coasters from the tray so smoothly, so swiftly, it was almost as if she were automated.

I knew then she was the figure I'd seen as we were driving in, moving with the same mechanical precision.

"Yes," Jed said, his face coloring. "I mean, good to see *you*. It's been so long."

"And this is your bride." She turned to me, sharp jawed and her eyes narrow and piercingly blue. A woman of unplaceable middle age who looked so cool despite her heavy hair, deep red and gathered tight and high, despite her formal appearance, the crisp white shirt, collars and cuffs blade-sharp, a stiff long skirt, full and feminine.

"Jacy," I said, extending my hand. "And you're . . . um . . ."

"Sorry," Jed said, flush-faced. "Mrs. Brandt's the . . ."

"Caretaker," she said, stepping back from the coffee table, hands crossed at the wrists in front of her, like some kind of courtier, a dusty, mysterious formality.

The central air in the house was supposedly on, or so it seemed from the perpetual low hum, the sweet, cloying smell of Freon. But it still felt warm, sitting on the heavy damask furniture, the minty tea gone tepid, watching Jed's fumbling (*We're breaking even. The shop is. And we're looking for a bigger place....*), and sitting under the glow of Doctor Ash's attentions made me even warmer, bleary.

"Everything's fine," I assured Jed when he asked, but he, too, bore a sheen of sweat.

Only Doctor Ash looked cool, his madras shirt unbuttoned from the top. (*A button too many*, my mom would say, *but there's no accounting for taste.*)

"I've been thoughtless, greedy," Doctor Ash said. "You need some rest. Let's get you settled, comfortable. Jed, you know where the guest room is—"

"Is that—"

"That one, yes. And Mrs. Brandt should have set some towels and things in there for you both."

Smiling, so handsome, his tan knuckles rapping on my forearm. "I've been greedy."

It was only later, in the guest room alone, twin beds pushed together sweetly and the central air booming now, that we could relax, even if we still thought we had to whisper, both of us giddy and Jed laughing finally, being himself finally, joking about his father's distaste for our rental car. *Never pick an economy model. Pay the extra forty bucks, Jed.* A furtive scolding in the kitchen and Doctor Ash's lowered voice, *This is your family here, son*, and gesturing less toward me than to my belly as I pretended not to hear.

And most deliciously, Jed admitted, as we reached across the pushed-together beds, that he'd had a dire crush on Mrs. Brandt as a boy. All through his childhood, she'd lived in the house alone all winter as a caretaker and then when Doctor Ash and Jed came in the summer, she'd move to the guest cottage.

Once, they'd arrived a day early and he found her soaking her unmentionables in the laundry room sink. It turned out that under her stiff, tailored garb she wore lingerie. He never forgot watching her fingers untangle a swarmy knot of silk and lace, creamy and jet-black and intricate. He wasn't even sure what some of the items were, a garter belt he took for a pair of ribbon-thin suspenders—well, it was all too much.

"Maybe I imagined the garters," Jed said now, laughing.

"Or maybe not," I teased. "What lurks under those long skirts..."

"I was dying for her to step away, just for a few minutes," he whispered in my ear, his fingers moving down my neck. "So I could sneak my hand down in that sink. Jesus."

"She let you see them, isn't that enough?" I said, breathing harder now against his neck, his hips leaning against me.

"Let me? Do you think she knew I saw her?" Jed's hands, their roughness. Every callus, all of it. His hands.

"Of course," I said, my voice catching in my throat, waiting for him, his hands down there.

NIGHT TWO

Dinner was at the big slab of dining table, the doors open to the deck and the twitch of cicadas. Just we three, Mrs. Brandt nowhere to be seen.

"I would have helped," I said, rubbing a sheet crease on my face. Feeling lazy, though Jed had not lifted a hand either, dozing greedily with me upstairs.

"Not at all. I like to cook," Doctor Ash said, carrying a large platter, steaming and strong. "Never had the chance till I hung up my cleats. That's old-man code for retiring."

A family dinner, I thought as we sat down together, jazz playing somewhere, softly. I'd always heard of these but never had them growing up, my mom and I snipping open the microwave bags, hunching over the steaming TV dinners at the long L of the kitchen counter, the TV blaring and my mother rubbing her feet, heels kicked and clattering across the linoleum.

But this was the real thing, Doctor Ash even saying a secular grace so quickly a cracking branch in the distance swallowed it, and demanding we enjoy.

Whitefish baked on a plank, roasted potatoes and green beans slick with butter, a basket of puffy rolls, all very simple and old-fashioned and soothing, like going to dinner with my grandparents at the Old Mill Inn, with its cloth napkins and bowls of rolls with big butter pats and entrees like trout almondine with potatoes mashed and piped into little rosettes, and I'd always drink two Shirley Temples, my lips maraschinoed.

"Sometimes, there's a comfort in old things," Doctor Ash said as if reading my mind.

After, we sat overlooking the green haze of the backyard, a yard that wasn't a yard but was *property, acreage.*

There were beers for father and son, and later the bourbon Jed brought from the city, as we settled in low lawn chairs on the deck—nearly too low, I thought, feeling suddenly more pregnant by the hour, like the pregnancy had finally just fully arrived and asserted itself, made me hot, dizzy, unsteady on my feet.

At first, I felt a little sad not to be able to join in. But then Doctor Ash appeared from the kitchen with an elegant cocktail glass, the kind you see in old movies, stems thin as toothpicks.

"A virgin cocktail for the mighty mother-to-be," he said, setting the glass in front of me, steeped in crimson and topped with creamy fizz. "Bubbly water, strawberry syrup, the Ash family's signature rhubarb bitters."

"My goodness," I said, lifting it to my mouth. "Thank you." And it was delicious, herbaceous and flowery at the same time, like walking through a cool garden.

"When did you become a mixologist, Dad?" Jed asked, eyebrows raised in surprise.

"Oh, that's an old trick," he said, waving his hand. "Your mother loved them. Made her feel cared for."

"I didn't know," Jed said softly, his face sweetly red from the bourbon.

"Well, then," I said to Doctor Ash, taking another sip, "that makes it all the nicer."

29

He smiled at me and squeezed my hand across the table as if we had formed a little bond already. As if we were the special ones, the ones with social skills, a desire to put others at ease.

"It's the schoolteacher in you," he said, offering me a dish of astonishingly blue ice cream.

I was too full, my hands on my belly and feeling so warm and content.

"Son," Doctor Ash leaned back to say to Jed, "she's gonna be such a great mama."

And Jed was already smiling, smiling with all his teeth, and suddenly all that I wanted was to be upstairs in the guest room with him on that sunken, lumpen mattress, my hands on him, his breath in my ear, bourbon sweet.

Could I possibly be drunk? Can you be drunk from merely sitting with drinking people when you're not drinking at all? Or is it possible the air is thinner up here? I wondered woozily, as if the Upper Peninsula might ascend upward into the sky like a Colorado mountain range.

Maybe it was the phantom feeling of the road still beneath me, the whir of the tires, or maybe the hypnotic churn of their matching voices. The Ash men voices.

Or maybe it was the oddness of knowing him so well—and I did, despite what my mother loved to imply—and to be married without ever really seeing Jed the son, Jed the member of a family with its own history. Peering suddenly into this new part of him, the very center of him, which our childhood, our family, always is, whether we want it or not.

It was like the final piece was falling into place.

Every story they told was one I'd never heard before. Jed and his father, together and jubilant, a dozen tales of long-past summers, of leech bites and broken ankles, of snagging walleyes with jigging spoons and racing a cache of firecrackers all the way up from across the state line, the sizzle of a Roman candle and the origin of the smiley scar on Jed's palm.

"You told me that was from work," I said, surprised, taking Jed's hand in mine, flattening his fingers, tracing my finger along the scar, like a wriggling worm.

"Did I?" Jed said distractedly, taking his hand back, punching his thumb into his palm, into the scar. "I have a lot of scars."

"Trade hazard, eh?" Doctor Ash said casually.

"Tell your dad about your new restoration job," I said, Doctor Ash looking at me now, eyes crinkling over the rim of his highball glass. "The toothpaste sign." It was a beauty that had hung for six decades in downtown Trenton on the Delaware River, turning to rust. And Jed had made it alive again, a vivid thing: a giant neon tube squeezing and unsqueezing.

Doctor Ash nodded, eyes darting from me to Jed. "And now where will it hang," he asked, "to sell more toothpaste?"

I could nearly feel Jed's shoulders sinking beside me.

"It's stunning," I continued. "You should come see Jed's shop one of these days. See him work. Maybe after the baby—"

Doctor Ash started to say something, but Jed rose abruptly.

"It's getting late," he said, setting his own glass down. "And you wanted me to look at that grill wiring, right, Dad?"

"Sure, sure."

I guessed Jed didn't want to talk about his work, that sneaking suspicion his father didn't understand it. *He's never even seen the shop*, Jed had confided early in our relationship. *I'm not sure he thinks it even exists.*

A signmaker. Jed always described himself that way—to my colleagues, census takers, the bank. Or he'd call himself a tube bender, like he did with my mom and which she has never since stopped talking about. *Tube bender, what did he expect me to say? I mean, really, Jacy.*

But a man of science like Doctor Ash—surely he might understand, if Jed let him. After all, what was neon if not an alchemical mix of art and science? One type of inert gas plus one type of glass coating becomes searing color. *It's just writing with light, drawing with light,* Jed said, but his signs looked like no one's but his. Lush, lilting but also lurid somehow. He was famous for his mouths, tongues, teeth.

"You should just sit," Doctor Ash kept saying, a dish towel tucked at his waist, a makeshift apron. "Sit and keep me company."

"No dice," I said, a pair of the dessert dish stems laced between my fingers as I stepped into the kitchen to help while Jed fiddled with the grill, convinced the uneven heat meant the burner ports needed to be cleaned.

Doctor Ash was sealing the top of the ice cream tub, its impossible blue color like an iridescent smurf.

"I've never seen ice cream that color. What's the flavor?"

"Blue moon," he said, showing me the label.

"But what's the flavor?"

"Blue moon," he repeated, eyes twinkling.

"Are you trying to do an Abbott and Costello routine with me?" I said, laughing, feeling slightly dazed, punch-drunk. Was it possible he was flirting with me?

Plucking the top from the container, revealing a sear of chemical blue, he smiled at me.

"Go on, take a lick." He reached for the counter, a spoon. "Or a bite."

"I don't know," I said, laughing still though I wasn't sure why. "Maybe one."

The cold spoon in my mouth, I felt a swirl of candied tastes on my tongue, raspberry Jolly Rancher, sugared lemon drops, starchy-sweet vanilla pudding jiggling in a plastic cup.

"It tastes . . ." I started, trying to pinpoint it.

"I always thought it tasted like a circus," he said, a wistfulness drifting into his voice.

I took another bite and smiled. I'd been to a circus exactly once, age five, and remembered only the elephant smells and the fistfight that broke out between two dads in the stands.

"It's delicious," I said and he laughed.

"You are a good daughter-in-law," he said, patting my hand.

I realized suddenly who he reminded me of, with his cuffed trousers and gallantry, the merriment in his eyes when I spoke. My English teacher in high school, my first big crush, his celery-green suit everyone made fun of but that my mother knew—and mentioned, after parent-teacher night—was stylish, was very "big city." I sat in the front row, imagining myself as his wife, mother to the three towheaded children I once saw him with at the Rite Aid.

He was, that day, fitting them all with flip-flops for the city pool. I watched him between the blow-up pool toys, my breath going fast like it used to all the time back then. I wanted him to fit me with flip-flops, imagined him sitting me down on the stool, touching my feet, looking at me, fingertips up my ankles. Hidden behind the party pinwheels, the sunscreen twirling rack, I wanted so many things I couldn't name.

But then, with a sharp burst, his children took off, slapping down the aisle with their new footwear, and I saw his face unanimate itself, his shoulders slump slightly, and a far-off look in his eyes like he'd lost something, or it had gone away, but maybe he could have it back. Maybe.

Looking for Daddy, my friends have always teased me. Maybe I was, then. But nothing's ever that simple, after all.

Thinking this all the while cleaning up, stacking dishes, unfurling plastic wrap, the whitefish stuck to aluminum foil, curling upon itself in the heat, the sink filling.

"Now, that's enough of that," Doctor Ash was saying, because maybe there was a queasiness on my face, the cascading stench of fish bones and gristle, the oven fan churning mercilessly, trying to steal it all away.

And Doctor Ash was helping me to a chair, his hands on my arm, guiding me, settling me there, his forearm brushing, just barely, my stomach, my belly.

"Sorry," he said, pulling his arm away. "So sorry."

And was that even a little blush?

"Once a doctor, always a doctor," he said. "But that's no excuse. So many people think a pregnant woman is theirs to touch."

"You can, if you want," I said without even thinking. I don't know why I said it.

But he merely smiled, turning away.

"Truly," I said. "I mean, that's your grandchild."

My mom, I thought, would cringe at this, maybe I would too. *So it's his property, which makes you his property, giving him permission to—*

Tentatively, he slung his dishcloth over his shoulder and, just barely, placed his hand on my belly.

The kitchen felt hot, everything was hot and suddenly strange somehow.

"Why'd you give it up?" I blurted, the faint pressure of each fingertip, his palm spread wide. "Medicine."

He sighed and looked at me, pulling his hand away, "It never felt right again after Jed's mother. You know."

His face drawn suddenly, looking older and graver and glassy-eyed, and I was sorry I'd said anything at all.

"Jed doesn't really talk about it," I said. *I don't remember anything*, he said, the few times I brought it up. *Not even the idea of her.*

"Well, I don't see how he could," he said. "He told you, right?"

"Yes," I said, unconfident. "I mean, he told me that she died when he was a baby."

"During childbirth."

"Right," I said, lying. My brain racing. *In childbirth.* Had Jed told me this and I'd missed it? He didn't talk about his mother, so I never pushed.

"But it was the right thing, leaving medicine," Doctor Ash said. "I never could get the thick skin, the rawhide over my heart that you need. The ego too."

I nodded, not knowing what to say.

"You have to think you can do no wrong," he added. "And after seeing my wife on the floor, swimming in her own blood . . . well, I could never think that again."

Swimming in her own—

A loud crack came, a singing sound, my head blurring with confusion.

Crack! once more.

Through the patio door, I could see Mrs. Brandt outside, her face white in the dark deep of the yard.

Mrs. Brandt, in her arms a rifle, its butt in the air as she peered through the soaring security fence.

"Damn, that's loud," Doctor Ash said as we pushed through the screen door. "That your springer, Mrs. Brandt?"

But she didn't say anything, still staring out into the impossible darkness.

At the grill, Jed stood, his arms streaked black, his gaze fixed on Mrs. Brandt.

"Remember," Doctor Ash said to Jed, "how I used to warn you not to surprise Mrs. Brandt after sundown?"

35

Jed started to laugh, then saw me, saw something in my face.

"It's nothing," he assured me. "Just an air gun."

"What happened?" I asked.

"Mountain lion?" Doctor Ash said, looking at Mrs. Brandt.

"Maybe," she said.

Mountain lion, I thought. *My god.*

I looked up at the security fence. *The tallest I've ever seen outside of a prison, or a nuclear waste facility,* Jed had told me earlier, saying it had to be a code violation. There were laws about fences, even up here.

"But that fence has to be twelve feet high," I said. "Fifteen."

"Funny how mountain lions don't care about our fences," Mrs. Brandt said.

"I saw one once in California," Doctor Ash said. "Leapt from the ground to a treetop in a blink of an eye."

"Do you think you hit it?" I asked Mrs. Brandt.

She shook her head. "Wasn't trying to."

"They're protected," Doctor Ash said, drifting back toward Jed, who was back to fiddling with the grill.

I couldn't move quite yet, my head still whirring. An earthy, wormy smell coming from the humid black beyond.

"A new fence is like a fresh invitation," Mrs. Brandt said, looking at Doctor Ash.

"Last year, one bent the top of Hicks's fence like a tin fork," Doctor Ash said. "All with a baby hare in her mouth."

Who's Hicks? I mouthed, looking at Jed, approaching. *Family friend,* he mouthed back.

The gun still in her hands, Mrs. Brandt didn't move, standing sentry, peering out into the heavy black.

"Could it still be out there?" I asked, staring at the top of the fence.

"No," she said. "But you never know what they're up to."

She turned and looked at me for the first time, the floodlight on her.

"They're very secretive animals," she said, her mouth like a zipper, straight with teeth glittering. "The worst kind."

A mountain lion is the same as a cougar is the same as a panther is the same as a puma, I remembered, my skin quilling, staring into the dark.

It was a lesson plan I'd created last year. I'd led my students in making papier-mâché wild cats—tigers, lions, bobcats, leopards, ligers. Second graders loved big cats.

We spent a week making hind legs and forelegs from cardboard tubes and torsos from cereal boxes, cutting holes with safety scissors, sliding in tails and heads and going through sixteen rolls of masking tape and gallons of slurried paste. Two full days of drying time later, they began slathering on gaudy gesso, in yellow, gold, and bronze. I wandered among them, my back hunched, neck curled, kneeling and squatting with the ease of my unpregnant body, helping them with the whiskers, the googly eyes.

I don't like Diego's, said Amelia, which meant Ellie and Lilly didn't like it either.

Poor Diego, our sweet, pursed-mouth little worrier, always the most ambitious, envisioning projects far too great to accomplish. His fingers still stiff from Tuesday's glue, Diego was trying to re-create Queenie, a 150-pound, seven-foot-long mountain lion he'd seen two years before at Six Flags. The result was an unwieldly two-cereal-box torso that made his Queenie look like a horse just born that can't stand on its legs yet.

It's weird, one of the boys added. *Diego always makes weird things.*

But I couldn't stop looking at it, squatting low to look closer, Diego standing beside me, his hand reaching, carelessly, for mine.

Its eyes were eerily hollow, deep-set holes painted black inside, a slick, flat black you could see yourself in, or see something darker than you ever knew.

Queenie likes you, Diego whispered in my ear, once the other kids had moved on, their stubby hands and soft forearms spangled with paint, their faces bright with excitement.

She'll kill you like this, he said, his face grave, his fingers reaching out, pinching the base of my skull. *One bite.*

The next morning, I opened the classroom to find poor Queenie fallen from the craft table and split in two, gold paint spattered and slick on the floor, the smell everywhere of flour, glue.

Before I could try to put her together again, Diego had slunk beside me, looking down at her, his sneaker caught on Queenie's tail.

Look what Queenie did, he said, softly as ever.

It was an accident, I said. *Probably one of the custodians—*

She tried to get away, he said, shaking his head. *She tried to run away.*

Until nearly midnight, I lay in the twinned bed, body still churning from the thunking road, from all the evening's excitements.

On the bedside table, I found a fat paperback, its cover cracked and swollen with time, humidity. *Bedtime Tales of Suspense*, it was called, its pages yellow with tiny print.

I wondered if Mrs. Brandt had left it for me. It had a great spooky cover of a woman in a long white gown hanging off the side of a bed, her neck bare, her eyes closed, her mouth open.

I opened it to the first story. It began, like they all do, with a carriage ride to a grand old house. An ancestral manse.

But my mind kept drifting.

I wanted to call my mom and tell her everything, but there was no service anywhere I could find. *We'll be off the grid*, Jed had warned me. But wouldn't that be nice for a few days?

Sure, the school might call, except they wouldn't. It was summer and I was pregnant, and no one would bother me with supply orders, stray incoming parent questions.

There was a landline in the kitchen and in the upstairs hallway. But no TVs or computers I could see. Maybe back in Doctor Ash's study, tucked somewhere in the center of the house. But I doubted it, not among all those bound medical books, that fancy rosewood chessboard with all the pieces laid out . . . the faint smell of old tobacco, fountain ink, wood soap . . .

Maybe it was better not to talk to my mom right now anyway. She didn't like the idea that we had to go all that way to spend time with Jed's dad, that he lived in such a remote place and, as she put it, made us come to him. *Does he live in a bunker stocked full with canned goods and semi-automatics?* she'd teased in that way she had.

Maybe we should have invited her too, Jed had said, with a forever-keen understanding of those who might feel left out, forgotten. Lone wolf recognizes lone wolf, after all.

But wasn't it more peaceful just to listen to the low hum of Jed and his father on the deck outside, their voices drifting up through the fraying window screen, fireflies like plugs in the sky?

Because whatever fear or trepidation Jed had wrestled with on that long drive seemed to have slipped, magically, away.

Wasn't it always like that with family? Once home, you're back in it, good or bad. You're under its spell. You're eight, twelve years old again, when everything feels so big, epic, life-altering. Except this time it can make your heart ache, too, knowing how long past it is and how you were wrong about it all anyway.

❧

In the dark, Jed came to bed, finally, the screens humming from the window fan.

Jed, Jed, I thought. Watching him tearing his tee shirt over his head like a boy—like I could imagine him doing at age ten, running through the woods to jump in some nearby water hole, cool and deep.

I'd wanted to ask him about what his father had said, what he'd told me about his mother, but now I couldn't bear to break the mood. It was so rare to see him so young and light and playful.

Kissing me, his mouth hot and bourbon-sweet. "You taste," he said, "like sugar."

"From one taste of blue moon?" I said. "That stuff must be powerful."

Jed made a face, chuckling to himself.

"Your dad talked me into it," I insisted. "He made it sound so good."

"Really?" he said, giving me a funny look, sitting down on the bed, his tee shirt still half-caught around his fists. "Did he . . . he didn't tell you what's in it, did he?"

"No. Why?" I asked, because Jed was really laughing now, and I told him he was drunk and tried to press a pillow over his mouth.

"Beaver musk," he said. "That's what's in it. That's the taste, the aftertaste."

"No way," I said, my face flushing suddenly, unaccountably. "That's some Michigan urban legend."

But Jed just kept laughing. "It's the gland under the beaver's tail," he insisted, gesturing with his hands and both of us now covering our mouths, shaking with trying-to-be-quiet laughter.

"I'm so glad you're feeling better," I said, my finger pressing against the vein in his arm, the one that always reminded me of the first time I saw him in his studio, wondering over all his scars, his mysteries.

"What do you mean?" he said, finally letting his tee shirt drop to the floor, settle over his bare feet.

"The drive up," I said. "The motor inn. How you wanted to turn around and go back."

He pulled back from me slightly, kicking his shirt to the corner of the room.

"You must've been dreaming," he said, with that same vague, bewildered look he'd had earlier, when we first arrived. "This is my favorite place in the world."

DAY THREE

The next day was a trip to Pictured Rocks and it flickered by like a Technicolor dream.

Doctor Ash drove. For a man so refined, his truck was surprisingly showy, a great black tank of an SUV that seemed like it might roll over our toothpaste-white Chevy rental, its matte-black wheels nearly as tall as me, its grille glinting in the sun.

At night, I thought, *it must look like a submarine.*

There was something awfully fun about it, like riding in an oil tanker. We were high, so high, and the air conditioner gusting and all the controls lit like in a movie spaceship.

"Don't judge me, Jacy," Doctor Ash said, patting the dashboard. "First full winter I spent here humbled me. Come November, that sky goes iron-gray, all bets are off. One spin in a whiteout and I knew I'd better arm up or perish."

The ferry bobbed us along the shoreline until we turned one last bend and came upon a landscape nearly psychedelic.

Fifteen miles of sandstone cliffs, all mineral streaked with colors hallucinatory. Hot magenta and glowing green and searing pink. Like those William Blake visions I'd studied in art school.

"The red and orange—that's iron. The copper's blue and green," Jed was explaining. "The darker strands are manganese."

The sandstone kept shifting, revealing new shapes and formations.

They were the result, the tour guide told us, of wind and wave erosion, but to me it was as if some hand had fashioned them, sculpting out a series of caves, arches, mounds.

"There she is," Doctor Ash said, pointing to one cliff at least two hundred feet high.

"Miners Castle," Jed said, tugging me under his arm.

"Jed always saw castle turrets. Too many dragon books as a kid."

Jed kept laughing this high laugh, this little boy laugh I'd never heard before, except on our wedding morning trying to tie a tie before we remembered he never wore ties.

"The Pictured Rocks were always Jed's favorite," Doctor Ash said.

"It makes sense," I said suddenly.

Jed looked at me with a curious smile. "What do you mean?"

And Doctor Ash was looking at me, too, waiting.

"How you shape and sculpt light, color," I said. "You know."

A flicker of something in the air and I thought again of my mom. *Jacy's tube bender husband. How's the tube bender?*

That morning, I'd asked Jed, "Does your dad not really get what you do?"

But Jed only shrugged, disappearing behind the medicine cabinet, hunting for floss. "I don't know. I guess he's old-fashioned."

That word again, *old-fashioned*, which seemed to contain multitudes.

At this moment, however, it seemed Doctor Ash did get it.

"Shape and sculpt light and color," he repeated my words back to me, then looked out on the rocks. "Isn't that something? Like the hand of god, one might say."

And I smiled and Jed sort of smiled, as if he wasn't quite sure.

Boys are forever trying to please their fathers, I supposed. It explained all Jed's nerves, his earnestness, the adolescent Adam's apple when he swallowed.

"Get thee a woman who understands thee," Doctor Ash added with a wink. "Jed, my boy, aren't you the lucky one."

The ferry took one last turn and we saw one of the plainer cliffs.

"Is that it?" Jed asked softly.

"Yep. Bridalveil Falls," Doctor Ash said, pointing to a lacy spray of water tumbling down the cliff. "Not much of a veil this time of year."

He turned to me. "That's where Jed's mom and I were married."

As if on cue, we approached an overlook where a woman in a wedding dress and swirling veil scurried to the cliff edge, her groom hurrying after her, and the photographer following them, swinging a tripod and reflector umbrella in his hand, a nervous mother running behind and crying out, "Hold her hem, Donny. Hold my baby's hem and train!"

We all laughed, the whole ferry laughed.

Except Jed, who was staring up the cliff face, quiet and pensive.

"I wish we could see it better," I said. "It must have been a beautiful wedding."

Doctor Ash cleared his throat and nodded. Smiled.

"There's a trail that'll take you damn close, but I wouldn't dare let Jed tantalize you up there. Especially not in your condition."

"That's how all the shows my mom watches begin," I said, reaching for the railing as the ferry canted right. "A man is always taking his pregnant wife to the top of a cliff."

Doctor Ash laughed, and I did too, shaking Jed from his reverie. He turned to look at me.

"Are you okay?" he said, putting his hand on my arm.

"What do you mean?" I said, still laughing—maybe a little too loud now.

"Jed's gonna be one of *those* expectant dads," Doctor Ash teased. "The kind with sympathy pains."

On the ferry ride back, the guide was telling us to come back in the winter when the cliffs freeze into long curtains and fine columns and narrow daggers of blue, pale green, and metallic white ice.

"We'll get you back here in the winter," Doctor Ash said. "When the little one can see too."

"Maybe," Jed said, a clouded look on his face. "But Jacy has school."

But Doctor Ash ignored him and started describing how, in the winter, you take an ice screw and hurl it into the waterfall and then you climb up, up, up.

"You press your ear against it," he said, softly and only to me, "and you can hear the water rushing underneath."

⚘

The evening was another grand meal, this one with Mrs. Brandt in the kitchen, managing a fish fry that somehow didn't put one speck of oil on her immaculate apron.

"Won't you join us?" I asked as she set down a platter of battered whitefish.

"No," she said, her voice low and fine. "No, I won't."

And then Doctor Ash appeared and she disappeared.

"This is probably her laundry night," I teased in a whisper to Jed as Doctor Ash turned the speaker on, Frank Sinatra, and began squeezing lemons over all the fish.

Instantly, Jed reddened, his hand on my thigh under the table and in an instant my heart was in my chest. I wanted to be alone with him.

I still didn't like to share him with anybody, any place at that stage.

It was embarrassing but true.

Enjoy it while you can, my mom would say. *Eat it all up, sweetie. Gorge on it if you can.*

In some ways it felt like being this much in love—you had to hide it, tell no one, keep it to yourself.

NIGHT THREE

Mom—

   Having a great time. Ready to scale the waterfalls
this winter!
   We miss you.

   XO Jacy

Writing postcards on the bed, my legs sore and swollen, the bleachy smell of the bedspread, old Bactine.

Downstairs, on the back lawn, Jed and his father talked alongside the bug zapper, their bourbon already a nightly routine.
   The way their voices sounded so close, thrumming in my ear.
   "Do you have a name yet?"
   "No, I told you. We don't even want to know the sex."
   "And you call me old-fashioned. Like father, like son."
   "Like father, like son," Jed repeated, slapping his arm. I imagined a mosquito that drew blood.

Drifting in and out of sleep, I read one of the *Bedtime Tales of Suspense* and the last thing I remembered was Jed coming to bed and my telling him the story.

It was about a man who keeps asking the same beautiful young girl to marry him and finally he throws himself at her feet, promising he loves her so much that he'd even return from the dead if she wanted. Then, the day of the wedding, the groom is late, hours late, and when he finally arrives, he looks so pale and there's a funny black mark on his head.

It's only after the ceremony that they learn the groom had died on the way to the wedding, and she'd married a corpse!

"That doesn't make any sense," he said, laughing, setting the book back on the table. "You're dreaming."

"You always say that," I said, one hand on my belly and the other on him. "I can't always be dreaming, can I?"

It was a perfect sleep, the two of us cocooned so tight, the window screen glittery from a late-night shower. The breeze like a long hand stroking across us both, casting a spell.

Perfect, I wanted to say out loud, but was too sleepy to.

Perfect, I finally whispered to myself, drawing Jed closer. It was tempting fate, though, wasn't it? I see that now.

DAY FOUR

I woke up with a start, sliding out of bed and stumbling into the hallway, tugging down the tee shirt I slept in, one of Jed's that felt soft as the back of his earlobes. Back when we first came together and all I wanted was to touch him and touch him. All that crazy stuff you say and feel at the beginning of things. *I'd like to take this earlobe with me, put it in my pocket like a rabbit foot . . .*

The hallway blazing with light, tee shirt riding up between my thighs, I hurried into the bathroom, my stomach pitching, sinking to my knees in teetering fashion, nearly slipping, my arms circling the toilet bowl.

"Are you okay, honey?"

Jed on the other side of the bathroom door, a husky whisper.

"Just a little sick," I said, my mouth wet and pungent, that acid taste I remembered only from a few crushing hangovers as a teenager, the humiliation of my mother behind the door, jiggling the handle and demanding to know what boy gave me all that Southern Comfort because she would like to call his mother.

All night the taste had sat inside me as I tried to sleep, a slurpy roiling giving over to an oily heaving the minute I stepped into the hallway and smelled smells, any smells, all of them—slowly roasting coffee, the whisper of last night's fish, the fleet of plug-in air fresheners that seemed to be emanating "spring linen" in concert.

"But you haven't had morning sickness before," Jed was saying, sitting me down on the tub ledge and gently pressing a wet washcloth on my neck, under my ears.

"I haven't been pregnant before," I said vaguely, holding on to his shoulder.

Jed looked at me, his brow pulled tight.

"I'm fine, Jed," I said, more firmly now, trying for a smile. "It happens. All the time."

My phone stared blankly back at me. No Wi-Fi, no cell service. I kept forgetting.

My mom, surely hungry for all the details about Doctor Ash, would have to wait. And, too, her questions about his house and if he had a girlfriend and how many acres did he own. I hadn't even put a stamp on the postcard. And where did one find a mailbox up here?

My mom was a woman who insisted on specifics of everything, once giving me a forty-minute lecture on the loss of power inherent in a specific sexual act: *Some women say they like it, but they're lying.* I could never tell her I liked it.

I want a full report, she'd said before I left. *And take a good look at how he's aged because it'll be a window into Jed's future.* My mom and my aunt laughing together on the phone, teasing me. *Does his belly hang over his belt loops? How about his hairline? They say that comes from the mother's side, but it never hurts to check. How many cups of coffee in the morning? How many sniffs of scotch at day's end?*

Does he respect women?

Does he even like women?

Men of that age, they said, *we know.*

All those questions felt ridiculous in the face of Doctor Ash, his hair silver as a fish fin, summer-brown skin, smiling eyes that reminded me of the bachelor uncle on that old TV show, or so many old TV shows.

Everything would be fine without a phone. It was only a few more days and wasn't it nice to not be so wedded to one's devices, one's regular life, the outside world?

I closed my eyes, just for a moment. The bedsprings pinged.

Mrs. Brandt's face large above me. She set down a glass of ice.

"Sometimes this helps," she said.

I thought for a second I was still dreaming, the early hour and the bedroom door inexplicably wide open.

"It's so early," I said blearily. "Do you live nearby?"

I wasn't sure where the question came from and for a moment she just looked at me.

"Near enough," she said, straightening her pale shirt, smoothing it flat.

I looked at the glass of ice, its mineral tang in my nose.

"I never had it . . . morning sickness," I said. "Or I didn't before now."

"It isn't always that," she said, watching me closely. "Try the ice."

Obediently, I picked up the glass, the shock of the cold.

"Do you have children?" I asked, unthinkingly. Then feeling embarrassed. "I mean, you seem to know . . ."

"No," she said, her face unreadable. "I'm the caretaker."

It was such a funny answer, to another question, not the one I'd asked.

And with that she turned toward the door, disappeared into the hallway.

I took a breath, aware suddenly of how I looked, wearing only Jed's tee—a faded picture of an electrode—soaked from sweat and riding around my waist, the sheets thrown back.

Since the eighth week I couldn't sleep with anything resting too heavily on my body. Everything felt like one of those radiation blankets they lay over you at the dentist for the X-rays.

I put one of the discs of ice under my tongue. A jolt from my gums, my nerve endings humming.

I'm the caretaker, I whispered to myself, letting the ice do its work. It felt so good, its coldness tapping my gums. T-t-t-tapping as my teeth nearly chattered, the ice like a metronome clacking, like a telegraph in an old movie, its key humming, rapping out an important message for someone who needed to see it.

Moments later, my eyes opened again and Mrs. Brandt's shadow became Jed's, now hovering near the bed.

"Where does she live?" I murmured, my mouth gurling from the melted ice.

"Who?" Jed asked, reaching for his shoes.

"Mrs. Brandt."

"Out there," he said, pointing at the window. "I told you. The guest cottage."

The shudder from the ice.

"Where?"

Twisting my neck, looking through the spiney screen, I could barely see it. A tiny house up the back slope, through a knotted twist of tall trees. One story, it was anchored by a stubby stone chimney. Unlike the Ash house, it looked like a real cottage. Small and unassuming with its faded yellow shingles and graying eaves.

Suddenly, as if the cottage itself were listening, I thought I saw the curtains twitch.

"With a husband?" I asked.

"No," Jed said, surprised. "She lives alone."

"Oh," I said, eyes squinting at its single picture window, wide and paneless, half hidden by peach sheers.

Near enough, Mrs. Brandt had said.

Nearer than that, I thought, noticing the heavy willow tree dangling above it, its corkscrew branches nearly clawing the roof like an arcade toy.

So close, maybe five hundred feet, but you wouldn't see it if you didn't know where to look.

Jed turned and smiled down at me.

"You look pretty," he said, taking my hand.

And suddenly I wanted to cry.

"Hormones," Jed kept saying, wiping my tears away, my wet, wet face, both of us laughing, sort of.

"I hate the hormones," I cried out, laughing harder, like a hiccup that hurts.

❧

Outside, the sky was squint-bright and the humidity that tended to fall like a curtain by midday hadn't appeared yet.

An hour had passed and I was feeling better. The ice like a jolt to my body, a bright, piercing jolt.

"Are you sure you're up for a hike?" Jed asked, the back of his hand on my cheek.

"Of course," I said. "I ate and everything."

A bowl of oatmeal care of Doctor Ash, steel cut and soaked in cream. I couldn't get enough of it. A lilting shiver of déjà vu, one of my few memories of my dad, whom my mother divorced when I was three and who died a year later, a cancer that ate away at him before he even knew it was in him, twining around his spinal cord.

My dad in a Steel Wheels tee shirt, reading stories to me as he made breakfast. Standing at the stove, making cream of wheat with three lumps for my three years, just like I liked it. Cream of wheat, pale and smooth, a curl of butter swimming on top and both of us eating over the kitchen sink, me on a stool, matching bowls and a spray of black pepper for him and the smell he had always of instant coffee crystals and Benson & Hedges and dad sleep.

"We gotta spray," Jed said, a can of Repel rattling in his hand. "There's a lot of bloodsuckers in the woods."

I stretched out my arms, but then he paused.

"Is it safe? For the baby?"

"I don't know," I said. "Maybe safer than malaria?"

"Or West Nile," he said. "Or Lyme."

He looked at the back of the can, a wrinkle over his brow.

"Jed," I said, "your dad told me about your mom."

I don't know why I brought it up in that moment. Maybe it was because he seemed so jittery. Worried that I might start vomiting again, worried we might be poisoning our baby.

At first, he didn't say anything, shaking the can, scattering the sticky insecticide along the backs of my calves, slapping it on the back of my neck.

Hiss-hiss-hiss-hiiissssss.

"What?"

Hiss-hiss-hiss-hiiissssss.

"I didn't realize," I said, trying to turn my head around as he knelt behind me, the warm mist of chemicals on my ankles, "that she'd . . . that she'd died *during* childbirth."

Craning my neck, only seeing the top of his head, his bent knee.

Hiss-hiss-hiss-hiiissssss.

"What difference does that make?" he said finally.

"None, I guess," I said, taken by surprise. "But you never told me."

"What is there to tell?" he asked, rubbing my legs, averting his eyes.

That she was swimming in her own blood. That's what I thought.

But I couldn't say it, his posture stiffening, the can tight in his hand.

Hiss-hiss-hiss-hiiissssss.

My legs, my arms, my neck, tacky, sweet. "I think that's enough."

"I think so too," Jed said briskly, and when I turned around he was already out the door, pounding down the stairs like a lurching teenage boy, or something.

⌁

Redruth, Mrs. Brandt's Irish setter, licked at my fingers as we all waited for Doctor Ash to pull his truck around to drive us the six miles to the trail. The same great black monolith that had taken us to Pictured Rocks the day before.

The plan was to go for a hike, a "lake loop," five miles around the glittering surface of a body of water so peaceful it would cure all ailments and soothe even the most tormented soul.

"At least that's what the realtor promised when I bought up more land here," Doctor Ash said.

We were all going, even Mrs. Brandt and Redruth, her "outdoor dog," who also seemed to be Doctor Ash's dog even though he wouldn't let her sleep in the house.

"They like it in the rough," he said to Jed, adding out of Mrs. Brandt's earshot, "but they bring in dirty things."

The truck carriage seemed even higher today, so high that Jed had to help me inside, nearly lifting me like you might a child, a bulbous, awkward child.

Mrs. Brandt watched from below. Then, once I was safely ensconced, swung one leg up and rose with the grace of a dancer, an equestrian.

"Glad you're feeling better," Doctor Ash said, looking at me in the rearview mirror.

"I'm fine," I said, looking at Jed. "Really good."

Jed and I sat in the back, Redruth quivering between us. Behind my sunglasses, I couldn't help but watch Doctor Ash and Mrs. Brandt in the front seat, wondering about their silent ease with each other, or was it something else? It seemed impossible to tell.

Their eyes always flickering at each other, looks passed, messages received.

The road seemed to corkscrew, the front bumper leaping and landing soundlessly.

"If anyone feels sick," Doctor Ash said, his eyes on me in the rearview, "give a holler."

The trail was labyrinthine, dense, but Doctor Ash was a consummate tour guide, leading the way under impossibly verdant tree canopies, across worn-wood bridges, pointing out birds I couldn't even see, up high in the ancient trees, and the occasional skitter or scurry of something—a fox? A hare?

An hour in, something wonderful happened: We exited an endless canopy of virgin white pine to come upon a clearing and the distant swoop of what looked like a prehistoric raptor.

"Bald eagle," Jed said, his voice high and boyish.

"Sure is," Doctor Ash said.

Soaring. Now I knew why they always said "eagles soar." Watching it, its astounding proportions, its elegance, its grandeur, I felt my breath catch, my ankle turn slightly.

Jed turned, looked at me. He didn't miss a thing.

"I'm fine," I said. "It's just . . . it's beautiful."

I pointed up, but the eagle was gone.

We kept going, a half hour more, the sumptuous mineral smack of the lake tickling my nose. At a clearing, we sat and passed around hardy apples, some sort of jerky that looked like a tongue. Mrs. Brandt didn't eat anything, checking Redruth's mane for ticks.

"Are you sure you don't want to head back?" Jed asked, looking me up and down as if searching for a crack in my seams. "The trail is pretty uneven. If you tripped—"

"Jed," Doctor Ash said genially, "she's a woman, not a hothouse orchid. Listen to what she's telling you."

And then holding his gaze on Jed, who said nothing, a sulky look on his face like a little boy. Didn't we all become our childselves with our parents if we were with them long enough? With my mom, I was forever an impudent, outraged thirteen.

Back on the trail, we'd gone only a few yards when my foot landed in a mound of leaves and came up wet, slick.

"Jacy," Jed called out, pointing at my leg, a sluice of ruddy brown on my calf.

Looking down, I nearly slipped.

Beneath my foot, there was a funny little face there, a ruined animal, a tangle of fur and bone, its skull crushed.

"What is it?" I burbled, my voice high and faint.

"Snowshoe hare," Doctor Ash said. "Two, I think."

Jed was standing over me, an almost-satisfied look. As if to say: *I told you so.*

"I couldn't even tell," I said without thinking, my mouth feeling funny, tingly. "What it was. What was left."

Suddenly I was perched on a log soft with moss. I barely remembered sitting down, my legs somehow curling beneath me, my hands reaching out before I could faint, the thought of fainting too humiliating.

Thankfully, Jed didn't see, kneeling down to look at the animal. Doctor Ash and Mrs. Brandt stood a few feet away in their proper shoes and poker faces, looking down at the bone and hair, tufted, the impossible white of its torn eye.

The smell from the animal—strong, bloody, metallic—filled the air, Jed covering his mouth with his hand. But it didn't bother me. After all those hours in the house, sealed so tight, the mingling odors of lemon cleaner and vinegar, it was a relief. It was like how exiting the frigid and dark interior of a movie theater, your body clenched for two hours, into the sunlight of a sweltering day feels like a relief. At least for those first few minutes of heat and life.

The smell also made me hungry.

"It's the iron," a voice hummed in my ear.

I turned and it was Mrs. Brandt.

"What?" I asked, but she had already looked away.

Had she seen something on my face? I wondered, feeling like she'd caught me naked, indecent somehow. Like the time my high school boyfriend's crazy mother shook her finger at me, claiming she could smell me on her son's sheets. *I see you! I know you!*

Doctor Ash bent down to the ground near Jed for a closer look.

"Bobcat get him?" Jed asked.

"Or mountain lion," Doctor Ash said, lifting his head, his eyes landing on me.

"Another mountain lion?" I said.

"Or the same one," Mrs. Brandt said.

"If they don't finish off their meal in one sitting," Doctor Ash said, "they cache their kill like this. Hide it under leaves, come back later and feed again."

"We should ask Hicks when he comes by."

"Who's Hicks?" I asked.

"I told you," Jed said, his voice clipped. "Family friend."

For a second, I thought he might say: *pregnancy brain*. Which was something Jed would never say. But he was being so brusque with me. *I told you where Mrs. Brandt lives. I told you who Hicks is.* It's from concern, I assured myself. And everything. Maybe even my bringing up his mother.

"Never used to see mountain lions up here," Mrs. Brandt said. "But last dozen years . . ."

"I've always thought they've been here all along," Doctor Ash said, looking at me, then down at the savaged hare again. "Folks just thought they were big cats."

"Maybe," Mrs. Brandt said. "But the screams. There's no missing that."

I looked at her, my hand on my belly.

"The female cats scream," Doctor Ash said to me, a smile lurking. "Sounds just like a woman."

It was all alarming, in a way, but there was something fun about it, like he was trying to spook me, like a dad telling his kids a scary story.

"That's the female in heat," Mrs. Brandt said, crisply. "They leave their stench to draw the males, to entice them."

"Used to scare Jed at night," Doctor Ash added, grinning at his son. "Boy, did it."

I tried to keep up, Mrs. Brandt ahead of me, her spine straight, head high, her swirl of red hair like a siren, the cherry top on a police car.

She moved with such elegance, such regality.

It made me think, fleetingly, of my mother's hip-swinging gait, the opposite of all this, my mother's curves and fleshiness. A different kind of power.

My eyes landing in the center of Mrs. Brandt's bun, a hairpin dug there, its teeth glittering in the sun whenever the tree canopy thinned. A dark wood hairpin with some obscure symbol carved in the top, too intricate for me to see.

Wondering at the brain behind it, the thoughts churning through Mrs. Brandt's head. Was she thinking about the trail ahead, her duties at home? Was she thinking of the mountain lion, or the slaughtered snowshoe, its sloe eye glaring at us?

Mrs. Brandt, in her heavy boots even in the summer heat.

Does she like me? Such a funny question to pop into my head, but there was a feeling I had. That I was added work, an encumbrance, a trespasser. It was nothing she said, maybe it was everything she hadn't. The way she looked at me but didn't say anything. Or when she said something, she never looked at me.

I pictured her suddenly at her dressing table, her bathroom mirror, sweeping her hands up her hair, pulling the pin, letting it fall to her shoulders with such solemnity. Staring at her bare face, never a skim of cosmetics, its paleness and set jaw, and letting her fingers slide through her locks, shaking them loose, like a shampoo commercial, a movie moment, something private and female and hidden behind closed doors, in the little cabin behind the house, silent and hers.

We were getting ready for a late lunch, cold salads and honeydew, some leftover chicken thighs. Jed even let me set the table.

"Are you sure I can manage it?" I teased through the screen door. "These napkins are awfully heavy."

But Jed didn't hear, or pretended not to, his head bent over the grill outside, replacing a sooty tube, still trying to fix it.

Napkin left, fork left, knife right, then spoon, I could never remember, my mom's endless melted trays of Lean Cuisine, the steaming bags of vegetables, the butter packets oozing. *Any plastic forks left in that drawer, Jacy? How about a spork?*

On the old sideboard, I spotted yet another photo of young Jed, this time in his graduation cap, a sprig of acne on his neck and a brooding look to him, the shiny emerald satin of his robe, the golden tassel. The kind of boy I myself at that age would have wondered over helplessly at parties, hoping he might make room for me in the car with his friends, and I'd have to sit on his lap, hold on to his knee when the car made all those sharp turns, the pinball pleasure, those sad eyes turning to desire.

"Future serial killer, eh?"

I looked up and Doctor Ash was grinning, a bag of briquettes in hand.

"Aren't a lot of serial killers doctors?" I teased.

"That's why I left medicine," he said. "Devote more time to my real passion. Murder."

It occurred to me suddenly I hadn't seen a single photo of Jed's mother on all these walls, or perched in the bookcases, wedged between all the ones of Doctor Ash and Jed holding up big-eyed basses like a Hemingway story, or riding matching blue Jet Skis.

Once, I'd seen a photo of her, the only one Jed had. A Polaroid he kept tucked between the pages of a book on "cold cathode lighting techniques." You could barely make her out: a dark-haired woman in a smocked dress posed sidewise, the better to see her pregnant belly, her hands cupping it in the manner of a classic painting. Her chin dipped slightly, eyes lowered, shy smile. Shy or sly, it was impossible to tell.

Oh, he'd said when he saw me looking at the photo. *Yeah, that's her.*

I told him she was pretty, lovely, but Jed looked uncomfortable and instantly plucked the Polaroid from my fingers.

I'm sorry, he said, handling it with care as if I might have left an oily thumbprint, something. And he looked at the photo again.

She gets fainter every year, he murmured, and I reached for his arm. His fading Ghost Rider tattoo.

Everything dims, he added, and it was only then I realized he was talking about the photo. *Vanishes.*

It just slipped out, my asking.

"I mean, if you have any around," I said, following Doctor Ash outside, the humidity like a hot breath in my ear. "Jed only has one photo of her, so . . ."

"Oh," Doctor Ash said, eyebrows lifted. "Well, of course you'd be curious. Of course."

"I mean, if it's no trouble."

For a split second, I thought I saw a flash of something on his face.

"Of course," he said quickly, wanting to assure me. "You love my boy. I'll have Mrs. Brandt dig out some musty albums." He smiled again, such glorious teeth. "Of course."

And suddenly Mrs. Brandt was there, standing behind the patio screen, her red hair even redder in the sunlight. In one hand a flashlight I'd seen her carry before, heavy and aluminum, red tipped like a lipstick.

"They're in the garage, in one of the crates," she said, scraping open the screen door and moving swiftly outside as Doctor Ash drifted over to the bar cart.

"Oh," I said, following Mrs. Brandt. "No need right now. I didn't realize . . ."

She was ahead of me on the gravel path, a quiet, cool pocket between the house and a grove of trees, when she stopped abruptly and faced me.

"It's hurtful to him," she said, low and quick, her face close to mine. "Don't ask him. Ask me."

"Ask you . . ."

"About her, the past," she said, the vivid green of a low-drooping tree branch hanging in front of her like a hat veil. "It's hard enough seeing you."

"Me?"

"Pregnant, fulsome. Fecund, ripening," she said, her eyes hidden, her voice a low murmur. "Your skin is bright and you're carrying low. You'll bring a boy, you know. Jed's boy."

Hard enough seeing you. I should have thought of it, my face reddening. It made sense there would be some echo. *But, really, Jacy?* I imagined my mother asking, rolling her eyes. *That was long ago, and you're not his wife.*

But how about for Jed? I thought again.

I need to be more careful, I thought.

You need to be more careful of Mrs. Brandt, I could hear my mom say. *She wanted you to feel bad and guess what? It worked.*

Mrs. Brandt said she couldn't find the boxes. She'd look again later when Hicks was here.

"Unless you're in a hurry," she said, looking at me.

"No hurry at all," I replied. "Later's fine."

It was only when we sat down that I saw it. I'd set the table, but someone had reset it. Everything rearranged, the knife turned the other way, a whole new set of forks I hadn't seen, linen napkins for paper.

"Oh," I said softly, my fingers on one of the fork tines.

Looking up, I saw Mrs. Brandt watching me notice. She wanted me to see.

"She likes it done a certain way," Jed whispered when I asked him later. "It's a Midwestern thing. Or a Cornish thing."

Because Mrs. Brandt was of Cornish descent, like so many up here. The descendants of miners who arrived nearly two centuries ago. Jed had told me that and I'd forgotten, I guess.

What that had to do with table-setting, I didn't know, but I kind of laughed, or something. A barking noise that reminded me of my forever-working mom at school meetings when my teacher would say, *Maybe you'd like to volunteer to be a den mother this year?*

The lunch was so fresh, crisp, but the only thing that tasted right was the melon, cold and slimy, an acid tang. I ate three, four slices of it, Doctor Ash finally teasing me about it, heaping his slice and Jed's both on my plate.

I found myself wanting, obscurely, to call my mom, which made me think I was a little sunsick. Maybe that was why the strong smell of the whitefish salad made me sweat. Made me keel slightly to the right, one of my sandals falling off under the table.

"It's only seventy-eight," Jed was saying, mopping his forehead and making me feel relieved, "but Michigan humidity."

"I'll turn up the air," Doctor Ash said, rising. "I hadn't noticed."

"You're always cool," Mrs. Brandt murmured, looking at Doctor Ash over her iced tea. "Always so cool."

"Hicks is here," Mrs. Brandt called out. "Don't let him track his feet in."

I saw him through the screen door. A snowy-haired man with a snowy-white moustache waiting outside a truck the color of pea soup.

"Hi, there, little miss," he said, tipping his cap at me through the window screen.

I said hello, stepping outside as Jed approached.

"You look just fine to me," Hicks said, walking toward me with a slight limp that gave him a John Wayne gait.

"Oh?" I said.

"Mrs. Brandt said you looked a little, well, peaked."

I wondered when they had talked.

"I'm fine," I said firmly. "I'm pretty sturdy. I—"

Jed put his hand on my shoulder. "You can go upstairs, take a rest if you like."

"No," I said. "I'll come." Even though I didn't even know where they were going.

The men looked at each other. A shadow lingered at the screen door.

"I think she looks just fine," Hicks repeated, looking at Jed. "And I think it's gonna be a boy."

✌

I was putting my shoes on, Jed hovering over me.

"But, really," Jed was saying. "Just stay here, okay?"

It was something in his tone, and the way he was watching me, like you'd watch a toddler near the stove.

A door shushed open and Doctor Ash emerged from his crimson study, mahogany gleaming behind him.

"We won't be gone long," Jed said to me. "The bait shop isn't that exciting."

Doctor Ash laughed and made a joke about ice jigs and musky lures, but I didn't say anything.

"I'm fine," I repeated, giving Jed one of those looks, those married-couple looks that say STOP. Jed caught it and went silent. An awkward silence.

"Well, it's natural to be more tired," Doctor Ash said, his eyes darting between us, trying to broker some kind of accord. Then, turning to me. "Your body is adjusting to this hurricane of hormones."

Jed looked at me, gratified. "It's true. And why take a chance?"

"I'm fine, Jed," I said again, now for the third time. "Really."

"But what do I know?" Doctor Ash said suddenly, eyes flickering at me. "I was only a GP and I've been out of the game a long while."

"Oh, it's not that," I said quickly. Had I hurt his feelings? *Men and their feelings*, my mom always said, every time Mr. Panarites cried in his car in our driveway before going home to his wife. "I'm sure you're right. Better safe than sorry."

Jed's eyes on me, reaching tentatively for my wrist, which felt cold under his hot fingers. Was he hot, or was I suddenly so very cold?

"Caution is the better part of valor, right?" Doctor Ash said, patting my back with surprising vigor. "Soldiers need their strength."

Through the upstairs window I could see Hicks still leaning against his truck, his Ray-Bans glinting, one leg bent, his left shoe resting on the rear bumper.

I watched Jed and Doctor Ash join him, slapping each other's backs, the ballgame on the radio echoing up.

I no longer knew if I felt tired or not. Weak or not.

It's the hormones, Doctor Ash had said.

It's the iron, Mrs. Brandt had said. And I hadn't been vigilant about supplements.

Honey, prepare for strange hungers, my mom had told me when I first gave her the news. *I gorged myself on chicken livers and sucked on ice. Nine months later, you came out!*

There was nothing wrong with needing iron, I reminded myself.

Or being hypersensitive to smells.

Was I anemic? I wondered. No. No. Just because the iron smell of the animal's blood hadn't bothered me. Had made me hungry.

But how had Mrs. Brandt known that? Seen that?

The back of my hand on my cheek, it felt hot.

Iron, blood, beast. It was all so embarrassing.

ԓ

Upstairs, the bedroom—which smelled so magical at night, the window screens humming with what my aunt Laraine always called, with a roll of the eyes, *country air*—smelled like mildew by day. Bleached sheets, dried calamine, dust between the floorboards, like the one time I suffered through camp: a platform tent with a dead bat hanging in one corner, a torn condom like an old balloon in another, a dried milky spatter.

But, yet, there was somehow a stillness in it too. A sense of nothing happening and best you rest, the faint squeeze of old springs as I turned on the mattress, my cheek on the softly pilling sheet.

A dream came, decades thick, of rubbing buttercups on my chin with my dad, the brush of his moustache, his big teeth and faded jeans.

He never had a moustache, my mom always said. But he did, that last year, after the separation and before he died, six weeks to the day his doctor found the hourglass tumor passing through his spine.

And then a memory of Jed, that time he showed up at school during my last class of the day. Jed, looking a hundred feet tall inside P.S. 313, holding a bending tray of takeout coffee, hair sticking up from a day, head bent, goggles on, bending and splicing, lost in his head.

That dazed look he always had after a day of intensive work, like a baby bird plucked from its mother's nest.

"This is Jed," I said to my grinning second graders. "He's an artist of light."

And they oohed and ahhed as he showed them how to make shapes with glowsticks and how to experiment with neon paint on black paper. And he promised to give them a big neon tube-bending demonstration at his shop.

Field trip! Field trip! they all cried out, surrounding me with a *Lord of the Flies* intensity.

"Maybe," I said, smiling, curling my hand around Dani Koplin's pigtails, tugging them as the dismissal bell rang, its electronic ping.

"I love you, Miss Jacy," said little Miles Farhad, blinking his long lashes as he lingered at the door.

After the students spilled out, their hands smelling like the same pink soap, we stayed in the darkened classroom, drinking deli-sour coffee as I showed Jed things, Jed bending down, peering into the glazed castles my students had made, poking his finger through the lopsided drawbridges.

"I can't believe I've known you this long and never knew this," he said, a whistly whisper.

"Knew what?"

But he didn't say anything, only smiled, peeking through a turret window at me, like a king in his castle, waiting for his queen. Like a princess in her tower, waiting for her knight.

"I should never have waited this long," he said, his fingers curling around one of the shellacked turrets, "to see this. To see you like this."

We've only known each other a few months, I nearly said but didn't.

He circled the big slab table, coming for me. Oh, my heart skipped, my chest trilling. Wondering if there was time to lock the door. Pull the blinds.

"You should never," I agreed, my legs shaking as his hands found my face, neck, "have waited this long."

Within a month, we were married.

Maybe I'd close my eyes, a moment.

Doctor Ash, hair like soft ash, soft to the touch. Thicker even than Jed's, which went fine at the crown and sometimes I could catch him looking at it in mirrors, fingertips touching his scalp lightly as if it were a delicate thing, his youth, his young manhood.

This is a dream, I thought, *watching the doctor watching me from the door, ajar. Watching me through the sliver, eyes glittering.*

He puts cinnamon oil in his hair, Mrs. Brandt whispered in my ear. *Like General Custer.*

NIGHT FOUR

"We could always drive to Doctor Craig's office," Jed said. "Just to make sure everything's okay."

He'd returned and found me asleep in the twin bed. And I guess it had happened that I'd laid down to rest and now it was three hours later. A deep sleep I hadn't known since my teen years, like sinking into some far-off place. A dream about a baby doll my mom showed me once, hers as a little girl. An anatomically correct boy with a button-mushroom penis that squirted warm water.

"Who's Doctor Craig?" I asked, lifting my damp shirt off my skin, fanning myself over the air conditioner vent. "You smell like an old-man bar."

"The bait shop," he said. "Those guys just hang out, beers and smokes, cutting bloodworm collars. Aren't you sorry you missed it?"

I wanted to smile, but something oily rose inside me, my stomach twisting.

"You look really pale," he said. "Listen, Doctor Craig's a GP, a friend of Dad's. He's only a half-hour drive and—"

"Jed, there's nothing wrong with me. I just fell asleep. I'm fine, I swear."

He didn't say anything. The ceiling fan whirred above. The room full of sounds and neither of us speaking.

"Okay," Jed said, his hand on my leg, stroking it gently. "You're fine."

Under the showerhead, I kept turning and turning, the water slow and scalding.

There was nothing wrong with taking a nap on a vacation. It wasn't a sign of calamity. Of wrongness. Of a disordered body, worse. It was natural, organic. Common among pregnant women, as Doctor Ash had said.

Then, reminding myself I feel—I felt—fine.

And wasn't it lovely to have Jed so attentive, like Jed that very first night, feeding me broth, rubbing my stomach . . .

Coming out of the shower, wrapped in one of the thin towels that someone—surely Mrs. Brandt—seemed to have ironed flat, I caught Jed by surprise. He had my sundress in his hands, like he'd brought it up to his face, pressed his nose into it.

It was unexpected, and stirring. So intimate, a naughty boy.

"Naughty boy," I even said softly, pushing him back on my bed.

His smile, my wet hair slapping at him, as he slid his fingers under the towel, into me, so deep it was like the center of me. It was the center of me and my heart skittered hotly, one bent leg shaking like a twitchy rabbit and my eyes pressed shut. My belly between us, but nothing stopping Jed, flipping me on my side and pressing into me, his fingers still tickling and twisting, making me nearly cry. Then his lurches, breath hot in my ear, and how large he felt, almost monstrous, and strong, the stitchy scars on his arms rubbing hard against the soft of my back, and *god, would he ever come inside* until he did, pushing my face into the limp pillow with the heel of his hand on my crown. The pillow slipping, my chin landing on the old rattan headboard, its peeling rungs. My teeth knocking against it

71

and my mouth filling with salt, bile, blood. *C'mon, c'mon,* I said, in a voice I didn't recognize. *Harder, harder than that.*

Something in me wanted us to go someplace we'd never been, where no one could follow us. Beyond any place we'd ever go again, this baby coming and any nerves or growing pains, any sneaking doubt or parental caution over, behind us.

It was nearly seven and I stood by the kitchen door, wanting a glass of water.

But inside, Doctor Ash and Jed seemed deep in conversation, low voices, a soft chuckle. Jed was drinking a beer as Doctor Ash *thuck-thucked* with his fish knife, like a wet seam ripping, the water running in the sink.

"Business is going really well," Jed was saying, his voice looser at last, as if the sex and the beer had burned off all the anxiety. "Really well."

But Doctor Ash didn't say anything, taking a slippery whitefish between his hands, its scarlet gills like wet petals, lopping off the head, slitting the thing open, its glittery scales like a dress unzipping, digging his fingers into its scarlet center. The headless thing, washed white under the faucet, a gaping hole where its head had been.

My foot, a squeeze of the floorboard.

"Hi," I said. "Sorry to interrupt."

Both of them, sun-burnished nearly to red in the humid kitchen, looked at me.

"Never. How you feeling, sweet girl?"

"Great," I said, my hand on my belly again. *When did I become this woman, her hand forever on her womb like some dauntless sister wife on the plains?*

Doctor Ash looked at Jed, who set his beer down and walked over to me.

"I'm sorry about before," he said, taking my hands. "About all day, how I've been. I don't know what came over me."

"Thank you," I said, resisting the urge to say, *It was nothing, nothing at all.*

At the sink, Doctor Ash washed his hands, shook them dry, watching us, enjoying it.

"Jed always was a worrier," he said. "Even as a little kid."

Jed shrugged genially, pulling me into his arms. Jed's beer breath in my hair and the softness of his shirt.

"He used to save the baby birds from the fallen nests," a voice hummed behind me.

Mrs. Brandt in the doorway, her mouth a slit. "A soft boy for a hard world."

Everyone buzzing around me, readying things, knowing where things went and how they should go. I tried to pitch in, but there was no place for me, Jed rarely leaving the grill, smoke surrounding him like a skein, the way heat distorts things, refracts things, and was that really Jed or some kind of wavy mirage.

As if sensing it, Doctor Ash appeared, his arm gently around mine, asking if he might borrow me. There was something he wanted to show me.

"We gotta be quiet, though," he said, whispering, guiding me by the shoulders to the footpath that snaked around the house.

And there they were, a pair of green hummingbirds ambling around a teetering feeder.

"Always the same two," he said. "Or so I tell myself."

They were tiny and lovely, with violet patches like bathtub puffs on their throats.

"Very rare in these parts," he said. "But they're all over the Southwest, Mexico. Cloud forests."

"Cloud forests . . ." I started, because it sounded like a fairy tale, but then something happened, a flutter inside like one of the hummingbirds had landed in my belly, flapping its iridescent wings.

"Is he kicking?"

I looked up. How did he know?

"Not a kick. Just a little . . . something." Then, realizing. "But we don't know, you know. The sex. We decided not to know."

"My grandchild," he said, his eyes shining. "Oh, Jacy, I can't tell you how happy it makes me. And how glad I am it's you."

I felt a pinch over my heart.

"That's so nice," I burbled, moved. "My mom, she never . . . She's happy, I know, but, well . . . it's all happened so fast for her."

"She'll come around," he said. "She misses you, I bet. If you need to call her, the landline is all yours."

I smiled, suddenly afraid I might tear up.

Turning back to the hummingbirds, their wings like little motors, the feeder tilting, a spatter of sugared water on my ankles, feet.

"Oh," I said, touching my belly, a whirring feeling inside. "Oh."

Dinner was ready and I hurried upstairs to use the bathroom. The downstairs powder room felt too close to everything and everyone, and had no discernible lock. Like the one I'd grown up with, having to listen to any man who came by—Mr. Panarites, Uncle Nick, a high school boyfriend, the occasional handyman—urinate through the thin wall. As a kid, when Mr. Panarites came over, I used to run the water in the sink while I peed until one time I heard him say, "Is that your little girl in there or a racehorse?"

Passing the bedroom, I stopped short. Instead of the swirl of sheets we'd left behind—*our muffled afternoon clench, the wheels on the twin beds scraping, Jed pressed against my back, a mouthful of pillow, his fingers so deep inside I . . .*

The beds were lined up straight as soldiers, freshly made with new starched blue sheets tightly tucked, hospital corners, pillows puffed to faint life.

My face grew hot imagining Mrs. Brandt seeing the telltale stain from Jed's and my afternoon interlude, even as I'd meant to scrub it away with a wet washcloth. *You're a prude at heart*, my college roommate used to say. A *prude after the fact*.

"Do you think she heard us?" I asked Jed when he appeared in the doorway.

"Who?" He rubbed his face, flushed from the heat, all that still air, or the beers over badminton before the mosquitoes came out.

"Mrs. Brandt," I hissed.

"Mrs. Brandt doesn't change the sheets," Jed said, changing his shirt, dropping his sweaty one to the floor. "She's not our maid."

"Jed," I said, looking down at his discarded tee on the hook rug, "your dad did *not* remake our bed."

Jed paused, thinking, pulling back the window curtain and looking out.

"This house means a lot to her," he said. "All those years she was caretaker. Before I was even born."

"That makes sense," I said, peering out, too, through a tangle of trees to Mrs. Brandt's cottage. The sunlight fell across its large picture window, swathed today in peach curtains shivering from the air conditioner wedged beneath. And was that a cinder block for a front step?

It reminded me of the makeshift setups older siblings sometimes had, or guys like Toby, to whom I'd lost one lazy summer in my late teens, the ones stuck in community college or a dead-end job after high school and they move in the musty room over the garage, smelling forever of gasoline and low-grade pot. How glamorous it all seemed, and how temporary.

It seemed so sad to ponder. For years, Mrs. Brandt lived in such a fine, spacious house eleven months of the year and then her employer retires . . . and now she's in that shabby little cabin.

"Dad offered to get her a house of her own near town," Jed said, as if reading my thoughts, "but she likes—"

"Likes to be close," I said. As if on cue, I thought I saw a heavy shadow behind the peach curtain. A trick of the light.

"When I was a kid," Jed said, "we used to have one day together every summer where she'd take me over to Kitch-iti-kipi, the Big Spring. I can't wait to take you there. Anyway, we'd take one of these rafts they had on cables to the center and you could look down through bubbling water and see the bottom, green as emeralds. And after we'd get ice cream at Dairy Kream—"

"Blue moon?" I teased.

"More of a soft-serve situation," Jed said, grinning. "By the time I was thirteen or fourteen, I'd be a pain in the ass about it. But the truth was, I always had a good time. She paid so much attention to me. Asked me all these questions. And she smelled so nice."

I smiled.

"And every year, we'd do the whole Kitch-iti-kipi thing. You're supposed to put a drop of honey on a piece of birch bark and dip it into the spring and if you give it to the one you love, it'll make them true forever. She took it very seriously, so I started to too. Whatever girl I had a crush on—"

"Like Molly Kee?" I teased.

"What?"

"The girl you told me about. From summer camp."

But Jed wasn't listening, still caught in his memory, a dreamy look in his eyes.

"And then after we got our ice cream, we'd drive out to the big red Breakwater lighthouse in Manistique and take the picture."

"The picture?"

"Yeah, every year, she made me stand in front of the lighthouse and wave. Same pose, everything." He laughed a little. "She must have taken fifteen or twenty over the years. The metal years, the acne. I wonder what happened to those pictures."

Jed looked back out the window again, cracking his knuckles distractedly.

"One year, you gave the birch bark to Mrs. Brandt," I guessed.

Jed laughed. "Sure, I was eight. She was the only girl I knew."

"What did she do?"

"It's funny. She started crying."

I didn't say anything. I didn't know what to say.

"The only time I ever saw her cry," he said, letting the curtain fall from his hand.

We were quiet for a minute, thinking of Mrs. Brandt, and her sink of lingerie and her air gun and her darted skirts.

"Are they . . ." I found the words slipping from my mouth.

"Are they what?"

"You know, involved. Your dad and Mrs. Brandt."

His eyes widened. "No. No way." Then, "Why would you say that?"

"I didn't *say* anything," I said, surprised. "I was just asking. They're around the same age and—"

"Dad doesn't do that."

"Do what?"

"It was only ever my mother," Jed said, a surprising tremor to his voice. "Just ask him, anyone. He was devoted."

"I'm sure, but it's been more than thirty years—"

"Women were always throwing themselves at him," Jed said, a faint harshness to his tone I'd never heard before. "At conventions, on work travel. Friends tried to set him up. He wouldn't have it. They were relentless, but he would never do that."

"Well, that makes me sorry for him. All those years without . . ."

But I could feel my voice growing smaller, disappearing. Like I'd found myself stumbling into dark woods. Like in a dream when you open a door in your house and find yourself suddenly in a place you don't recognize, an extra room you never knew was there.

"You miss her," I said, my hand on him, his skin rough and burn mottled, "your mom."

I knew firsthand how you could miss someone you never knew, my dad and his crushed hard packs and his cream of wheat technique. Reading stories to me as he stirred it. Tilting the saucepan over the deep brown bowls with the drip glaze around the rim, and the butter swirling, steam rising, and *tut-tut-tut, wait a minute, baby girl, that's hot-hot-hot.*

"I guess so," Jed said, his voice just above a whisper. Then, "This is the sign you're looking for."

"What?"

Jed grinned. "Oh, just a sign I made for a client once. It said, 'This is the sign you're looking for.'"

"You have that in the shop," I said. It was behind the cash register, in hot pink cursive.

"He stiffed me," Jed said, laughing. "So the sign is mine."

Dinner was served on the deck, planked whitefish thick enough to choke a bear, ribboned with piped duchess potatoes.

Hicks stopped by again. Same white moustache, same aviators, but this time with a paper sack of thimbleberries, which I'd never heard of but which grew wild up here.

"Stay for a bite," Doctor Ash insisted, and Hicks did, and we all tried the thimbleberries straight out of the bag, fuzzy and cartoon-red and tart enough to make my tongue burn. Red enough to stain Hicks's white moustache, and Doctor Ash started calling him Yosemite Sam.

The heat still vibrating, the smell of slathered bug spray, a sun-warmed bottle of Bactine squeezed empty, I started to feel a little woozy as the three men began debating the mechanical origin of the suspect smoke coming off the grill. The blackflies and deer-flies and mayflies and midges flitting behind my ears, it was hard to follow what they were saying, and I had to turn away from the strong smell radiating from the whirring lazy Susan of white-fish dip and headcheese spread and crackers Mrs. Brandt had brought out.

It felt like a wedding, overserved at the cocktail reception and you really never knew how to drink hard liquor, least of all that Manhattan someone handed you (*two cherries to match your lips*), and somehow you end up at your appointed seat and suddenly, there's wine pouring over your shoulder and everyone sticky with prime rib at one end of the table, while the other end has already moved along to cake white as Ivory soap, big wedges of it, and ro-settes smearing and you think, *I can't eat anything or I'll die—*

But now Jed was tearing at the fish beside me, talking loudly over a distant spray of backyard fireworks to his dad, reminding him that he, as someone who works in neon, ought to know a thing or two about ignition systems.

And Doctor Ash laughing and telling him to relax and enjoy himself—after all, it wasn't a contest—and Jed knocking his beer over, all of us jumping to our feet to sop up the foam, foam every-where and licking the edges of the fish platter and I jumped up too fast, too-too fast, and why did I think jumping would—

A hand on my shoulder, steadying me. A cool, clean voice in my ear.

"Come with me," Mrs. Brandt said, taking my arm as I rose.

We were in the kitchen, which was remarkably cool.

I felt better already.

Quiet and dark and Mrs. Brandt taking something out of the

icebox—that's what she called it, which reminded me of my grandmother—a foil-wrapped packet she set before me.

"I don't think I can eat."

But she didn't say anything, uncrimping the foil to reveal a small hand pie, glossy and golden, its crust crimped.

"It's so cool in here," I said. "How is it so cool in here?"

"Cross-breeze," Mrs. Brandt said. "Eat."

"I don't . . ." I started, but the pie looked so plump and cozy and it didn't smell at all, and before I knew it, I was picking at the crust, then lifting it to my mouth.

I didn't think I'd ever tasted anything so good, the flaky crust giving way to soft potato tinted pink from the pickled cabbage. I finished it in silence, in four bites, the snap of the crimp last.

"You can get a good pasty most places up here," she said, "but Jed always liked mine best."

"*Pass-tee*," I repeated back, trying the word out. "Well, I can see why."

"Don't tell him I gave you one," she said, rising and pouring me a glass of icy milk from a pitcher. "He made me promise they were all for him."

I smiled, not sure if she was joking or not, or if Jed was.

"Should be hot, with gravy for some, but he was only ever here in the summer, so . . ."

I found myself picking at the crumbs like some kind of animal. I stopped myself.

"The crust was meant to be a handle, right? For miners?" I said, remembering now that Jed had mentioned them on the car ride, the pasties, brought here by the Cornish miners long ago, taking them down in the quarry for their lunch.

"Had a use." Mrs. Brandt nodded. "Meant for gripping, but also kept 'em from poisoning themselves."

I looked at her, letting the last crumbs fall from my fingertip.

"The arsenic on their hands," she said. "They all had arsenic on their hands. So they'd toss the handle after eating."

I smiled at the strange detail, how strange it all was, and the pasty somehow still filling me, fortifying me. Picturing a deep iron mine, at the bottom a towering pile of crimped, poisoned crust.

By then, Mrs. Brandt was back at the icebox, handing me another foil packet "for later."

"Why is it so good?" I asked, gulping the milk, which tasted like snow, or how you imagine snow will taste, splaying your tongue toward the sky.

"Secret ingredient," Mrs. Brandt said with a grin.

"Not arsenic," I said, laughing. Wishing for more milk, like a four-year-old suddenly.

And Mrs. Brandt looked at me, her grin fading and eyes narrowing, her face like a window slamming shut.

"No," she said, moving toward the door. "Lard."

❦

The flies had gone with the sun and now it was the eerie pagan rattle of the cicadas.

Hicks had left and the evening seemed to be winding down, but then suddenly it wasn't.

"Boy, you wouldn't recognize her now," Jed was saying as he slid open the screen door. "Had three kids, as big as a house. A big house."

The rolling laugh came, sung with the cicadas. *Jed, how could you—*

But, thankfully, it wasn't Jed and, honestly, could never be.

It was a man in a baseball cap, tufts of ice-blond hair sticking out, rangy and grinning, a longneck hanging from long fingers, and he had his hand on Jed's shoulder, both of them slapping at each other like schoolboys until he saw something in Jed's eyes and turned to see me. "Oh, I'm a goddamned idiot."

"Jacy, this is Randy the Ripper," Jed said, stepping forward, pulling a chair back for me.

"Randy Pascoe," he said, doing a funny little bow in front of me. "Local troublemaker, cryptocurrency enthusiast, and all-around bad influence."

I smiled, swatting a mosquito away.

"And you must be Jacy," Randy said, pulling off his baseball cap, its brim sweated through. "Jed and I go way back. Townie and troll, teaming up to get into trouble."

"Oh," I said, a little dazed. "I've never met any of Jed's old—"

Jed slid his arms around me. "Isn't she the prettiest?" he said, a huff of beer in my ear, old memories of a frat boy over the keg.

"I'd expect nothing less from you, Jedidiah," Randy said, and the two kept giving each other looks and it was like seventh grade, which boy would try to slide ice cubes down your back in the cafeteria, which would try to snap your bra during assembly.

"These two gave me untold grief," Doctor Ash said, appearing suddenly from nowhere. "Teeth knocked out jet-skiing. Bar fight over in Manistique. Drunken Bigfoot hunting in the middle of the night."

"Bigfoot was never drunk!" Randy shouted. "If he had been, we'd've caught him."

"Not with the Whistler," Doctor Ash said, winking at Randy, who let out another peal of deep-throated laughter. "He'd have blown your cover."

"The Whistler! I forgot!"

I didn't know what anyone was talking about, some secret boy code.

And when I turned, Jed's face had gone bright red like I'd never seen before.

"Jacy, your boy wasn't always the dutiful son," Doctor Ash said. "Sometimes he didn't want to go fishing with his old man. Can you believe it?"

He explained how Jed had tried to get out of a planned fishing trip because he wanted to go off swimming with a girl.

"I went, didn't I?" Jed said. "I just had other stuff on my mind."

"He got a bite, went to pull the line and reel when it snapped and the bait and lure and bitty tungsten weight came back on him like a slingshot right to the mouth," Doctor Ash said. "Knocked his two front teeth out."

I winced, looking at poor Jed.

"And he didn't just lisp. He practically whistled. They called him the Whistler."

"We sure did!" Randy crowed.

Jed looked at us, poker-faced. Doctor Ash's eyes glittered at me. We both started to laugh a little.

"Oh, Jed, c'mon," I said, my hand on his chest. "It's adorable. You're adorable."

It was irresistible. Jed could be so reserved, inscrutable. But seeing him with an old pal helped fill in all those empty spaces. And Randy seemed okay, settled down now and sitting beside me, showing me pictures of his two boys, six and eight, a pair of bruisers, fair-haired and pigeon-chested, holding high a fish big as the younger, both of them making duck faces at the camera.

"They look very mighty," I said, feeling Randy's eager smile, slapping his wallet shut again and whacking Jed on the back once more.

"That'll be you soon enough," he said to him, "taking your son out there to snag some champion pike."

"Maybe," Jed said. "We don't know if it's a boy or a girl."

"Best fisherman I ever knew was Mrs. Brandt in there," Doctor Ash said, eyes flitting toward me.

"Hell, Stacey!" Randy said, then turned to me to clarify: "That's my lady."

"Sometimes," Jed said, smiling at Randy.

"Sometimes?" I said, smiling at Randy too. Wanting to play along, to not be the straight man, the old lady.

"Sometimes," Randy said, averting his eyes, a cool glint there. "When she doesn't decide to change the locks."

Finally, Randy said he had to go, had a date with a nine-ball over with some pals—*yes, remember your old buddy Tommy Tickler*—at Eddie's Teepee.

"Oh, boy, Eddie's Teepee," Doctor Ash called out from the grill. "Jed's favorite."

"My favorite," Jed repeated, looking at his dad. "Boy, I forgot all about that place."

"Eddie's Teepee," Doctor Ash said, "where Jed had his first taste."

"Those days, they'd serve you at twelve," Jed said.

"You mean beer, right?" Randy laughed. They all laughed, I laughed too.

Everyone seemed to know a thing or two about Eddie's Teepee and finally I said, "Are you sure this isn't a strip club?"

They all laughed harder now and seemed very pleased with me. I was one of the boys, or something. It was funny seeing Jed this way, Jed who had no close male friends I'd ever heard him mention.

"Eddie's still family owned?" Jed asked.

"It is, friend," Randy said, his eyebrow raised.

Doctor Ash cleared his throat and there was an awkward pause.

I could feel a question hovering in the air. Jed asked Randy if they still had the purple felt and the old air hockey tables and would their old euchre buddy Wheedy be there, gosh, he hadn't seen him since he flipped over on his dirt bike fifteen years ago and literally broke his neck.

"Why don't you go too?" I suggested, because Jed's longing was so visceral it moved me. Because Jed never had any nostalgia about anything, scant friends even from college, and he had never mentioned his past life as a Midwestern good old boy until Randy appeared to inspire it. Or until this place did.

"Oh, no," Jed said. "I'm not leaving you here."

And it sounded funny when he said it. *Leaving me here.*

"Don't be silly," I said. "Your dad can entertain me."

And Jed, looking at me with beer-blurred eyes, boyish and charming, looking in my eyes to make sure, really sure.

"Get outta here now," I said, shooing at him like a cartoon wife until finally he guessed it'd be okay for an hour or two if Randy was game.

And Randy, grinning, pushing his hair back with his hat, was game.

"Now you're stuck with the old man," Doctor Ash was saying, dragging an Adirondack chair down the slope for me.

"Hardly," I said, smiling. Enjoying the new quiet, even the cicadas retreating as the husky heat gave over at last to a starry coolness, the trees shivering and the smell everywhere of that wild mint Mrs. Brandt gathered for the iced tea, studding the fruit salad.

"How you feeling?" he asked as we sat, my body releasing itself from untold tensions gathered through the day, so long and strange and sunstruck. "Can't be easy, a trip like this, with child. All these eyes on you, everyone with their opinions."

And suddenly I felt my eyes go soft, unfocused. It felt like such a kindness for him to notice and to say it. So simple and yet.

"You must've had a great bedside manner," I said, the words slipping from me and sounding odd, inappropriate.

He smiled in the blue light, looking younger, far younger and so much like Jed, but with a kind crinkle at his eyes, a crinkle that said he knew about things and was sorry.

"Do you ever miss it?" I asked quickly. "Practicing medicine?"

"I never wanted to be anything other than a sawbones," he said. "My old man practiced family medicine in Romeo, Michigan, for forty-six years. I loved watching him pack and unpack his beat-up leather bag. Every time, I'd ask him to explain what this was, what that was. One day, he turned the tables on me. One by one, he'd hand me an instrument and I'd say, *That's the plessor.* Or the tongue depressor. The blood pressure cuff. Even the tourniquet." He laughed. "I can still remember how that bag smelled, like rubbing alcohol and Starlight mints and my dad's secret cigars. The ding in the handle from the time he underestimated a ninety-year-old woman's reflexes."

I was nodding and nodding, thinking of my perfectly sensible ob-gyn, Doctor Anwar, a year younger than me and forever swiping her fingers on a tablet for the seventeen minutes of our visit, my body swallowed by the paper robe and its stringy ties, my legs veinstruck under the fluorescents.

"I had every intention of being a GP until I keeled over, just like my dad," he said. "But I was only a year out of my residency when . . ." His voice thickened and he cleared his throat, looking off into the blue-black distance, past the branches still heavy with summer heat and into the cool woods beyond. "Somehow, after Jed's mother passed . . ."

I felt a twinge. But in the closeness of night, the grass tickling my ankles, I thought, *If not now when,* and the words tumbled from my mouth. "If you don't mind . . . I mean, Jed doesn't talk about it. What . . . what happened?"

"Blood clot. Her blood pressure spiked and spiked, even the feeling of the cuff on her arm. . . . She was in such agony." He paused, cleared his throat again. "And then suddenly, I just saw it. Her face. It changed. It looked so calm, so . . . blank. I said her name and nothing except this panicked look in her eye. Pulled her blankets back and scraped the bottom of her feet with my fingernails. And she didn't move. At all.

"That was when her face changed again. Like she was seeing something so . . . so unfathomable."

He turned to me, his jaw tight.

"She didn't make it through the hour. We held hands the whole time. Her hand seemed to dissolve in mine. That's what it felt like. Like a pillar of salt.

"I took six months off, strapped my boots on, and threw myself into taking care of Jed. He needed me.

"Finally, the hospital came calling. Everyone told me it would be good for me to return to work. They said it'd all come back to me, once I got back into it. But in the end it never came back. Instead, there was this dread."

He shook his head.

"I'd just look at my bag, the one my dad had given me when I graduated—hand stitched, brass clasps, just like his must've looked like a few thousand strep throats ago. It had been sitting by the door since the night I took Jed's mother to the hospital, her water breaking on the kitchen floor. And every time I looked at the bag, I just saw . . . loss."

I could see it as he said it, the air humming between us. The bag, black as coal, square-mouthed, its handle gleaming like a smile, a leer.

"So, I moved over to the dark side. Big pharma. Then med tech. It was good to be surrounded by people. It was good to . . . be useful. To let go of ego. This notion that I was there to save everybody. Because the only one I needed to save was Jed."

He looked down at his hands and added, more softly, "We needed each other."

. . .

It was late and the mosquitoes were climbing up and down my legs, but we'd put the radio on and were just finishing a nightcap. Doctor Ash made me something for my stomach, a virgin cocktail called a Femme Fatale, bitters and soda water, a splash of grenadine.

"How fatal can she be," I asked, "without the booze?"

"Oh, far more so," he said with a grin. "She's saving the liquor for her mark, her stooge, her hapless patsy instead."

We started walking toward the house, a pointy golden triangle up the slope.

"Or she slipped him a mickey," I said, smiling, too, sipping the last of it through my tiny red straw, pretending I was at a swank nightclub somewhere.

"Ah," he said, still smiling. "I knew it! There's a man-eater in there!"

And it was so funny because it was so ridiculous.

When I looked up at the house, windows blazing, it seemed stuffy and wood-warped and airless. I didn't want to try to make myself comfortable in the bed upstairs, the mildew tang, listening to the bugs and the squeaking floorboards.

But, as if on cue, a song came on the radio, crackling through an open window as we headed toward the patio doors, the opening chords of a jaunty, soft rock song I could remember from childhood, a duet between a honey-voiced man and a raspy-voiced woman. One of those swaying, snapping songs you'd see on old variety shows, singing with such lightness, even carelessness, about laying their wounded hearts on the table and stumbling into love.

"I remember this!" I said, some distant memory of childhood, parents dancing at the summer block party, Aunt Laraine with her shoes off and her feet black and my own mom smoking a Benson & Hedges on the porch, a rind of watermelon in my sticky hand.

I found myself swaying slightly and Doctor Ash reached out to steady me, and then we both fell into a gentle, stutter-step spin.

"You can dance," I said, surprised, and he twirled me one last time, and I was laughing, so gentle scarcely his fingertips touching me, and my own legs so clumsy, my right foot landing on his, my ankle turning and Doctor Ash reaching out to steady me once more. "But I can't."

"Oh, you do just fine," he said, smiling at me.

"My body doesn't feel mine these days. Well, I guess it's not. Or at least not just my own. My bones feel like taffy."

"It's the relaxin. It's a hormone your body releases when you're pregnant. It loosens your pelvis and hip joints. Softens and widens your—*one's*—cervix." Was Doctor Ash blushing a little? It was hard to tell in the blue dark of the lawn, but I found myself smiling.

"It's not really called relaxin, is it?" I grinned.

"Doesn't it put your mind at ease?" he said. "And yet some women find it . . ."

He turned and the porch light came on.

"Find it what?" I asked.

Then I saw it, the flush on his neck.

"Well, let's just say they like it," he said.

A giggle slipped from my mouth. To see him so courtly and boyish.

I felt my own skin burning, too, and my hand reaching for the screen door, Doctor Ash behind me and his reflection in the patio glass.

Both of us clearing our throats and then a nervous titter from my mouth.

"Well, Jacy," he said as we stepped inside, "we are so lucky to have you."

And I turned around in the dark interior and smiled and wanted to say something, too, about how welcome he'd made me feel, how cared for.

My face still burning and the chug of a fan somewhere and Doctor Ash reaching for the light and his arm brushing mine and—

The house lit up, suddenly, the twin beams of Randy's SUV and, through the front window, Jed stumbling out, pushing open the front door.

⁊

There was brief, slurry chatter of what a good time Jed had had, how much he needed that, and how grateful he was, his arms slipping around me, tangling with mine.

It was maybe the first time I'd ever seen Jed truly drunk and it was good and not surprising to know he was a sweet drunk, a little embarrassed and full of apologies.

You're the best wife, he kept saying, *so much better than I ever deserved.*

I stayed downstairs a few minutes, turning off lights and getting water for Jed. I could hear him above, lurching loudly from bathroom to bedroom. I wondered if he was getting sick, because he'd said something about shots of some blue raspberry vodka concoction they called the Methadone and wouldn't it be something if we'd both thrown up in the same chipped porcelain toilet in the same day?

Pouring a glass of water, I could smell Doctor Ash's aftershave on my hands, like fresh-cut limes. I could smell everything now, it seemed, even the carpet glue, the wood paste in the staircase post, the one Jed told me that he knocked off as a kid after one too many of his sneaking swoops down the railing.

But the aftershave was nice.

When was the last time I'd danced, had Jed or I ever danced? And Doctor Ash's ease, a twirl, making one feel slight, girlish, good.

Then I remembered, the weight in my pocket, and it was Mrs. Brandt's pasty in its foil.

Without stopping or thinking, I unwrapped it and ate it standing up, the house dark around me.

I ate the whole thing and it tasted even better than the first.

Just as I began to tiptoe up the stairs, I saw Mrs. Brandt looming at the top, the air vent blowing behind her, her red hair burning under the chandelier.

There was something white billowing in her hands. Ghostlike.

"Mrs. Brandt," I said, my hand on my belly in surprise.

"I noticed you didn't have a robe," she said, moving away from the air vent, the whiteness settling into her arms. "Jed thought you might like one."

"Jed?" I whispered, climbing the stairs toward her. Why was she upstairs at this hour? Or in the house at all?

"He explained how you were cold at night. And it's not an en suite bathroom, so . . ."

"I can't take your robe," I said as she rested the garment in my hands. It was white eyelet, with a ruffle down the front, like something you might find in a country store.

"It's not mine," she said. "We had one on hand. It's never been worn. If you don't like it—"

She handed me its package as if in proof, a plastic sleeve yellow from what I guessed were years in the linen closet.

"I . . . I just don't think I need—"

"The choice is yours," she said, heading down the stairs past me. "Good night."

And she was gone.

"Hit me if I snore," Jed said, collapsing on the bed.

"What if you whistle?" I teased, throwing the bedspread over him.

He was silent for a second, as if he'd forgotten that I knew. *The Whistler.*

"He did that," he mumbled heavily into the pillow. "He did that on purpose."

"Who?"

"Dad. When my fishing line started shaking, he said, *Look at those girls sunbathing on the shore.* I turned and the line snapped."

I looked down at Jed, his burnished neck, his face hidden, dented deep into the pillow.

"Why would he do that?"

"He wanted to teach me a lesson."

I thought maybe he was dreaming. It didn't make any sense.

"What was the lesson?" I asked.

But he didn't answer.

"That doesn't sound like your dad," I said, the lime smell gone from my hands.

"You don't know my dad," he murmured. "You haven't even met him yet."

"What?" I said. "What?"

But Jed was silent, drifting into sleep, his breath coming fast and desperate.

It took me a long while to shudder into sleep, Jed's beery breath in my ear, the shivers of the branch against the window, all the strange house sounds.

It was all so heavy, Jed's mother, everything that had happened. It explained so much about Jed, the heaviness always inside of him, the hunger always for love. There was a desperation in it. Once, a few months in, I'd had to cancel plans and Jed hung up on me, brooded from a distance for days, and I'd had the thought: *There's a hole in him I can never fill. Never.* I'd forgotten about that, hadn't I?

Finally, the sleep came, like a cool sheet across me, and I was dreaming I was back outside in the blue-black grass with Doctor Ash, and he was telling me stories of kissing girls in white dresses in the dark pool house. . . . We sat in a gazebo, we rocked on porch swings, and I wore a white flower in my hair, petals tickling and he was whispering in my ear, the cinnamon oil in his hair tingling in my nose, and I kept saying to myself, *There's nothing wrong with this, there's nothing wrong with this. . . .*

The crash came, thunderous, like a tree had landed on the house, nearly splitting it in two.

"Don't move," Jed was saying, loud and voice shaking. "Don't move."

And he was standing at the window. Staring out, glassy-eyed.

"It was just an animal," he said.

"Just an animal?"

"Maybe that mountain lion."

"We're on the second floor," I said, wondering if I was still dreaming.

"They can jump really high," he said. "And that sounded like its scream."

"What scream?"

But then I remembered I'd heard it, made it a part of my dream. The porch swing rocking and something in the dark of the lawn and the flower falling from my ear and where had Mrs. Brandt gone and was she behind the bushes with her air gun now? Why was she crouching behind the bushes, watching us?

He puts cinnamon oil in his hair, like General Custer, Mrs. Brandt's whisper in my ear. *That's how you know he's coming.*

I'd shut my eyes and reached for Jed, the crazy thought coming in my head:

Captain Murderer! Captain Murderer!

␟

We fell back asleep, somehow. Drifting off and at the same time my heart was still thudding. Was it real? Did that happen? Or had it all been part of one long dream?

But no more dreams came and I fell deep into a bottomless sleep, where everything beneath you is a coolness, seductive and endless.

DAY FIVE

The smell woke me. Sharp, earthy. Coffee beans, coffee grounds. A smell so strong and enticing, I rose instantly, my chest, my back sweat-wetted from the night.

Sitting up, the smell stronger. Suddenly oily, fishy even. My mouth wet.

I remembered something about pregnant women and coffee, something chemical, attraction and repulsion, but then there were so many things about pregnant women.

Pregnant women and soft cheeses, deli meat, tuna, raw eggs, uncooked sprouts, hot tubs, oven cleaners, electric blankets, cat litter. It went on and on. I had tried reading the books, all the ones people had given me. Stacked high back in our apartment, they became the place from which Jed's dirty shirts or socks or jeans hung.

The number-one thing pregnant women were supposed to avoid was stress. But what those books caused was stress.

Still, the smell . . .

Don't be sick, Jacy, I told myself. *Don't.*

I closed my eyes, pushed it away.

The robe Mrs. Brandt gave me sat on the foot of the bed. It was so funny to think of it now. Had she thought there was something unseemly in the oversized tee I wore to bed, or on the way to the jiggle-handled bathroom?

I put on the robe, stiff-starch against my skin, too long, too everything, like a costume, or one of those voluminous disposable wraps they give you at spas, the spindly ties twisted from heavy laundry.

Inside the bathroom, Jed was coughing up a death rattle. He never could drink, could he. *But then again, you haven't known each other that long.*

What a strange thought, like my mom invading my groggy brain. We'd known each other more than two years, after all.

Coffee. Its acid gasp now impossible to deny and I stumbled down the stairs to sneak a quick cup.

There at the kitchen table sat Doctor Ash, sparkly eyed, freshly shaved, impeccable seersucker shirt. And Mrs. Brandt beside him, holding the coffeepot. Good mornings, good mornings.

"I have to get some of that," I said. "The smell! What's your secret? Some special UP blend?"

Reaching for a mug, I saw the jar behind her. Taster's Choice, a jar, freeze-dried crystals. How was it possible?

But Mrs. Brandt's eyes were on me, and now Doctor Ash's lashes flickered, both of them looking at me now, a curious twin gaze.

"Oh," I said. "The robe. Thanks again. It's a little big, but—"

"I'll call Doctor Craig," Mrs. Brandt said to Doctor Ash, rising.

"Is something wrong?" I said, holding out the mug. Wouldn't anyone let me have a cup of that coffee?

But there was the look on Doctor Ash's face now, his tanned fingers thumping on the table. A tight, funny look, not like himself at all. Like someone else.

Mrs. Brandt was dialing now, the old rotary phone on the kitchen wall.

"Jacy," Doctor Ash said, rising too now.

"What's wrong?" I said again. Then, "What's wrong with me?"

Because now I felt it, too, the warmness on the back of my leg, the stickiness I'd taken for sweat.

I looked over my shoulder to see the back of the white robe sheeted red.

Bright red, clown red.

"Did you hear the crash?" I found myself saying, my head light. "Last night. Was it a mountain lion?"

"Let's get you sitting down," Doctor Ash was saying, his arms around my shoulders as my legs started to twitch, a tingling in me, my body pitching right.

"But it doesn't hurt at all," I told them, in a high, odd voice, not my own.

There were towels, so many towels, a sticky pile at my feet and Jed was pulling the car around.

"It stopped," I kept saying, backing away from them all, moving toward the stairs. "Just let me go change."

No one wanted me to change, but I changed, pulling on a sundress because it was easiest, trying to wipe down the browning blood between my legs.

Downstairs, Jed was shouting from the doorway that we had to go to the doctor, we had to go now.

No one wanted me to change, but I changed.

⁓

Doctor Ash insisted on driving his black colossus, smoothly managing every bump and crevice, every salt-pocked pothole. He knew them all.

"You're going to be okay," Jed kept saying, even though I knew I would. The bleeding had stopped, the unsnapping inside snapping up again.

Bleeding happened, of course. I'd heard about it, hadn't I?

God, the body was a nightmare, a miracle, both, I thought, my hand on my stomach.

"Could be a hematoma," Doctor Ash was saying, with Jed rattling off questions to me: "Are you cramping? Do you feel any pressure?"

I gave him a look, but he missed it, too busy with his questions.

"Has this happened before?" he asked.

"No," I said. "Do you think I wouldn't tell you?"

"Maybe you didn't want me to worry," Jed said. I could see Doctor Ash watching me in the rearview mirror. "I don't know."

"No," I repeated, "it's never happened."

Both of them watching me, Jed reaching for my hand.

I kept telling myself I should feel flattered, these nervous knights in dented armor.

But I didn't, quite.

✌

Doctor Craig opened the door with a smile, big-chested with a silver crewcut, his voice booming as he greeted me.

"Come on in, little lady," he said, moving to the sink to wash his hands. On the back of the door hung a fishing hat festooned with feathers and glittering hooks.

I was in another robe, a paper one this time, and sitting the only way you can sit in those robes, like a prim church matron, except my knees wouldn't lock.

Doctor Craig was talking, telling me how he went to medical school down in Ann Arbor with Hank Ash back in the day and that any daughter-in-law of Hank Ash was a daughter-in-law of his own, except his own daughter-in-law hadn't waited until her thirties to have kids, though now, four kids later, he kinda wished she'd stop—but who wants to listens to an old man, eh?

I nodded vaguely. It all felt a little haphazard, like the time I had a UTI on spring break and my friends summoned the "hotel doctor," a man in a sherbet-colored sports shirt and Bermuda shorts with a duffel bag of pills and rum on his breath.

Don't be a snob, I told myself. Just because Doctor Craig was a "country doctor"—was that the right phrase?—didn't mean he wasn't a good one. In fact, he was probably better. Better bedside manner even, right?

But what did that matter anyway? And what did it matter if no one had yet asked me if I wanted to come here at all? I was bleeding and that was what mattered. The only thing that mattered.

Doctor Craig squinted at me, as if sensing something, then dried his hands quickly, reaching for his clipboard.

"Now, I know you're upset," he said, looking at my intake forms.

"I'm not upset—"

"—but many things can cause bleeding in pregnancy. Many harmless things. Hormones, a minor infection. Intercourse."

"I'm not upset," I repeated.

Intercourse. Flashing on the sneaking moments with Jed on the pushed-together beds. The roughness, the scrape of the bed's wheels.

"I know it's common," I said. "I'm sure it's fine."

"Me too," Doctor Craig said, clicking his pen with one hand and patting the exam table with the other. "Now, hop on up here, eh?"

⚘

In a private waiting area, a curtained-off corner, I drank water, twenty-four ounces of it.

"Gotta get that bladder full up," Doctor Craig said jollily.

He wanted to do an ultrasound. *Janie, roll out the clicky-clackedy!*

The cart jangling down the short corridor.

Through the curtain, through the wood-paneled warren of tiny rooms, I could hear a constant low thrum of male voices. I could see, through the curtain gap, an ajar door, the seated knees of Jed and Doctor Ash, jeans and khaki, Styrofoam coffee cups in their curled hands.

I drank more water, tepid and sweet.

Doctor Craig wanted to do an ultrasound.

My stomach slicked, Doctor Craig loomed above me, whistling along to the Muzak piped through the drop ceiling.

Whoosh-whoosh, the machine hummed. Doctor Craig's tongue clicking. The smell of old coffee.

I wished it were my doctor, Doctor Anwar, cool, tight-lipped, unflappable, the rings on her hands glinting. Her pretty hands.

I'd never thought anything was wrong, even feeling the blood sticky on my thighs.

Inside, I knew nothing was wrong.

But now, after the car ride, after Doctor Craig, after peering out into the waiting room and seeing Jed, his leg jiggling ceaselessly, his father beside, speaking softly, saying things I couldn't hear. Reassuring things, I guess. *Don't you worry, son.*

Whoosh-whoosh-whoosh-whoosh.

My eyes fixed on the grainy screen.

What if, what if . . .

It was taking too long. I thought suddenly of that time with Jed, the one we'd decided was when we'd conceived. It was on Jed's birthday.

I came to the shop after hours, ready to take him out to dinner. Jed, moody, said something about a difficult client, an uncomfortable exchange, something. *What happened,* I asked again and again, but he kept shaking it off, sitting in his wheeling desk chair looking surly, mean. Finally, I'd climbed onto his lap, trying to soothe him.

How fast it had turned, and exciting, his hands gripping my thighs, fingers rough. It was quick, intense. Only his desk lamp on, the darkness of the shop at night, the glowing edges of the neon, the sign above blinking, THIS IS THE SIGN YOU'RE LOOKING FOR.

I have to get it, I kept saying, meaning my diaphragm. But I didn't have it with me and he wouldn't have waited and I didn't want to either.

Happy birthday, Jed. Happy birthday to you.

Later, the feelings still shuddering inside me, we laughed about it. It was like being on drugs, he said. And that gash on Jed's forehead from hitting the desk corner, and later, my taping bandage after bandage on it, because they kept falling off and both of us laughing at the bathroom sink, laughing so hard because it was like a freebie. We hadn't meant to do any of it, least of all skipping my diaphragm, because I'd wanted to wait at least a year or two before we even tried.

This is the sign you're looking for This is the sign you're looking for This is the sign you're looking for. . . .

I guess I never did find out what he'd been so mad about, so upset when I got there. I guess I'd forgotten and never asked.

Because now we were having a baby. And the baby would be beautiful, ours.

Whoosh-whoosh-whoosh-whoosh.

The screen seeming to sizzle, pop.

Whoosh-whoosh-whoosh-whoosh.

· · ·

By the time he found the heartbeat, I burst into tears.

"Well," Doctor Craig said, gliding the instrument again and again, staring at the blurry screen beside him.

A long pause, then, "Well, well. He was right. Old Hank was right."

It had to do with my placenta.

My placenta was in the wrong place, doing the wrong things.

"I've never heard of this before," I said, making me think again of that stack of books at home, unread.

"It's fairly common," he said. We had moved now, it seemed, from *common* to *fairly common*. "Your placenta's lying low in the uterus. As the uterus stretches and grows, the placenta can shear off . . ."

He saw my wince and cocked that head again, lowering his reading glasses on his nose. There weren't jokes anymore, no more folksy bits.

". . . and cause bleeding. And if the placenta continues to migrate over the cervix, we'd need to do a C-section. Or your ob-gyn would."

A cesarean. I knew several women who'd had them, of course, including Jen, my friend since we took studio art together in college. Jen, who'd elected to have one at week forty of an endless, fraught pregnancy, and everything had worked out, her charming two-year-old Minnie, with her mother's flossy black hair, snub nose, her fists forever reaching for me when I visited, clambering up my legs.

"But how did it move? The placenta," I said. "I've been careful. . . ."

"I'm sure you have," Doctor Craig said.

My brain flurrying, remembering lifting those cubbyholes at work, and were all those paints truly non-toxic, the paints that constantly covered my hands and dappled my forearms, shook onto my ankles? Hadn't I used a weighted blanket once? Was that time I cleaned an out-of-town friend's kitty litter box before or after I got pregnant? Had Jed and I done things in bed we shouldn't? Had we been too rough. Had I been careless.

Maybe he saw something in my face because Doctor Craig looked at a slim page stapled to a manila folder.

"Well," he said, "certain behaviors put you at higher risk."

"Behaviors?"

"Smoking. Cocaine."

"Never had money," I joked.

But he didn't seem to hear me, continuing, "Over thirty-five."

"Is that a behavior now? I'm thirty-two."

But he knew that, didn't he? He saw it on the page before him.

"Or other things," Doctor Craig said, more coolly now. "Uterine scars from past surgeries."

I didn't say anything.

"Fibroids, for instance. Or an abortion."

I didn't say anything.

He looked at me, nudging his reading glasses down. Squinting at me, his thick eyebrows knotted.

"And women who've committed two or more abortions," he said evenly, "have twice the risk of developing placenta previa."

I paused. *Committed.* Had he said that?

But he was writing in his folder now, slant-wise and illegible. Then I remembered the intake forms the receptionist had me sign, the one about permission to access medical records.

I shifted on the paper beneath me, looking around. The wall calendar, the faded anatomy poster, the tufted tub of wipes.

"But are you sure?" I said. "About the placenta. I mean, it wasn't that much blood and—"

"Some women don't bleed at all, but that doesn't mean we don't pay attention," he said, a slight sharpness in his voice. "But we'll need to do a transvag to confirm." His eyes flitted up at me. "A transvaginal ultrasound, that is."

"Okay," I said. "Let's do that."

He nodded, a thin-lipped expression.

"It'll take a few days. We'll need to get our sonographer to come over from Marquette. With these cases, I use her. Nice girl, very sharp. We can get her tomorrow or day after. Or after the holiday. Or you can go there, but you really shouldn't be in a car if you can help it." Adding, a hint of a smile, of his folksier self, "Not even with Hank's suspension."

I nodded, feeling sticky under the paper gown.

"And avoid sex," he said, his eyes averted. "If you can help it."

Everything had changed so quickly. It was subtle, but there. Women knew the difference, a hair's-breadth and yet everything.

I'd come in as his friend's lovely expectant daughter-in-law. Now he seemed less sure what I was.

When I came out of the exam room, the waiting area was empty.

The receptionist looked at me a long minute before pointing to Doctor Craig's office.

The door open a sliver, I could see all three of them huddled close in there: Doctor Craig at his computer, Doctor Ash leaning toward him, his face animated, Jed cracking his knuckles, that nervous tic.

All three of them in there, talking about me.

This isn't right, I thought. Not right at all.

"What's going on here?" I said, knocking on and pushing in the door.

All three of them turned their heads, looking at me. Me in my wrinkled tangerine sundress, flecked at the thighs with browned blood.

"Honey, we just—" Jed started.

"Jacy dear, this is on me," Doctor Ash said. "When I called, I'd mentioned placenta previa and Whit here—Doctor Craig—was only confirming—"

"Jed," I said, "may I talk to you privately?"

The only place was the stark white restroom, Jed leaning against the sink and trying to explain. That this is how doctors of a certain generation worked, especially old colleagues, and why were we wasting time on this when, after all, it was my condition we should be focusing on.

"But, Jed, they're connected," I said. "It's my body."

"Of course it is," he said, his face so red, sunburst or hungover from his night with Randy. So red in the white-tiled room, a slick of foamy white soap on the mirror behind him.

"It's your body," he repeated. "And our baby."

"Don't do that," I said, my voice wobbly, all of it crashing through me now. "Jed, you shouldn't be in there talking about my body without me there."

But he had his arms wrapped around me now.

"I was afraid of this," he whispered into my hair.

"Of what?"

But he didn't say anything, and I could feel the sonogram jelly still slathering me, warm and growing.

It turned out the sonographer was available, after all. Or another one was. Because by the time we came out, the receptionist wanted to escort me back to the exam room.

"Sandy's a class act," Doctor Craig was saying. "And why wait a day or two, right?"

"If that's what Jacy wants," Doctor Ash said solemnly. Looking at me, "Is that what you'd like? Get it over with, avoid the to and fro, the wondering?"

I paused, wishing suddenly, improbably, that my mom was there. What would she say, do. *Tell me again why you need to do this?*

"Tell me again," I said, "why you need to do this?"

Because of course I would do it. I wouldn't wait. I wanted to know. But I didn't like how things were operating, didn't like the closed doors, the sidebars, the confabs while I was in another room, closed off, shivering in a paper gown, my feet just moments ago in the air.

"It's the gold standard for detecting placenta previa," Doctor Craig said, a funny hitch in his voice, his eyes darting past me to Doctor Ash.

Sandy the sonographer stood over me. Her pastel pink mask sucking in and out, she asked me how I was enjoying the Yoop, how she hoped the Yoopers were treating me well.

Sandy was nice, gentle.

The wand, pale gray, like a flashlight, a vibrator. So different from the one Doctor Craig had used on my belly, shaped like a sweater shaver.

I looked up at the ceiling again, the pocks in the drywall.

Snap! went the condom Sandy stretched over the wand.

The *wand*, the *probe*. Wand sounded so sprightly. Probe seemed a better word.

Transducer, that was the real word, like something out of science fiction.

Probe was the right word.

. . .

The hum of the machine, imagining the sound waves bouncing around inside me, making pictures of the inside of me.

Pictures of the inside of me, giving away secrets, if I had any. We all do.

"Now, we're being real careful here," she said, "don't you worry."

"I'm not worried," I said, my voice creaking with worry.

"It's real common," she said. That word again.

"No one ever told me," I said softly.

"My sister-in-law had it at five months," Sandy said. "By month eight it was gone."

"Really?" My neck bending, trying to look at her. "It goes away?"

"Most of the time the placenta shifts back where it belongs all on its own," she said.

Why didn't Doctor Craig tell me that? I thought. It would have been nice—important, even—to tell me that.

The placenta shifts back, like those old ideas about the "floating womb."

I could feel myself breathing again, listening to Sandy's voice, hearing the slur of the machine.

Sandy was nice, reassuring. I thought about Sandy and her sister-in-law, both of them around a kitchen table, a forelocked baby in a bounce chair, both of them drinking Lipton tea in stone mugs and remembering how worried they were, and now all the worries were gone.

Soon enough, it was over, Sandy handing me packets of wipes, smiling sunnily.

"And see? No blood," she said, smiling above me.

"Blood?" I asked, fumbling with the wipes.

"Not everyone wants the transvag," she said, "in case it disrupts the placenta, makes you bleed."

"Oh," I said, the words not quite landing. "No one told me that."

"Tell Mrs. Brandt, I sure could use a tin of her pasties," Sandy said. "Mine never come out half so good."

"I'll tell her," I said, my eyes dry and aching from the fluorescents. I guess everyone knew everyone up here. "Thank you."

"I'm glad I could help," she said. "I don't usually work Wednesdays, but when I heard how upset you were—well, moms gotta stick together."

Her smile spreading.

"So what does this mean?" I asked, dressed once again, my sundress rippled, stiff.

"Vigilance," Doctor Craig said briskly. "These babies tend to get out one way or another."

"Okay," I said. "But what do I need to do?"

Outside, Jed was pacing the waiting room. His worry, his pitched anxiety, seemed to hum through the wall.

"Regular ultrasounds to monitor it," he said, writing something down with a thick brass pen. All the folksiness was long gone. In its place, the vague aura of an assistant principal. "And, well, the safest path is bedrest."

"What?" I said. "By bedrest you mean . . ."

Bedrest sounded so serious, severe. It called to mind Victorian women cloistered in canopied beds, in beds swathed in mosquito nets, choking from malaria, tuberculosis, smallpox, cholera, neurasthenia, wandering womb.

"I'm not *ordering* it—"

"I need to talk to my ob-gyn," I blurted.

"Of course," he said, capping his pen, shoving it in his pocket. "Of course you do."

I nodded tightly.

"The bedrest is to help with the biggest risk: bleeding," he said. "Especially once we get into the third trimester."

"Okay," I said. Third trimester, it seemed so far away. And Sandy's sister-in-law, well, it just went away. Third trimester and we'd be back home, with Doctor Anwar and our apartment and my placenta drifting—

"And there's other possible complications we'd like to avoid."

"Like what," I said softly.

"The placenta doesn't attach to the uterus as it should, slows your baby's growth. Or preterm birth, which can bring its own complications. Or, potentially, birth defects." He clicked his pen again, watching me. "But that's not gonna happen, sweetheart."

Then, handing me a booklet, something, he started talking, kept talking. Guidelines, do's and don't's, *How You Can Make the Most of Your Bedrest.*

Sandy had been so reassuring. Sandy had told me how common it was, how often it resolved itself. Sandy hadn't said anything about the baby's development, about birth defects.

". . . any questions?"

I looked up, rubbing my eyes, straightening my back. "I'm going to talk to my doctor."

"You do that," he said, rising.

I nodded and rose, too, taking his proffered hand, his pale hand, smooth like a baby's.

But for a second, I couldn't move. He held the door, a flicker of impatience.

"You didn't tell me," I said. "No one did."

"Tell you what, dear?"

"That it might go away. The placenta previa."

"Didn't I?" he said, distracted.

"And that sticking that thing inside me might make it worse."

"The transducer? Oh, no," he said dismissively, his hand in the air, "never with Sandy. She's got the magic touch."

⁂

On the endless crawl home, the speedometer never exceeding twenty-five miles per hour, I never said a word.

My brain was buzzing, distracted. Everything about it was confusing, these papers still clasped in my fingers. I couldn't figure out where to sit my thoughts, where to rest them and sift through them.

I couldn't stop thinking about that moment after the diagnosis when Jed and Doctor Ash first saw me. How—as I entered the waiting room, my hair disheveled, my breasts oddly cinched from dressing so quickly—they'd looked at me like a naughty child, something. A body on display, a criminal in a lineup, a squirmy specimen under glass.

Jed, like he didn't recognize me. Like I was a stranger.

And Doctor Ash, like he'd known me a hundred years or more. Like he knew all about me.

Not really, of course. But that was how it felt.

But then, back in his office, there had been Doctor Craig's change in tone, demeanor. After the ultrasound, then again after the diagnosis.

Women who've committed two or more abortions.

It was a statement, not a question. But it felt like a question and, vaguely, a trap.

Because it was possible that, by then, Doctor Craig had already received my medical records. A click of the button these days.

Two or more? No, not me, I might have said, truthfully.

But that felt like giving something away. And I didn't want to give him anything.

I've only had one, I might have said. Because he might already know it, a checked box or an entry in my medical history. *Pregnancy termination.*

But even if he knew, he didn't really know. He didn't understand.

That was part of being female, wasn't it? Intuiting, each time, what men didn't want to know.

All the things men really didn't want to know.

It was so long ago, nearly a decade.

He was my boyfriend for a few months, both of us twenty-three and still figuring everything out.

He was a bad boyfriend. Not my only bad boyfriend, but the one who hung most darkly in my head, not because of the abortion but because the wanting was so great in me in ways I could never explain or fathom. We'd met at the beach, on the long pier, a misspent day with girlfriends, cans of beer in little paper bags, twirling curly fries around our fingers. He tried to bum a smoke, though none of us were smoking. He took a beer instead, and we spent an hour at the arcade. He had a wicked pinball arm and we played for hours, hips pressed against the machine, the lights blinking, bells whirring.

After, he saved all our beer can pull tabs, bending them together into a necklace he draped around my neck. *Like a queen,* he said, blinking through his cigarette smoke. *Like a goddamn empress.*

He lived in Long Island and rather than make his way back to the LIRR that first night he came home with me and stayed off and on for weeks, smoking in our windowless bathroom and driving my roommates to distraction, drifting into the city for work—something in sales—and coming home with six-packs and Chinese food and borrowing forty dollars once, twice, and sometimes disappearing for days on end while I texted him to thumb-numbness and clamored after him whenever he emerged.

It was never going to be anything, but he was good at talking and at kissing—long, lingering kisses, his fingers dappling over me. He had a tattoo of Hot Stuff, the little devil from comic books, on his forearm, and he liked to pinch me hard and sometimes shove my head into the pillow, once so hard I chipped a tooth, and I imagined him for a short while to be far more interesting than he would ever be, and far nicer.

I was crazy about him, I was crazy. I cried when he left, every time he left.

I was young and dumb and believed everything he said.

I was young and nine weeks along, and I made an appointment at the clinic, but the night before, he came over in a sweaty panic. *This doesn't feel right*, he said, and I was surprised how glad it made me, not because I felt ready to have a baby but because I thought he meant, *Let's not do this. Let's have a kid, why not, we could go the distance.* I thought he meant *I love you.* But I had it all wrong. At four in the morning, he shook me awake, his keys already in hand. *Get dressed*, he said. *It's time.*

I didn't even have time to tie my shoes. We both cried the whole way there. He wanted to pay cash. The girl at the desk drew a map to the nearest 7-Eleven that had an ATM.

He wanted to pay cash because, it turned out, his girlfriend would see the credit card bill. See, he meant to tell me. About his girlfriend, in Long Island. She was the jealous type, he admitted. Oh, and by the way, they'd been together a long time, and hell, he'd probably have to marry her someday. She was Catholic. And he guessed he still was too. Or something. And that had gotten him all confused about everything.

He told me all this in the waiting room, his voice husky and a bottle of beer in his jacket pocket.

By the time they put the rubber mask over my face, I was glad we were doing it. Or that I was. He wanted it to be over. He wanted it all to be over. Twenty minutes later, it was.

I wanted him to be over.

The drive home, the radio over our silence, a thick seeping pad between my half-numb legs, he started humming along to the music, drumming his fingers on the steering wheel, for several minutes until he caught himself and stopped. Until I started screaming, and then he stopped. Until I started sobbing and then he stopped.

I'm so old, I kept thinking. *I'm suddenly so old.*

But I was twenty-three and it happened, and I don't regret it, only him.

The truck dipped slightly, Doctor Ash steering us off the paved road onto his drive.

Jed's hand reached for the dashboard, his knuckles white, his eyes finding me in the rearview mirror.

"Are you okay?" he asked, a crack in his voice.

I felt a squeeze over my heart.

It was serious, or was to be taken seriously, but the feeling of solemnity in the car felt outsized. I'd never seen Jed so upset.

Maybe he's still hungover, I thought as we arrived back at the house, Doctor Ash pulling his truck all the way up to the screen door on the side of the house. He turned off the engine and no one moved or spoke.

This was serious, but it wasn't calamitous. It wasn't catastrophic.

Or was it? I'd been so caught up with Doctor Craig and how it had all unfurled, and what he knew and did it matter, the bad boyfriend, the appalling *suck-suck* of the mechanical pump. But had I ruined myself? Had I imperiled my future baby a decade ago?

You didn't imperil anything, I could imagine my mom saying.

That pop-up clinic you went to did. That baby-faced medical resident did. If you'd called me . . .

But I hadn't called her and in fact never told her about the abortion at all. I knew she would say she never liked that boy anyway, even though she never met him. She never liked any of them before Jed and I had the feeling she was still reserving judgment on him.

Yes, it was serious, it was all serious. Bleeding, it was serious. But it wasn't fatal.

"Sweetheart," Doctor Ash said finally, looking at me in the rearview mirror as if reading my mind, "everything's gonna be okay."

"I know," I said. "It's very common." That refrain, our new refrain.

"It *is* very common," Doctor Ash said, "and you are very dear."

And he smiled at me. A strange, sad smile. Melancholic, mysterious. A smile not that you give but that a private thought summons.

A strange, sad smile like the kind when you're really saying goodbye.

꙳

As Jed helped me out of the car, I felt something warm between my legs and the sudden, antic fear. *No. No. Not again.*

Inside the house, I slipped into the powder room off the kitchen, my heart skittering.

The terrible feeling that everyone outside was listening: *Is she okay? Is there more blood?*

Pulling up the dress, the skirt ballooning around me, I looked down only to see my legs sluiced with dried gel, gluey and crackling. Reminding me of that party I'd taken Jed to, the first time he met any of my friends, how he'd been so miserable and we'd had that fight in the parking lot, so loud we climbed into the car so no one could hear . . .

. . . and then how it turned, Jed pulling me onto his lap and there I was, my thighs tight, like when I was six bouncing like a spring toy at the playground and after, going back into the party, sticky under my skirt from him, sticky from him and from us. *No, Jed's having a great time. He's so glad he came.*

No, I wasn't bleeding. It was a phantom feeling, like when you're afraid you're pregnant and keep feeling something there, keep hoping your period has finally come.

No, there was no blood.

But, this time, it was good. Was a relief.

Through the door, I could hear Jed and his dad whispering.

"What about stairs?"

"Just take it easy. Help her, Jed. Be a man. That's your wife."

Be a man, that's your wife.

Jed and I tramped up the stairs, me taking one step, then another, like a toddler.

The blast of pungent bleach wafted from the bathroom, the white robe hanging wetly from the shower bar, the stain blooming from a pinkening man o' war, then burnishing into a lion's mane.

Jed sat on the bed, watching me change, then asked if he could help. My arms above my head, he gently pulled the dress over my elbows. As he'd done thousands of times, taking my dress off—cotton dresses, sundresses, shirtdresses, my one fancy dress, slippery as an eel.

We lay together on the pushed-together beds for a long time, Jed nuzzling against my neck as if to say, *I'm sorry I'm sorry I'm sorry* for how everything had gone, how he'd handled things, clumsily.

"It could be worse," Jed said, nuzzling against me. "You'll be well taken care of here."

115

The phrase, so odd, sent a shudder through me.

"What do you mean?"

A look of vague alarm came over his face.

"I don't know," he said softly. "I never know what to say."

I'm not ordering *bedrest.* That was what Doctor Craig had said.

"But, Jacy, he was pretty clear," Jed said now, an hour later. "No heavy lifting, no exercise. Until they get this . . . thing under control."

"Under control?"

"The placenta," Jed said. "He showed us pictures. If it starts to cover the cervix, you'll have to have a cesarean. And that can cause all these complications."

"He showed you pictures?"

"While you were getting the second ultrasound."

A heat was rising in me, everything was. The room so small and who could hear? Doctor Ash? Mrs. Brandt? Anyone.

"I don't know why," I said, a loud whisper, "Doctor Craig thought it was okay to talk about my body to you and your father while I wasn't there."

"We're family," he said, surprised. "And they're old friends. He's known me since I was a kid. A baby."

"I don't care. It's so inappropriate."

"Look," Jed said, "you have to look at it from my position." A phrase I'd never heard from Jed. Jed the artist, Jed who never had a savings account until he met me, and always filed a tax extension if he remembered to file the extension.

"Your position?"

"My wife was bleeding all over the kitchen," he said, that desperate crack in his voice that made me want to cry. "I just want our baby to be okay."

A pause, a long one, the tiny room, the walls gluey with humidity.

Then, finally adding, "I just want you to be okay."

❦

When you get pregnant, no one ever tells you the real things. The secret things. No one talks to you about how your hair might change, thick with oil and not your own, and your nipples might darken and jut under your shirt. No one tells you about creeping placentas at all.

Instead, they tell you of the miracles and mysteries of life resolved. Of a deeper, ineffable meaning unreachable without giving birth, becoming a parent. They share tender portraits of their newborn's hand curled like a seashell around Daddy's finger.

No one ever tells you this before. Or they do, but it doesn't matter.

❦

"I need to call Doctor Anwar," I said, the bedrest pamphlet clammy in my hand. "And my mom."

"Of course," Jed said, jumping to his feet. Wanting to be helpful, trying.

"There's never any signal and I need to—"

"Not a problem," he said. "The landline. There's one in the hallway and another in the kitchen."

"I'd like some privacy."

"From me?" He gave me such a look. A stunned expression, like a spanked child. The worst thing you can ever see, a child in the park or at the store and an angry father or overwhelmed mother with their hand raised.

"Well, no, I . . ." I said. "I mean . . . it's just that anyone could come in. Your dad, or Mrs. Brandt, or . . ."

"Of course," he said. "Of course."

A moment of relief, his firmness, his head nodding as if to say, *I get it. I'm sorry. I get it now.*

But then he stood up and opened the door and stomped down the hall, his heavy tread, the whole house creaking, and then a clatter and the burring of metal. The faint drag of cords, wire on the floorboards.

"All yours," he said in the doorway, holding a big beige rotary phone he'd yanked from the hallway, the spray of its fraying cords.

"I only meant . . ." I was trying to talk, but a queasiness kept coming, my body feeling enormous, wet, split open and shut only half-closed again.

"Dad and I are going for a walk anyway," Jed said. "He heard that noise last night too. He wants to check that fence again."

I nodded. In my lap, I held the phone, heavy, metal-footed, like a doctor's kit.

Jed, now on his knees, hunted out a jack.

The most private place in the house, the only private place.

I sat on the toilet, the robe dripping bleachy water onto the tub bottom.

Doctor Anwar spoke in that calm, even voice of hers.

She, like Sandy, told me it was very common, one in two hundred pregnant women. She, like Sandy, said it often resolved itself. And that many women never even know they have it, or had it.

I rested my head against the tile and said, *Okay, okay, okay.*

She promised she'd review the sonograms as soon as she received them. That she was trading messages with Doctor Craig's receptionist, who'd assured her she'd get it to her before day's end. Before the holiday, before Doctor Craig's vacation.

Vacation. No one had said anything about vacation, and it was only then I realized July Fourth weekend was two days away.

"The main thing will be to make sure there's no placenta creep," she said. "We want to keep that cervix clear."

"But not bedrest?" I said.

"I'd recommend pelvic rest for a few days until we can get you in here. Just a precaution. To avoid another bleeding episode, especially while you're away from home."

"Pelvic rest?"

"That's doctor talk for no intercourse. We don't want anything going in that vagina right now."

"Except for the enormous wand they jammed in there today," I said.

"Well," she said. "Yes."

She wanted to say more, I knew it. I could feel it. But then, with a clack-clack of computer keys, she was on to next steps.

"Doctor Craig said bedrest," I blurted.

Doctor Anwar paused. "Well, that's an area where things have changed. There's no real evidence that bedrest has any benefits."

I felt my shoulders go soft with relief. I felt my lungs fill and gather themselves.

"I'll talk to Doctor Craig tomorrow," she said. "As soon as the sonogram results come my way. And I'd like you to come in next week. Let's find a time—"

"But can I do that drive?" I said, then immediately wished I could take it back.

"How long a drive?" she said. "*Where are you again?*"

A stitch of panic over my brow, I explained—about the thousand miles, sixteen, seventeen hours or more, the five-mile suspension bridge, all the potholes, the ones Doctor Ash kept talking about, the construction on the salt-scarred interstate adding a few, three states, or was it four, because the UP was so far, so far—it felt increasingly as if I were describing an expedition on steam train and coach through the Borgo Pass deep into the Carpathian Mountains and I started to lose my breath.

Doctor Anwar didn't say anything for a moment and my thoughts skittered wildly. *What about a plane? Surely there are airports up here. This isn't the wild, isn't Siberia and—*

"And you haven't experienced any more bleeding?" Doctor Anwar asked.

"No."

She paused, clucking her tongue. Then she started talking about how it was my decision, but that it made sense to stay put a few days to see if the bleeding returned.

"Let's touch base after the holiday," she said, and I could hear the shift in her voice. She was on to the next patient.

I'd forgotten all about the holiday. Independence Day weekend, a planned trip to Munising, Jed's favorite childhood tradition, a day of flag-raising, watermelon-eating, egg-throwing, the firemen's parade, a float contest, all leading up to a fireworks display to beat the band, as Doctor Ash promised.

We'd planned to leave the day after. I'd imagined us sunburnt and languid, ears humming from fireworks, caroming along the interstate in our searingly white Chevy, heading home, our hands interlaced over the gearshift.

Now it seemed so far away, farther than I could see.

My hand sticky on the plastic finger wheel, the only number I knew by heart.

"Jacy," my mom said, answering on the first ring, so alert, always ready for a crisis, "what's wrong?"

"Nothing's wrong," I said. "Except something's wrong."

And I explained. I explained everything except the parts I

knew would make her crazy. There was something in her always waiting, waiting to be enraged on my behalf, especially at the hands of men.

"I'm looking it up on the internet," she said. "And who is this doctor anyway?"

"He's just a doctor," I said. "A friend of Jed's dad. What does that matter?"

"Well, the bottom line is you need to get home. I don't like the idea of you out there in the wilderness—"

"It's not the wilderness. It's really beautiful up here and everyone's been—"

"Are you sure? Because this bedrest thing is just the sort of shit that doctors have been peddling since the days of the floating womb—"

The floating womb, the migrating placenta . . .

"Okay, Mom," I said. "I get it. I'm a few states away, not a few centuries. And Jed's dad's a doctor. I'm in good hands."

I explained again that Doctor Anwar didn't think bedrest was necessary but that it made sense to wait a day or two and after the holiday—

She let out a long, grand sigh.

"Jacy, you get to make these decisions. This is your body, your uterus, your goddamned placenta."

I could already hear how she'd talk about all this to Aunt Laraine, to Ilona, the secretary in her office, to Frank, the insurance agent she sometimes dated even though he was still living with his ex-wife and their daughter and her husband . . .

"Mom," I said, a hitch in my voice, one we both knew well. "Please."

And a pause, the click of her lighter. A stress cigarette.

"I know, sugar," her voice breathy and kind. "I love you, baby, and everything will be fine."

At the kitchen table, I drank glass after glass of water, impossibly hot, impossibly thirsty.

Mrs. Brandt kept pouring me more from a tall gold-veined pitcher in the refrigerator.

I was so, so thirsty, but I wasn't bleeding.

"I feel pretty good," I kept saying, wondering where the men were.

"They're still on their walk," Mrs. Brandt said, reading my mind. "Tracking down mountain lions."

Was that a twitch of a smile there?

"Did you hear it?" I said, remembering suddenly. "Last night. That noise."

"No," she said. "But it could be any animal. The patio door, the windows—sometimes they see themselves and think it's another animal, a predator. They charge at it."

I nodded, drinking more. There was something poignant about it. Seeing another lion and attacking and the only lion was you.

My stomach growled low and embarrassing, and then I remembered.

"The woman—Sandy—the sonographer talked about your pasties," I said.

Mrs. Brandt looked at me. "Did you eat yours? The one I gave you?"

"Yes," I said. "Last night."

She nodded and turned away from me, wiping down the counter.

Then she said the funniest thing.

"Maybe you should go home."

I looked over at her. The grim pull of her mouth.

"I'm not supposed to travel," I said softly, trying to understand what was happening.

Her eyes were hooded and she turned to put the pitcher back in the refrigerator.

I thought I could hear her take a little breath. A little antic breath. *Maybe you should go home.*

"Why do you think . . ." I started, but then the screen door swung open.

It was Doctor Ash and Jed, back from some adventure like in some old-fashioned novel of men swinging scythes and committing colonial atrocities while women back home waved palm fans over their sticky perfumed skin.

"Hey, there," I said, greeting them. "Mrs. Brandt and I were talking . . ."

But when I turned, she was gone.

Doctor Ash and Jed instantly took up all the space, opening and closing the fridge, cracking beer bottles while I sat at the table enjoying their vim and vigor. Maybe all that worry had passed, I thought. Maybe Doctor Ash had talked Jed down, assured him.

"How you feeling?" Jed asked gently.

"Just fine," I said, looking at him. He was wearing a royal-blue baseball cap, one I'd never seen before, so new the brim looked blade sharp. EDDIE'S TEEPEE, it said, with some cartoon logo: an eight-ball rack, two pool cues crossed like a teepee top. "I thought you'd come back with a wild beast slung over your shoulder."

"No beast, alas," Doctor Ash said. "Maybe a few slippery trout one of these days." Grinning at Jed. "We gotta get you out to Fox River, or the old Two-Hearted."

I thought suddenly of the story Jed had shared. His father distracting him so his fishing line snapped, knocking out his two front teeth. The Whistler. That story . . . could it really be true? I thought of myself, frightening my mom with tales of Captain Murderer, the boogeyman who haunted my dreams. It was true, to me.

"Sure, Dad," Jed said, hands gripping my shoulders hard, very hard. "But I've never been much at fishing."

I reached for his hands, discreetly trying to unclamp them.

"Did you get a little rest?" Doctor Ash asked, looking down at me, cocking his head.

"I feel brand new," I said.

"Really?" Jed said, his right hand now on my shoulder, curling around my neck.

"Really," I said. Again trying to gently shift his hand, hot and heavy and damp.

As if scolded, Jed pulled his hands away and turned to the counter.

"And you feel good about your talk with your doctor?" Doctor Ash asked, pausing. "If you feel comfortable sharing."

"Oh, yes," I said. "But I'll go see her as soon as we get back."

Trying to catch Jed's eyes, but his back faced me, looking out the kitchen window.

"Hmm," Doctor Ash said. "Well, good deal."

Slapping the table once and smiling at me with all his teeth.

"It's all good," I said to Jed later, telling him about my call with Doctor Anwar. "What's a few more days anyway?"

He looked so relieved, cupping my face in his hands.

"Isn't vacation a kind of bedrest anyway," he said, trying for lightness.

"Except I'm not staying in bed," I said pointedly.

A car horn trilled outside, loud and jolly.

"That's Dad," he said. "He's waiting."

They were going to the hardware store with Hicks. All these chores and errands, these men. They were looking for something called "predator lights" to ward off animals at night.

At the door, Jed turned to me, the biggest grin on his face.

"I knew," he said, "you'd make the right decision."

. . .

Those words humming in my ears after. *He doesn't mean that like it sounds*, I kept telling myself. *None of this is anything like how it sounds.*

I'm doing what I want, really.

And I was tired, anyway. The bed, sagging and soft, called to me. Insisted.

Lying back, I reached for *Bedtime Tales of Suspense*, wondering about the next haunted bridegroom, the next doomed bride.

NIGHT FIVE

Maybe you should go home.

On the bedside table sat a tall glass of water.

I guessed Mrs. Brandt had left it for me.

Maybe you should go home, she'd said. Hadn't she?

I'd fallen asleep, stiffly on the bed, my fingers tucked in *Bedtime Tales of Suspense*, my neck pasty with sweat, but suddenly, it was six P.M. and magnificently cool.

"Dad bought an air conditioner just for you," Jed said, smiling at the window, his hand on the brand-new window unit throbbing on the ledge. "He drove all the way to Marquette for it. So you'd feel comfortable."

"He didn't need . . ." I started, but the air felt so good, and Jed came over and set his hand on me and the hand was cold, too, like ice.

"I'm sorry about everything today," Jed was murmuring. "I was being a jerk."

I smiled. "That's a generous word for it."

He smiled, too, the back of his hand on my forehead. "You rest now."

My eyes started to stutter shut, but I was squinting at his cap.

That EDDIE'S TEEPEE cap. Eddie's Teepee, I finally realized. The bar he'd been to with his friend Randy the night before.

"A souvenir?" I asked.

Jed paused, his hand reaching up as if he'd forgotten.

"I guess," he said, then grinned. "Randy gave it to me. God, I drank too much last night. What an idiot."

It was the first time all day he seemed himself and it was so nice.

"I like it. The hat, I mean," I said, pulling him close for a kiss, long and open.

The cap fell to the floor with a soft shush.

Maybe we could go back, I thought. Had any of that happened? Doctor Craig, the wand drifting along my belly, all the men talking about me behind his office door.

Had any of that happened?

Maybe it hadn't, the robe dried to stiffness now in the bathroom. As white as snow.

✧

The smell was strong coming from the kitchen, some kind of Cornish stew that had been simmering on the stove for hours.

That mustachioed man Hicks was back again, hovering in the doorway, talking to Mrs. Brandt, an ice chest under his arm.

I don't know what made me hang back in the dining room, but I did, listening.

"Well, they're all unconfirmed," he was saying. "You know these summer folks. Three solid months of Bigfoot sightings. Dude really gets around."

Mrs. Brandt didn't say anything, busy at the hectic stovetop, her cheeks steamed pink.

"This guy who came in today," Hicks said, leaning forward, balancing the cooler on his knee. "He was so damn sure he'd seen one.

We took one look at his trail camera footage and told him it was just a dinky feral kitty, couldn't have been more than fifteen pounds. He said, well, maybe it's a *baby* mountain lion. I told him, *If you see babies, that was your head start.*"

Hicks's laugh rung out, loud and long.

"Shh," Mrs. Brandt said. "The girl is sleeping."

The girl. I guessed I was *the girl.*

She took the cooler from him, hugging it to her chest.

"Don't," she said as he moved to help her. "You smell like bluegill."

Hicks nodded and doffed his baseball hat. They all wore baseball hats, I guessed. His said DNR.

Do not resuscitate? I thought, but then I remembered Jed said Hicks used to work for the sheriff but now worked for the state, the Department of Natural Resources.

I turned to move away, back toward the living room, when the floorboard beneath my foot squeaked.

Holding my breath, I waited, a long silent second, no sound from the kitchen.

"The girl is sleeping," Mrs. Brandt said again, sharp and final.

Sitting on the musty screened porch, waiting, I wondered again about Doctor Ash and Mrs. Brandt, lingering closely in the kitchen. All these years and what might be between them.

Mrs. Brandt's clipped, closed face, Doctor Ash's easy, open one—it was impossible to tell.

Dinner was starting.

The pungent stew now sat on the dining room table. The saffron cakes, studded with currants, like little crowns nestled in a chunky braided bowl.

As I sat down, Jed reached for my hand under the table, squeezing it lightly, the grooves of his fingertips, the creases in his hand smeared by old burns. How I loved touching them all, the scar tissue like glossy glue gone hard.

"My mom had a bowl like this," I said, my fingers resting on its shellacked edge. "She used to dump a tube of Pillsbury rolls in it when we had company."

"That was hers," Mrs. Brandt said suddenly. I hadn't even seen her there, slipping in and out from the kitchen. "Jed's mom's."

"Was it?" Doctor Ash said. "I'd forgotten."

Her arms moved so swiftly, long and starch-cuffed, and she reached between Jed and me and flipped the bowl over, a golden confetti of crumbs, to show me its bottom.

"See," she said, hot in my ear. "There she is."

And so it was, WENDY branded on its bottom.

Doctor Ash watched, sipping his iced tea and looking unfathomably cool, the ceiling fan humming over him. "Mrs. Brandt," he said knowingly, "remembers everything."

And he reached out for the bowl, taking it from my hands gently, touching its edges, its lip, with such care. Running his fingers across WENDY like a lover's tattoo, like a lover's scars.

I thought I saw something else new in his eyes. Something lovely and lost.

The sneaking discomfort I'd felt over Doctor Craig, over the pressure at the doctor's office, in the car—it receded, at least for now.

"How did you meet her?" I asked. "Wendy."

Doctor Ash looked at Mrs. Brandt, a vague smile on his face. Mrs. Brandt didn't say anything, her gaze lowered.

"Rose introduced us," he said.

It was only when Mrs. Brandt looked up that I realized he meant Mrs. Brandt. Before then no one had even suggested Mrs. Brandt had a first name. *Rose.*

"Yes. That was long ago."

Swiftly, she stood, tucking a stray hair behind her ear, a gesture girlish and surprising.

"How did it happen?" I asked, eager for a story, for more about Jed's mother, for anything to take the attention off me, my body, its leaky parts and its failures.

Doctor Ash looked expectantly at Mrs. Brandt.

"We all knew each other back then," she said briskly, gathering plates, glasses, soggy napkins. Then, after she'd turned away, adding, "We ice-skated together, as girls."

I started to rise to help, but neither would let me, Doctor Ash insisting I sit back on my seat, a cushion tied to the chair rung. I noticed that my chair was the only one that had one. But it wasn't comfortable, its stiff tufts. *Who are you,* I thought, *the princess and the pea?*

Doctor Ash poured me more iced tea from a tall, slender pitcher.

"So Mrs. Ash was from here?" I asked.

He nodded. "A townie. And I was the interloper." Giving his eyebrows a rakish push. "But she was so beautiful. I'd come up here to ski and end up at the rink instead, watching her glide down a ribbon of ice."

"I wish I could see that," I said, my hand resting on my belly.

"Weren't we looking for those pictures?" Doctor Ash said, trying to catch Mrs. Brandt's eye, but she wouldn't look at him, stacking the dishes on the sideboard.

"I thought there weren't any pictures," Jed said, looking up.

Doctor Ash glanced at him. Mrs. Brandt disappeared into the kitchen.

"Well, probably a few," Doctor Ash said, then turned to me. "But, wait now, I hear you two have got a meet-cute story of your own."

I smiled. "Well, nothing as romantic as the ribbon of ice."

"Tell me," Doctor Ash said, leaning on his elbows handsomely. "I can't believe I haven't asked you before."

Both of them turned to me, Jed with an odd vague expression, as if he hadn't been there himself. As if he, too, wondered how we met.

"Well," I said, my mouth suddenly dry, "I used to pass Jed's storefront on my way to work. On my way home, the neon signs in the window were lit up and so beautiful. I remembered someone telling me once that there were less than two hundred people left in the country who still worked with neon. The real stuff."

"A rare bird, my boy," Doctor Ash said, winking at Jed.

"Then, one day," I said, "he invited me in."

I looked over and Doctor Ash was grinning, sneaking a glance at Jed, Jed's eyes averted. Jed shaking out his napkin, foot squeaking on the floorboard. The sounds of Mrs. Brandt loading the dishwasher in the kitchen.

"What?" I asked. "What's funny?"

My hands falling to my lap, eyes darting down at my lap as if I were bleeding again. Like when I'd been bleeding and everyone knew but me.

"Nothing," Doctor Ash said, reassuringly. "It's a grand story."

Jed, folding and unfolding his napkin, looked to the kitchen door. "I should help Mrs. Brandt."

"What's going on?" I said, an odd giggle in my voice.

Doctor Ash sighed, looking at Jed. Waiting for something.

Finally, he leaned toward me. One finger tapping my forearm teasingly as he said, "Are you sure you didn't sneak back there yourself?"

I felt my face flush instantly.

I looked at Jed. "Did you . . . What did you tell him?"

"Nothing," Jed replied, eyes wide and guilty. "Well, you said you were lost. I'd already seen you walk by so many times. It doesn't matter. You'd been partying that night—"

"Wait, so you two discussed this? And I wasn't partying, whatever that means."

Doctor Ash sat back, chuckling, watching us as if this were a charming couple's game.

Jed, his face gone dark and sullen, said that thing again about needing to help Mrs. Brandt.

"Don't you dare be embarrassed," Doctor Ash said as Jed rose and left the table. "I think it's wonderful. A woman courting. Taking risks. Going after what she wants. Going on the hunt."

The screen door made its stutter slam and Jed was gone into the green mist outdoors.

"The neon signs were so beautiful," I repeated to anyone still listening. "And I never said I was lost."

When I was in middle school, Billy Bieniek's mom caught me and Billy, his fingers inside me on her den sofa. She made me sit on the kitchen stool while she called my mother. *Only twelve years old, this sluttish behavior, the way girls today . . .* I could hear my mother sighing and bemoaning me as Mrs. Bieniek ranted breathlessly. *You know what I think,* my mother finally said, *your son's just lucky I don't lop off his diddle finger.* And how I dreamed for nights of waking up and finding Billy's index stump between my legs.

There was nothing to feel bad about then or now. And yet.

I'd seen Jed through the sooty window once, twice, five times. He was hard to miss, that husky intensity, his stretched-soft faded tees, a twitchy energy as he wrote out sales slips, answered the old rotary phone on the wall.

One day, after a few beers at a teachers' happy hour, I found myself pushing through the front door with the heels of both hands. *Why not.*

The chimes over the door had clanged, but no one came to the counter and when I rang the little desk bell no one came either. I heard a radio playing like a woman crying, a bluesy thing, the studio behind the store large and echoing, and the strange sounds like a vacuum screaming.

There he was, standing over a sprawling, battered metal table, a wall of colored tubes hanging like circus taffy behind him.

Like Oz, I thought dreamily, that first time. Dorothy stumbling down the long emerald hallway, gazing with wonder and fear.

I watched him for so long before he saw me, bulging headphones over his unruly hair, protective glasses, a fingertip on either end of a long acid-yellow tube laced through his mouth, turning it over the burner, a ribbon of fire at its center. I made myself small, like a keyhole, and watched. His hands, battered and brown, moved with such languor but such precision. The quick puff of air from the tiny hose hanging from his mouth like a cigarette. Blowing air in as he bent the tube. There was such tenderness to it all, such delicacy, as if it were a living thing counting on him to survive. I knew then that I had to have him. I knew it in a way I'd never known anything before.

As you bend, it'll collapse if you don't shore it up, he told me later. *So you blow on it lightly. In the end, your breath is in every molecule of it. My breath.*

I watched until he finally looked up and noticed me, lifting his glasses, his eyes unfocused. Softly tugging the hose from his lips.

"I'm sorry," I started, and that's when I saw the finished sign lit behind him, mounted high. A commissioned piece, tagged for the owner. A woman on her knees, her body an hourglass. In searing blue cursive slanting across her back, it warned, slyly: DANGEROUS CURVES AHEAD.

"If you didn't tell him, how did he know?" I asked Jed in bed that night.

"I don't know," Jed insisted. "He knows things. He figures people out. He guessed."

I didn't know if I believed him, but he was so adamant. I'd gotten it all wrong. It was dizzying.

"You fell for it," Jed said, rising, moving toward the bathroom. "He got you."

"That doesn't sound like your dad," I said tentatively.

"Well," he said, "you don't know him, really."

It was like the fishing line, Jed's front teeth. Maybe Doctor Ash did have another side to him, more traditionally masculine. Fathers and sons, it was mysterious, impossible to penetrate from the outside. Just like mothers and daughters, maybe. My mom so upset that I'd gotten married so fast, not enough time for her to come, that she'd sent me a bruising letter. *You've always been a selfish girl,* she'd written. The kind of words you can't take back.

"Jed," I said. "I believe you, I just . . ."

But he'd already disappeared into the bathroom, the shower shushing a moment later, washing everything away.

This is silly, I told myself, trying to fall asleep. There was nothing wrong with the story of how we met, no matter how it was told or why.

Waking in the blue middle of night, Jed beside me, sprawled, breathing heavily, like a little boy overheated, collapsing into sleep.

His left arm outstretched, the muscle heavy and hard and the elbow's soft inside.

I pressed my cheek against it, against that vein that always appeared at his elbow crook when he was working, creating. Whenever I saw it, from the first time I saw it . . . the way it hopped and shivered, like it might burst out of his skin.

And now feeling the throb there, the bend of his arm, his pale tattoo, his vein like a jumping bean, his heart beating fast, too fast.

Like that first time, sneaking into his studio drunkenly, my ankles teetering in scant-worn heels. His bare arm, inside the icy blue sliver of his vein pushing, jerking, so close to the skin and wanting, needing to put my fingers there, to feel the push of blood and heat.

What could be wrong with that. Nothing, nothing at all.

There was so much wanting, hidden and furtive.

A woman courting. Taking risks. Going after what she wants. Going on the hunt.

Women, so greedy, so hungry, our mouths forever open, wanting so much, too much.

THE DREAM

That night, I dreamt of the night we conceived, or decided we had. Jed's birthday, that unexpected, grappling encounter at his shop.

I'd arrived to find Jed spinning around unhappily in his desk chair, surly over something—a demanding customer, an unpaid bill.

Oh, what is it, honey, walking toward him . . .

The neon above blinked faster and faster.

THIS IS THE SIGN YOU'RE LOOKING FOR, it insisted, demanded.

When it happened, it had been thrilling, a little forbidden.

But in the dream, everything felt stronger, more intense—Jed's face dark and his fist curled and the hot flare in his eyes when I arrived. *What's wrong, Jed? You okay, Jed?*

He grabbed me so hard, the way men can, by the elbows and forearms, my breath catching, excited. So swiftly, tugging my skirt up and underwear down, the open desk drawer clattering, the desk lamp, its brass string swinging.

It must've sprung from one of the stories I'd read in that spooky paperback. Robber bridegrooms, demon lovers.

The way his hands had fastened themselves to my collarbone, gripped my throat.

Pulling me on his lap, his thumbs punched between my thighs, how the walls seemed to shiver around us and I could feel those thumbs inside me, and his scarred fingers and thick wrist and the heel of his hand and suddenly it was as though I was one of his creations—*a neon pinup girl, a burlesque cartoon, Eve with her apple, a mouth open*—as he was bending and blowing, turning my hot limbs like his glass tubes, Jed in shadows beneath me, his mouth open the whole time and teeth like sharp diamonds. His skin, quilled, felt like a snake's.

But it was his eyes most of all, eyes like glowing fuses, like neon filaments.

And was someone watching?

Suddenly I knew someone was.

Was it Mrs. Brandt hiding in the bushes?

Was it Doctor Ash, snapping a fishing line, twirling me on the porch, creeping up the staircase, padding to our door?

Click-click, like a chain pulled, the desk lamp behind Jed shutting off and on.

The last thing I remember, I looked down at my belly and suddenly I was glowing too. A neon charge inside me, lighting me up, taking me over, making me all his.

DAY SIX

"Did I wake you?"

My eyes opened to Mrs. Brandt in her white shirt, a gleam of white at her temples, that roseate mane of hair tightly braided.

She was standing at the bedroom door.

"Mrs. Brandt?" I whispered. "What are you doing here . . . ?"

And the new air conditioner throbbed back to life. *Chug-chug-chug.*

Her mouth closing, then opening again, a low whisper.

"Are you bleeding?"

In the bathroom, I brushed my teeth.

No. No, I'm not. My fingers now poking into the crotch of my underpants, double-checking.

She means well, I told myself. But *did* she?

Maybe you and Jed should go home. That's what she'd said.

I showered, delicately, my body feeling strange to myself. My body feeling like it wasn't mine but everyone's, with their questions and their probes and worries.

When I opened the door, towel pulled high, Mrs. Brandt was still there, holding out the robe for me to step into. Freshly laundered, the bloodstains miraculously gone, except in a certain light: the gray ghost of a spatter. Holding it for me like my lady-in-waiting, as if dressing the queen.

"Thank you," I said, taking it from her instead. Taking the robe and setting it on the bed. "But I don't need any help. Really."

She looked at me and I knew she could see through me. *No more pasties for me*, I thought. Though a pasty sounded very good just then.

"Doctor's orders," Mrs. Brandt said crisply, moving to the door.

"I'm not sick," I said. "It's just something we're keeping our eye on."

"Well," she said, pausing in the doorway, "Doctor Ash takes these things very seriously, after the last time."

After the last time. Those words hanging in the air.

Jed's mom, *swimming in her own blood*. I hadn't thought of it, not really, after the blood yesterday. Maybe I really was *a selfish, selfish girl.*

"Jed?" I called out, slinking down the stairs.

I could hear Mrs. Brandt outside, calling out for Redruth. *Get here, girl. Get!*

I could smell the coffee, singeing into the pot. "Jed?" I said again, wandering through the downstairs, empty and oddly dusty. A spiderweb visible now on the patio door.

It was like I could see—more like I could smell everything. And were those beetle holes in the floor?

In the hallway nestled in the middle of the house, I heard it. That odd sound, a *click-click, click-click*. Like my mom locking all the doors and windows when I was a kid and scared of the boogeyman. Of Captain Murderer. *Click-click, click-click, bolt.*

139

It was coming from Doctor Ash's study.

Carrying my coffee, I followed the sound, pausing at the study door, ajar. I could see its plush crimson walls like the inside of a mouth.

I pushed at the door, let it squeak open.

There was Jed, faced away from me at the large mahogany desk. Behind him on the wall: that mounted walleye and its gaping mouth.

"Jed, what are you doing?" I asked.

As he turned, I saw it in his arms: a gun, long and shiny.

No air gun like Mrs. Brandt's, no BB or pellet gun, it was a hunting rifle, long-barreled, with a glinting sight hooked on top.

"Hey, you," Jed said, a dazed look on his red, even redder face.

"Easy there, Dirty Harry," I said.

It was only then that I saw Doctor Ash, striding forward from behind the desk, waving me in.

"Good morning, darling daughter. Don't you look refreshed."

"You feeling okay?" Jed said, that crinkle back over his brow.

I nodded, trying to figure out what I'd walked into exactly, a tightness in the air between father and son.

"I'm sorry for interrupting," I said, though I wasn't sure what I interrupted, a slightly queasy feeling, like I'd caught them in something.

"You didn't interrupt—" Jed started.

"Jed," Doctor Ash said, reading something in my face, "show Jacy the empty chamber so she doesn't think she's married into a family of gun nuts."

"I'd never think that," I said, trying to smile. For years, my own mom kept a Taser her boss had given her in her handbag after she was mugged in the parking lot after work.

"Why don't you show her?" Jed said, handing his dad the rifle.

A look flashed between the two.

"I promised Mrs. Brandt I'd clean those AC ducts as soon as

everyone was up," Jed said, walking past me, his hand brushing gently on my belly, his kiss in my ear.

"Don't forget to turn the power off," Doctor Ash said. "And maybe run a razor on that face of yours later. Another day and someone'll mistake you for Sasquatch."

Doctor Ash turned to me, the rifle in his hands, all the mahogany and crimson damask seeming to cradle us, enclose us.

"He has his mother's thick, wild hair," he said. I wondered again if I would ever see those photos.

Suddenly, the desk lamp dimmed to darkness and the low churn of the AC ceased.

The small, busy room felt even smaller, like being inside a scarlet tufted box.

My eyes kept landing on the rifle, resting so easily in his hands. I'd never seen one that close. The nearest I'd come was a plastic six-shooter at the arcade.

"You can hold it," he said, "if you want to."

"Oh, no," I demurred, my hand instinctively going to my belly.

Holding it seemed forbidden somehow. A thought hovering: *Don't! You're pregnant.* Which was silly, and it was just a family heirloom, after all.

"Safety on," he said, gesturing, his fingers dancing along the rifle. "Trigger guard. And an empty magazine."

And before I could say anything, Doctor Ash had set the weapon in my hands. Still warm from his hands, Jed's hands.

It made me think of what Jed had said about his dad. *He knows things. He figures people out.*

"Bolt-action, matte blued," Doctor Ash said. "Nineteen sixty-seven, I think. One of my dad's. Hunting was the only time you'd get him to spend a day with his kids."

It was heavy, so much heavier than I guessed, and so long it felt awkward in my arms.

"I never use it," he said. "But it's a beauty, if you like that kind of thing."

I brushed back my hair to get a better grip.

"Feel the bolt," he said as my fingertips ran along its swirled pattern. "They call it jeweling."

He reached out and placed his hands next to mine on the stock, its soft, satin wood.

"Look here," he said, moving my hands along the barrel to its neck. "Still has the factory Cosmoline on it."

The amber wax felt smooth, hot, wet, like the inside of a tongue.

It still seemed forbidden, somehow, but I couldn't let go and the moment hummed in the air, electric.

"I used to go out with Hicks a few times during deer season, but I never fired it," Doctor Ash said, my ambered fingers tingling. "I should sell it, give it away. But I'm sentimental, I guess."

I smiled, catching my own reflection in the windowpane beyond.

"If Jed could see me now," I said, unaccountably flushed. "*If* I tell him."

Doctor Ash chuckled softly.

"Every woman should have her secrets," he said, taking the rifle from me.

I laughed. "I don't have any secrets."

"Oh, Jacy," he said, "you sure do."

And he was smiling so wide, teeth flashing.

Something crackled between us.

Outside, I could hear Jed calling Mrs. Brandt's name.

"But what were you two talking about when I came in?" I asked Jed, but he wasn't really paying attention, his head bent back in Doctor Craig's pamphlet, which I thought I'd buried in the bottom of the suitcase.

"Nothing," he said, digging his hand through his hair. *His mother's thick, wild hair.* "The mountain lion, I guess."

"Does your dad think that's what we heard the other night?"

"This says you shouldn't be drinking coffee at all," Jed said, holding up the pamphlet. "And no baths, only short showers."

"Jed—"

"I know," he said. "But you don't take baths anyway, do you?"

"I told you what Doctor Anwar said," I offered quietly, making a note to flush that pamphlet down the toilet when I could.

❦

The ring came like a thunderclap. The landline, the old yellow kitchen phone.

It was Randy calling for Jed. Did he want to go ATV riding over by the old copper mine? *The weather's sweet, c'mon, let's do this up.*

Even through the receiver, Jed curling the stiff phone cord around his arm, I could hear Randy's big, booming voice about what a spicy time it would be, *a super-whooped-out trail, lots of chop and grit, railroad grade, no shit.*

"You should go," I said, meaning it. "Nothing's going to happen."

"Mrs. Brandt and I will be here," Doctor Ash said. "Jacy doesn't need all three of us hovering over her all day. Just don't end up back at Eddie's Teepee."

He winked at Jed, who stutter-stepped, turning to me.

"Jed," I said, making him look at me, his eyes forever darting these days. "Go. Please. I want you to. Have a good time."

This was how it was going to be, of course. All our plans gliding away in an instant.

There would be no visits to Kitch-iti-kipi to dip a birch bark into the spring. No glass-bottom boat trips to explore historic shipwrecks, no souvenir refrigerator magnets from the Moose Capital of Michigan, no trips to the place that makes its own caramel and still serves cherry phosphates, whatever cherry phosphates were.

But it was fine. It was only a day or two, after all.

If I were at home, perhaps I'd be neck-craned for hours on my phone or a computer, trying to find out everything about placenta previa. And didn't that always make it worse? Here, I only had the skimpy pamphlet that Doctor Craig had given me, the one I would never read about how important bedrest was and how you could make it fun by taking up crafting or crocheting baby booties or catching up with your correspondence.

I had Doctor Anwar a phone call away, even if she seemed so much further, her sober, even voice.

I had my mom, who, now that she had the landline number, had called three or four times with second- and third-hand anecdotes collected from a cousin, a coworker, a new client, a mail carrier who'd "had it."

And maybe it would be a relief for Jed to go off, have fun. To have a break from his twitchy energy. To let him get all that out of his system, or whatever ATV riding did, or was.

Let him play, I thought. *Keep him busy.*

We'd be leaving soon, so what did it matter anyway.

I sat for a long time on the sleeping porch, snapping green beans, the only task Doctor Ash would give me.

In the distance, he was barely visible in the green haze, doing something with hedge clippers.

But just beyond the screen, Mrs. Brandt stood on the grass, hosing down Redruth, covered in mud.

"You never stop moving," I called out to her. "Let me help."

But Mrs. Brandt paused, the hose in her hand, Redruth looking small and haunted, her fur slack and dark.

"It's my job," she said. "I like it."

"More than driving a three-wheeler along a rusty rail trail with the boys?" I said, trying for a laugh, even the hint of a smile.

"The men who come up here now," she said, stepping back from Redruth, letting her shake, her fur like dark tassels, "the downstaters—they come for different reasons. They come to get away from change. To do what they want. That same land that gave up its copper, its silver to us all those years—they ride their motorbikes, their quads and rock crawlers, their sand rails and snowmobiles all over it. They smash their beer bottles, tear up the stream banks, the saplings, the forest floor."

She said it evenly but firmly, her hand on Redruth, untangling her fur with long fingers.

"You don't approve," I said.

"Never said that," Mrs. Brandt said, turning off the hose. "Boys will be boys. The one thing that never changes."

It was hard to imagine Jed amid such testosterone-driven fantasies, Jed who never seemed to care at all about the clichéd male pursuits: sports, cars, guns. It was hard, or it had been hard a few days ago.

Now it was all I could think of. Jed, out there in some steep, rocky terrain, in some tricked-out ATV of Randy's, reminding me of those high school boys you only dallied with once, careening around abandoned mall parking lots on two wheels, trying to impress you into the back seat, slippery tongues and the smell of Crest, dried-out condoms in their lumpy jeans pockets—

—trying to scare you into the back seat, and *go on, shotgun that beer for us. Show me and my buds what you got. Let's see you swallow. Go, go, go!*

BRRRRING. The kitchen phone inside rang, rescuing me from my reverie.

"I looked it up, Jacy darling," my mom said, the landline amplifying her voice. Like she was standing beside me, a tin horn between her mouth and my ear. "Ninety-five percent of placenta previa clears by week thirty-four."

"Is that true?" I said. "Where did it say that?"

"Of course it's true," she said. I could hear the hiss of her cigarette. She only smoked when she was nervous and I felt a wave of guilt. "So when are you leaving?"

"Mom, I told you. In a few days. And I'm not in the wilds. We're only twenty miles from the nearest hospital."

I knew because Jed kept saying it, even—that very morning—mapping it out at the kitchen table with Doctor Ash's atlas, just in case.

"And the doctor is even closer," I added. "Don't be a snob."

"Darling, how could I be a snob? I'm rolling a cart across the parking lot at T.J. Maxx as we speak."

A glimmer of light through the kitchen window, a rainbow flickering, and then a shadow. A creak of a floorboard and I knew Mrs. Brandt was there, lingering perhaps at the doorway. Wanting to give me privacy, or wanting not to.

"It's not about that," my mom was saying. "It's just . . . doesn't Jed want to get you home?"

There was something so lonely in that sentence. A deeper loneliness than I'd ever felt, my whole life. Far lonelier than all those years with no husband, no father . . .

"Of course," I said finally. "Of course he does, Mom. He's just being careful. We're just making sure."

Call me later, she said, which she always said. But there was no missing the worry in her voice as she said goodbye.

It made me think of something. How my mom had been happy,

so happy when I told her I was pregnant. But you always remember the first thing your mom says when you deliver big news.

So soon! she'd said, a look of alarm she couldn't hide.

Soon for what? I kept asking, but she wouldn't answer and it troubled me all day. I wanted to tell Jed, but I didn't because it felt like he might see it as a sign of something, about him, something.

When you're an only child raised by a single parent, especially one of the same sex, the bond can be so tight, the dependence so strong.

Like Jed. Like Doctor Ash and Jed.

❧

"I have an idea."

The voice came from behind as I hung up the phone.

It wasn't Mrs. Brandt lurking, but Doctor Ash calmly waiting at the kitchen door.

I wondered what he'd heard. *Mom, I'm not in the wilds . . .*

"I'm sorry for all the phone calls—" I started.

"Jed's out blowing off his steam," he said with a warm, conspiratorial smile. "How about we have some fun? What he doesn't know won't hurt him."

I smiled too.

❧

We were finally looking at family pictures.

Mrs. Brandt had dug out a dusty banker's box from a crawl space somewhere above.

We sat around the dining room table, a standing fan blowing across us, lifting the curling edges of all the photographs, snapshots. The ones Doctor Ash had kept promising and forgetting about. The ones Jed said, or thought, didn't exist.

On the table, there were sweet yeast buns called "Cornish splits," a dish of clotted cream to slather inside, and the pitcher of bitter iced tea I couldn't stop drinking. Doctor Ash had hooked up his old stereo cabinet and was playing what he called an appalling array of soft-rock hits.

"You're sure you want to see all of these?" Doctor Ash asked. "Or is this like when the neighbors pull out their vacation slides?"

I grinned. "I'm sure."

Mrs. Brandt flicked her eyes at me in that way she had but opened the first box anyway, a gust of mildew tickling our noses.

The first one was in a portrait sleeve, die cut. The faded browns and rusts of photos from the 1970s. There he was, Doctor Ash in his vibrant youth, looking much like Jed—the same lantern jaw, left dimple—his arms around a young woman in French braids with a mischievous glint in her eye, a freckle spray across her nose like in the snapshots of Jed in his sunbrowned teens. And that smile, the same one I'd noticed in the Polaroid Jed kept. Shy or sly, you couldn't tell.

"There she be . . ." murmured Doctor Ash. "Wendy."

The next photo was a formal portrait of Jed's mom on skates, this one with a caption: THE SOO LOCKETS, PERFORMING AT THE 1985 SILVER BLADES REVIEW. She was posed alongside another young woman, both with long, roller-curled hair like my own mom's blurry snapshots, with her feathered wave. *The Soo Lockets*. Both in matching silver outfits, long-sleeved with tiny, flouncy skirts, their right legs raised behind them.

The other woman looked familiar to me. And then I saw it.

"Rose and Wendy," Doctor Ash was saying, a burr in his voice, "Wendy and Rose."

Mrs. Brandt. That dark red hair half hidden under a shiny headband.

"She was Theia, goddess of light," Mrs. Brandt said, sitting down at last. "I was Diana, the huntress."

It was the softest I'd ever seen Mrs. Brandt. The photo had a kind of magic, transforming her into that young woman, the same flame of hair, the same poker face.

"Six coats of silver paint on those skates," Mrs. Brandt said, moving closer. "Wendy insisted. Shaking that spray can until there was nothing left."

"She had an iron will, that one," Doctor Ash said, flipping briskly to the next photo. Mrs. Brandt rose again abruptly.

These two, I thought. *What is it.*

The next photo was one of Jed's mom, baby-faced and dimple-cheeked, enclosed by the arm of a smiling Doctor Ash in a stiff checked blazer that looked like it might still have the tags on.

"The night before our wedding," Doctor Ash said.

"Bridalveil Falls," I said, remembering he'd told us when we'd visited it only a few days before.

"Took our vows overlooking that silver ribbon that plummets straight down a cliff face." He lifted an eyebrow at me. "Don't look too hard for the metaphor in that."

I laughed. "She looks so young."

"She'd just turned twenty," he said. "Her dad had just passed. Silicosis. The last generation of miners. And she was all alone in the world. Waiting tables to pay for classes at Michigan Tech. She wanted to be a nurse."

"Until she left," Mrs. Brandt said.

Doctor Ash blinked at her.

"I kidnapped her down to Ann Arbor with me," he said to me. "That's what Rose means. I took her far away."

"Those were different times," Mrs. Brandt said, moving quickly, so quickly the heel of her hand snagged the tablecloth, a photo of toddler Jed, towheaded and tanned, flying out of my hands, fluttering to the floor.

"Everything was perfect," Doctor Ash said, picture in his hand now, his thumb resting on it, leaving a mark. "Feels like a dream now."

It reminded me of one of those old books. The ones forever on the public library shelves. *Cherry Ames, Student Nurse.* Candy stripers and ice skaters. Long curling hair and smiles painfully open. Then one of the nurses—always the prettiest one of the most modest means—meets a handsome doctor in training . . .

The landline rang, but it was for Doctor Ash, who said he'd take it in his study, closing all the doors behind him.

Mrs. Brandt and I sat alone.

In an instant, the air itself seemed to change. All the power and mystery of the photos were still there, but heavier, thicker.

"I hope you got what you wanted," Mrs. Brandt said, gathering the photos back into tidy piles, retying them with old string.

"It was his idea," I said. "Doctor Ash."

She didn't like that, her mouth a straight line as she snapped a rubber band around a photo stack.

"If there's something you feel you must know," she said, "you can ask me."

Something in her face reminded me of what my mom used to say, *Women can't afford to be sentimental, honey. That's yet another male prerogative.*

But she didn't leave. She stayed, hovering there. As if, despite that hard line of a mouth, she did, in fact, want me to ask her things, or to ask her something quite specific.

"Is there something," I said tentatively, "that you'd like to tell me?"

"He thought Jed's mom might need a cesarean," she said. "Jed was breech."

On instinct, my hands rose to my belly. I shifted in my seat.

"So this was always going to be a hard time," Mrs. Brandt said. "Another pregnancy. Do you understand?"

"I think so."

"But we don't know that I'll need a C-section," I said. "And plenty of women—"

"'From his mother's womb, untimely ripp'd,'" Mrs. Brandt said softly, as if talking to herself.

"Ripped?" I said.

I felt myself twist, squirm in my chair. I wasn't bleeding. There was no more bleeding.

"Did Jed tell you about his caul?"

I looked at her dumbly, her eyes like two bright beads on me.

"Caul," Mrs. Brandt said. "C-a-u-l. Born with a veil. That's what they used to call it."

Caul babies. I only knew it from horror movies, or books about medieval royalty. I'd seen a picture of one once. They come out still inside the amniotic sac, like one of those balloons with a stuffed animal inside. Then they have to remove the membrane.

"It's like unwrapping a Christmas present," Mrs. Brandt said. "That's what my mother always said. She midwived. She had such delicate hands, far more delicate than any doctor."

It was painful to ponder a newborn Jed, small and purpled, a shiny eggplant, and such tender skin, the softness on the inside of his elbows still. (*How I loved to stroke the hidden vein there, tap it to life.*)

What a strange feeling to know you came into this life still protected, gusseted, hidden from the harshness of the world. And to be twice plucked from warmth and safety, the beating of a mother's heart, first the womb, then the caul. Torn, shorn away to the big, bright world, knife-sharp and dangerous.

"His face was violet when he came out, sticky and scared," she said. "The umbilical cord wrapped around and around him like a silver ribbon."

Like a silver ribbon, that phrase again. Doctor Ash and that silver ribbon racing down the cliff face of Bridalveil Falls.

"So you were there," I said. "When he was born."

"No," she said, looking away.

She's lying, I thought, though I wasn't sure why she would.

And Mrs. Brandt was already shoving the top back on the bank box, gaping with moisture, age. She was already on her feet, her face closed off from me.

"Of course, there's a lot of old wives' tales about caul births," she said, moving toward the door. "That you're born lucky."

"Not so lucky for Jed's mother," I said, the words slipping out before I could stop them.

But Mrs. Brandt didn't miss a beat:

"Well," she said, moving down the hall soundlessly, her long skirt so long she had no feet, no legs, "she was already dead by then."

⌁

The study door was closed as I passed it, but it hummed with Doctor Ash's voice.

I don't know what made me stop. Something in his tone, unfamiliar, clipped, wry.

"Yes, I got it. I'm looking at it right now."

The floorboard groaned under my foot. I stopped, holding my breath.

"I see. I see," he continued. "Well, it's their nature. She can't help it. Like a doe bleating to call in the bucks to rut."

A pause, and the scraping of a chair.

"No, I'm glad you told me. Good to know what we're dealing with."

Another pause, then a chortle, low and thick.

"Will do. Will do," he said. "You know what I always say, why hunt when you can trap?"

A long laugh hummed through the mahogany door until finally, abruptly, it stopped.

"So," he said. "Now we know. Now we know."

And another, longer silence stretching into forever. Until I gave up, retreating.

※

I was halfway up the stairs when I heard his voice behind me. Doctor Ash.

"Jacy," he said, smiling as I turned around. "I've been meaning to ask you something."

I smiled back. *Had he seen me, heard me listening?*

"Where did you find that robe?" he said. "The one you've been wearing."

I looked at him, confused. "Mrs. Brandt gave it to me."

"I see," he said. "Well, surely we can get you something better than that. I'll send her to the store."

"Oh, I don't—"

"You see," Doctor Ash said, looking up at me, eyes glinting, "it wasn't hers to give."

My face burning, I returned to our room.

Mrs. Brandt, I thought. *Why was she doing this to me?*

I would speak to her, I had to.

But something about it made me afraid.

NIGHT SIX

It was nearly nine when I heard Jed drive up, headlights flashing the living room.

He'd been gone almost seven hours.

Doctor Ash, Mrs. Brandt, and Hicks were playing three-handed euchre, Hicks slapping the table every half hour or so and shouting, "Thirty-two!"

"You can tell he's bluffing," Doctor Ash insisted, "when he twirls his moustache."

"Jed," I said, hurrying from the sleeping porch as he stomped in with such force the front windows shook and the newspaper sections on the dining room table fluttered and flew.

He looked different, changed. The sun, the mayhem, the wings and beers with the guys after and *summer traffic was a bitch.*

"Hey, kiddo," Hicks said, slapping Jed on the arm. "In that cap, you look like a local."

That EDDIE'S TEEPEE hat Jed had taken to wearing all the time now. That made him look like a frat boy, a teenager in a raucous pack.

Jed smiled vaguely at Hicks, but all his attention was on his father.

Doctor Ash finally lifted his eyes from his cards, giving him a dismissive look, cool-eyed and surprising.

Jed moved to me instead, crouching beside me, his hand, fingers spread, finding my belly and his head dipping against me like a big, misbehaving dog waiting to be petted.

He looked young—*so much younger than me*, I thought, wanting to laugh. His hair shaggy and wild and his eyes dazed or glazed in a way that made me feel like he was my teenage son coming home drunk or high, trying not to get caught.

"I kept texting to check in," he whispered in my ear, not looking at his dad.

"No Wi-Fi," I reminded him. "Remember?"

Hicks, watching us, broke out into a grin.

"I know who gave you that," he said to Jed, pointing to his cap.

Jed's face flushed instantly, tugging at the brim.

"His friend Randy gave it to him," I said.

"If that's what he told you," Hicks said, reaching over and knocking the back of Jed's cap playfully.

Suddenly, I felt something wet on my bare foot, and my heart clutched. *Blood. Is it blood?*

But it was only beer, an errant bottle wedged in Jed's hoodie pocket.

"Oh," he said, looking at it—a tiny pony, Miller High Life, suddenly remembering, "Randy gave me one for the road."

The AC cranked high, Jed buried under the stiff new sheets, the room dark and spinning for him.

"I'm sorry," Jed kept saying, "I can't drink anymore. I guess I never could."

"It's okay," I kept saying. "No one cares."

In the hallway, getting aspirin for Jed, I saw Mrs. Brandt, a glass of water humming in her hand, an Alka-Seltzer tablet spinning, spinning.

"Give this to him," she said. "It's what he needs."

"Is it?" I said. "Because he asked for aspirin."

Mrs. Brandt paused, a twitch of her eyebrow.

It was my chance and I took it.

"Mrs. Brandt, why did you give me that robe?"

She lowered the glass and looked at me, the light from the open door cutting across her face.

"Doctor Ash," I said, losing my nerve a little. "It made him upset."

"Did it?" she said flatly. "How do you know?"

"How do I know?" I whispered loudly. "It was obvious. He said it wasn't yours to give."

Mrs. Brandt lifted her chin, a hint of dismissal. "Well, he's wrong about that. I am sure she'd be happy for you to have it."

"She . . . ?" And then realizing it. Realizing it with an awful, sickly feeling. "Mrs. Ash? It was Mrs. Ash's robe?"

"Unworn," Mrs. Brandt said, lowering her eyes, stepping back, disappearing into the shadows. "It was a present. A baby shower present. Never worn."

I didn't know what to say, that hollow feeling.

"Mrs. Brandt," I started, trying to think. "I don't understand."

What was this, between the two of them? So mysterious, with an electric, almost erotic charge. But was it that? It would be easier if it was that, but somehow . . .

"I'll say good night now," Mrs. Brandt said, turning. Slipping quickly down the hall.

"Why are you doing this?" I managed finally.

"I'm sorry," she said, disappearing down the stairs. "It won't happen again."

*

Outside, firecrackers were sputtering and popping in the distance.

Jed was sweet—weepy, even—and I stroked his hair, grainy with sand, smelling of smoke, and told him everything was fine. That I'd spent a fine day reading, resting, even looking at some family photos. And I felt fine, I was fine.

Jed just nodded and nodded, and I felt drowsy now too, his body the impossible weight of a sleeping child, a remembered feeling from babysitting, how the sleep made them weigh ten times their weight, like iron pilings in your arms.

I don't remember even asking him.

I must've been half-asleep or hormone-drunk, because Jed was talking about the caul.

"Dad told me it was my armor. My armor for life."

I didn't say anything. I kept thinking of how sad it was, to be born without a mother, to be wrested twice from her. Plucked from womb, from sac.

"I never knew her," he said, as though reading my mind, "so there was nothing to miss."

"I guess not," I said, and then started to think of the time, age seven, my mother lost me at the public pool after disappearing for an hour to argue with Mr. Panarites at the snack stand, and the times she forgot to pick me up at the mall, and that summer night she ran over our cat, Frank, after one too many tequila sunrises at the neighborhood barbecue. All the ways mothers can make things harder, not easier.

⚘

Dreaming, dreaming. Thinking of poor Jed, a baby in a bag, a slick bag, like plastic wrap, its face pressed, lips bared. Its head like a great cloudy marble, a spaceman in his helmet, swirls of blue and gray, a dark churn of baby hair.

There was something so forlorn about it, about him. All alone in there, floating and lost.

. . .

"Go back to sleep," Jed said, his hand once more passing over my eyes, closing them for me. My eyes shut, Jed kissing both lids.

Like my mom when I was little, putting her cool hand over my sleep-crusted eyes.

The dream came back later.

Sneaking to pee in the middle of the night, the fireworks still cracking and popping outside, I remembered it.

I was suddenly downstairs, on the forest-green sofa, and looking down to my belly to find it larger, much larger, and my skin transparent.

Through the amniotic cloud, through the silver ribbon, like the swirl of a glass marble, I could see something moving inside. A whirl of hair, a toe, a flash of tooth.

My hand on it tight. Saving it from the slurry.

A baby, mine.

And then Doctor Ash was there, standing over me, watching.

My hands on my stomach, it felt thick and waxy, like Cosmoline.

May I? Doctor Ash said, that smile. His hands on my hands.

Doctor Ash's hands, large enough to cover everything.

It wasn't hers to give.

DAY SEVEN

I woke up to the smell. Coffee grinds again, sharp and humming between my teeth. And another smell, even better.

Peering out the window above the clammy AC unit, I saw Hicks down below, his right boot grinding out a cigarette in the mud.

My stomach throbbed emptily, a hunger fast upon me, making me dizzy, confused.

Slipping back down to the bed for a moment, clammy, too, forever feeling damp, the way summer places always are.

Last night had been odd, the sense of something rustling between Mrs. Brandt and Doctor Ash and then getting caught in it, ensnared. The robe, everything.

And Doctor Ash's voice so strange behind the study door.

Well, it's their nature. She can't help it. Like a doe bleating to call in the bucks to rut.

All these private conversations and somehow, in my fevered head, they all seemed to be about me.

I fantasized about leaving. Tomorrow at the latest. So we'd be back in New York right after the holiday. So Jed would be back in his store and I'd be at Doctor Anwar's office and she would assure me that everything was fine. And we'd get takeout at the place on the corner and pet the bodega cats and our phones would work and the windows would be streaked with city musk and someone would have stolen our mail.

We would be home and ourselves again.

But now it seemed so far away.

Sound asleep, Jed's mouth hung open, a funny kind of whistle coming from it, like a cartoon snore where a feather floats up and down with each breath.

He smelled like beer, barkeeper's friend, boy-sweat, reminding me of my first boyfriend, twelfth grade, always trying to pull my shirt up, my pants down, in the storage room at Little Caesars pizza between shifts.

That whistle, though, so forlorn. *The Whistler*, I thought, remembering that childhood nickname he hated so. The fishing-line story, his dad letting him get his teeth knocked out to prove a point. It seemed impossible when he first told me. Now, maybe less so.

Everything is different here, I thought. *Everything.*

In the bathroom, sliding down my underpants, that relief again. Nothing. Not a drop.

I looked in the mirror. My face slightly blobby, blotchy. The opposite of Jed, sun-kissed, taut, like a teenage boy, always moving, always ready.

I was brushing my teeth when I saw them. The tiny specks I thought were on the mirror.

Squinting. Were those freckles on my face?

Since when did I have freckles, I thought. I looked so different and my body no longer quite mine.

Turning on the shower, I noticed:

The robe was gone from the back of the bathroom door.

✌

Mrs. Brandt set a cup of coffee on the placemat in front of me.

I had drifted down to the kitchen, Jed still sound asleep and maybe for hours more.

"Thank you," I said. "I promise just one cup."

"That's not my business," she said coolly.

It struck me in that moment that Mrs. Brandt was the only one who never looked at my belly, my stomach. Not once at all. *That's not my business.*

The door swung open and everything shook as Hicks tromped into the kitchen with that funny cowboy gait of his, still smelling of cigarette smoke, my nose twitching.

"Tamp those boots," Mrs. Brandt called out.

So familiar with him, I thought. And he was so familiar with her, shaking his shoes with exaggerated force on the floor mat as she watched.

"Dropping off that venison I promised the doc," he said, heaving a cooler onto the counter.

Mrs. Brandt didn't say anything, reaching for a broom.

"In my freezer since last season," he said to me, because I was the only one who seemed to be listening. "He was in his velvet. That buck."

"Velvet?" I asked.

"Bucks got this soft fuzz all over the bone and cartilage that become his antlers."

"What does it feel like?" I asked, imagining those flocked animal figurines my grandmother used to collect, how I'd rub my fingers along the bunny's ear, the monkey's tail.

"Warm," he said. "Alive. They're still real vulnerable in that state. Then the testosterone kicks in and the velvet sheds or gets scraped away. The antlers get hard and dangerous. When the velvet's gone, they're ready to spar."

Giving him a look, Mrs. Brandt swept the wax-papered packages from his hands.

As I was reaching for the last of my coffee, her arm swung around again and suddenly there was a foil packet in front of me.

"Pasty?" Hicks said. He looked at Mrs. Brandt. "You sneaking her pasties?"

"That's our business," she said, before disappearing into the storage closet.

Hicks winked at me as if to say, *Lucky you.*

A half hour passed and Jed was still asleep, his head thunked into the pillow now, the whistle gone. All I could see was his tangled mane, that growing beard of his from five—was it six?—days unshaved.

Through the window screen, I could see Doctor Ash and Hicks with their morning coffees in the backyard, laughing at something, or so it seemed.

Shush-shush. Mrs. Brandt was sweeping again, somewhere.

The wind lifted and suddenly I heard it.

Yip.

My phone, resting uselessly on the dresser, yipped to life. Catching a phantom sliver of cell service hovering.

I reached for it like my life depended on it.

The voicemail icon pulsing. Seven messages, four from my mother before I'd reached her and given her the landline number and three from my doctor. Two from yesterday and one today.

This is Patrice at Doctor Anwar's office, following up on the sonogram. This number for Doctor Craig, can you call and confirm? He's not returning my call.

Then: *This is Doctor Anwar. We haven't received those sono-gram results yet. I've called, but maybe you can try. Let my office know.*

Then: *Doctor Anwar's office calling again about the sonogram. We still haven't received it. Please give us a call, ideally, before the holiday. . . .*

I tried calling back but only got voicemail.

Within a few minutes, I lost the signal, lost everything.

Moments later, I was yanking the heavy phone down the hall, the weight of it, heavy enough to bludgeon someone, these old phones. The stiff, twisted cord.

The bedrest pamphlet in my hand, Doctor Craig's phone number on a sticker slapped on the back.

One vibrating ring came before a click, then a reedy female voice: *Doctor Craig's office is closed in observance of Independence Day. We will reopen on July seventh. Leave a message at the tone. If this is an emergency, please call nine-one-one.*

⌇

"I don't understand what you're saying," Jed said, coming out of the shower at last, hunting for a tee shirt amid the dirty laundry.

"I'm saying Doctor Craig never sent Doctor Anwar the sonogram."

"It probably just got lost or something."

"Lost? How do you lose something like that? It's all electronic."

He didn't say anything for a moment. He let me stare at him as he folded his sweaty tee. It was an odd gesture, folding a dirty shirt. I watched him set it in the laundry basket Mrs. Brandt had left for us.

"Jed," I said finally. "Are you listening to me?"

"Let me call the doc," he said, reaching for the rotary phone, its cord now snarled on the bedpost.

"He's gone for the holiday," I said. "That's what I'm telling you."

"Oh, sure," he said, nodding. "He always heads up to his cottage in Ontario on the Fourth. Shake the tourists off. But he'll be back," he said.

I looked at him, said nothing.

"Or we can try his private number," Jed said. "Dad has it, I'm sure."

"Let's do that then."

He stared at me, his deep farmer's tan, a permanent press in his forehead from that baseball cap, his overgrown hair, stuck up in front.

"Okay," he said. "You mean now?"

⁂

"Sure. Spoke to him last night," I could hear Doctor Ash say downstairs. "What does she want to talk to him about?"

Jed's voice too low and deep and soft. I couldn't hear it.

"I see," Doctor Ash said. "Hmmm."

Imagining what Jed might be saying in reply.

"I talked to him yesterday," Doctor Ash said again, but this time his tone was different, his voice falling quiet. "He's a friend, you know . . ."

Then the sound of the screen door slapping shut.

Looking out the smeary window, seeing the two of them walking together, a hard diagonal across the back lawn, disappearing into the dark green of the tall trees.

Waiting, waiting, I unwrapped the extra pasty Mrs. Brandt had given me. The smell, deliriously good. Two bites and it was gone. A feeling came over me, rushing through me. So strong I had to lie down again, my feet twitching.

My hand on my belly. *Baby,* I thought, *my baby.*

"Dad left Doctor Craig a message," Jed said when he returned.

"But I wanted his number," I said. "*I* wanted to call him."

"Why?" Jed asked. "He'll get back to Dad faster. Besides, like you keep saying, he's not *your* doctor."

I opened my mouth, then closed it again.

It was exhausting, feeling like a flapping, screeching bird in everyone's ear.

They love to make you feel like that, Aunt Laraine used to say, by which she meant "men," but really Uncle Nick growling from his recliner. *Nag. Battle-axe. Ball and chain. Shrew.*

Be calm, practical, simple, I told myself. *That's the only way they'll listen to you,* my mom always said.

"Jed," I said, "can we start to make a plan? To leave."

He looked up at me, surprised. "Jacy, you know we can't. Not yet."

"Why not?"

"Because of your condition. It's risky."

"Everything is risky," I said. "Staying here, with no service, with no hospital for miles—"

"Dad's a doctor and he says it's risky."

"He never said that to me," I said. "We were together all day yesterday."

"Let's just give it a few days," Jed said, turning away. Something in his expression reminded me of those family pictures: the adolescent and sullen Jed, Adam's apple swollen, sweltering in a heavy polyester baseball uniform, the hat punched over his chunky hair, not answering the question. "It's the holiday anyway."

"I'm not saying we have to leave now," I said, as evenly as I could.

"But it's been two days since the bleeding and I'm fine. I think we need to make a plan."

He shook his head. "On that road? You remember."

"Maybe we could fly—"

He shook his head again. "You can't fly."

"It's barely my second trimester," I said. "I can fly. Where's the nearest airport?"

"Marquette," he said. "But you can't fly. What if you started bleeding on the plane?"

I didn't say anything for a moment, my thoughts racing, scrambling for an answer I didn't have.

"Look," Jed said, taking my hands, "let's remember what Doctor Craig said. Bedrest is the safest way to protect you and the baby."

I pulled my hands away. "Doctor Craig isn't my doctor."

"But he's the one who examined you."

"Doctor Anwar has the same information," I said. "Or she will, once she gets that sonogram. And Doctor Anwar knows my history."

"Doesn't Doctor Craig know your history?" Jed asked, pulling at his fingers, popping his knuckles.

"I guess," I said, blaming myself for bringing it up. *My medical history*, I thought. *The abortion*. But I pushed the thought away.

Crack, crack, those tanned knuckles of his.

"Jacy, listen," he said, rising, looming over me now, "you don't want to take any chances, do you? With our baby? We don't want to be irresponsible."

I looked at him, unsure I'd heard what I thought I heard.

"Says the guy who was out boozing with his buddies last night," I said. "I'm not being irresponsible, Jed."

"I know—"

"Jesus, you're making me feel like I'm a bad mom before I'm even a mom."

"You *are* a mom," Jed said.

It was something in the way he said it, not looking at me, cutting his eyes the other way.

It was there. I could feel it. That flickering sense that we were talking about something else. I thought again of Doctor Craig at his desk, Doctor Ash and Jed seated across from him. The three of them huddled around the computer screen.

"Not yet," I said. "Not a mom yet."

We looked at each other a long minute. One of those decisive moments in an argument with your spouse: *Will I keep going? Will I say the thing, knowing there may be no coming back from it?*

I wasn't sure what the thing was that Jed might say. Or even what I might.

But the thought crossed my mind: my medical history. Was it possible that was what was flickering on Doctor Craig's screen when I'd seen them in there?

ABORTION (1).

Every woman should have her secrets, Doctor Ash had said.

I don't have any secrets.

Oh, Jacy, you sure do.

We were on the precipice and both afraid to jump.

Jed sank down to the bed.

"I didn't mean that," he said. "Any of it. I'm just . . ."

"I know," I said. "Me too."

Jed looked up at me, a dazed expression, his mouth open.

"It's all so strange, though," he said. "Isn't it?"

"What?"

"All of this. It's like a dream you keep having."

I looked at him, wondering what was happening. Was it possible he was drunk, that woozy expression, but something beneath it, his left hand trembling like a fan shuddering, its blade caught.

"I'm sorry," he said, taking my hand again. His felt so hot. "I'm sorry about all this."

I said I was, too, but I wasn't sure we were talking about the same thing.

"Hey, kiddos."

Doctor Ash's voice came through the door like a cannon. How long had he been standing out there?

"Come get some sustenance. Jedediah, let's get some food in you."

The fight, the argument—whatever it was—was swallowed up by everything. First, by breakfast, by the big plates of sausage and bacon, the CorningWare dish of scrambled eggs slick with butter.

I couldn't eat anything, but Jed ate everything, the cloth napkin Mrs. Brandt had handed him tucked in his shirt like a little boy at a pancake breakfast after church.

I tried not to notice the bacon crumbs on the corner of his mouth, the smell of egg everywhere on him, the sausage grease streaked up his arm.

Instead, we silently sat at the kitchen table, doing the crossword puzzle. The way we always had, passing it back and forth like a hot potato.

"Maybe you should go out with your friend again today," I said. "Randy."

"No," he said. "I'm staying with you."

Mrs. Brandt looked at us, pausing with the coffeepot.

Doctor Ash appeared at the screen door. Behind him, I could see Hicks, blowing cigarette rings on the gravel.

"Good morning, Jacy," he said, but he was looking at Jed, his face now down over the crossword puzzle.

"Good morning," I said.

He glanced back and forth between us.

"Here's an idea," he said. "Hicks wants to show me something. How about we all go for a little walk, a half mile at most. Fresh air'll do the baby good."

"No hiking, remember—" Jed started, his pen gripped tight.

"Boy," Doctor Ash replied, a harder tone than I'd ever heard, "I think your old man knows the difference between a walk and a hike. Let your lady be."

Everyone was walking slowly, so slowly, to accommodate the pregnant woman.

But after all those hours in the house—the chemical hiss of the new air conditioner sweating Freon, the mildew tang from the window screens, the wafting dog hair sucked up by the *chug-chug* of the mini-vac Mrs. Brandt whipped out at a moment's notice—it felt glorious being outside at all. It felt glorious to be moving.

I told myself I wouldn't think about the missing sonogram, the fight with Jed, or whatever it had been.

But those words kept leaping back: *Risky. Irresponsible.*

So I found myself lagging behind, staring ahead at the pink ears of Hicks, the pale white ones of Doctor Ash, and the tanned ones of Jed, his baseball cap bill crisp and domed.

That EDDIE'S TEEPEE hat of his. I couldn't say why, but I was starting to hate that hat, and wasn't the use of *teepees* inappropriate, maybe racist?

"What did Hicks mean last night?" I asked, moving alongside Jed. "That he knew where you got it?"

"Got what?" Jed asked.

"Your favorite new hat," I said. "You never take it off."

Jed paused, looking toward his father, twenty paces ahead with Hicks and Mrs. Brandt.

169

"Well," he said, "it's the only one I have and the sun—"

"Get over here!" Hicks shouted, waving to Jed. "Let me show you the fresh tracks your dad and I found this morning. The claw marks look round to me, but your dad . . . Anyway, place a bet to see if we got ourselves a mountain lion."

Doctor Ash slowed beside me and we were alone for the first time since the night before. That strained conversation on the stairs.

"Thank you," I started, "for calling Doctor Craig about the sonogram."

"Of course," he said. "Of course."

"I'm sorry if you heard us . . . arguing."

"All couples argue," he said. "And you're dealing with a lot right now."

"Thanks," I said. "I feel okay, really. And my doctor doesn't seem worried."

"She shouldn't be," Doctor Ash said. Then adding, "And cesareans are very common."

"Cesarean?" I repeated. "Well, we're not there yet. I know Doctor Craig only said that was one possibility, but placenta previa, it goes away. For most women."

I felt kind of funny telling him, the doctor, but it also seemed like I had to keep saying it, to everybody all the time.

"That's the spirit," he said, turning away from me. "It's just a matter of precautions."

"Yes," I said, feeling the cut of a cool breeze through the trees.

Ahead, I could hear Hicks talking, opining, about "scent marking." *It means the bitches are in heat.*

"And I know you'd never do anything irresponsible."

Irresponsible. Just like Jed had said. The two of them echoing each other, passing the ball back and forth.

"Well," I said, as calmly as I could, "I never would."

We walked a few more paces, uncomfortably.

What happened to the warm, welcoming Doctor Ash, the Doctor Ash who made everything easier, who buffed and buffered Jed's hard edges, his sullen worry?

And there was something about the way he was looking at me, only occasionally, his gaze cutting across me quickly.

That feeling again: Something was turning, or had turned. His tone seemed different, had changed in ways I couldn't pinpoint.

Maybe it had started yesterday. The robe.

And: *I just spoke to him last night.* That's what Doctor Ash had said about Doctor Craig. *He's a friend, you know. . . .*

I wondered if that had been the phone call in the den I'd overheard the night before, Doctor Ash through the heavy wooden door to his study.

Yes, I got it. I'm looking at it right now.

Now we know. Now we know.

You know what I always say, why hunt when you can trap?

Those words, all those words sounding darker now, and personal.

Or maybe it had even started the day before, the doctor's visit, the bleeding.

That moment, coming out of Doctor Craig's exam room, the waiting room was empty.

The receptionist, head tilted, looking at me a long few seconds before pointing to Doctor Craig's office.

The door open a crack, Doctor Ash's concerned face, Jed cracking his knuckles raw.

This isn't right. Not right at all.

"After all," Doctor Ash said at last, turning to me, "there's risks with any kind of birth."

"Yes," I said, my thoughts racing now.

He smiled at me, that familiar smile. The one I'd seen as so warm. A smile that now seemed to have nothing to do with what he was saying, or everything.

"Hell," he continued, "there's risks with stepping out the front door. Turning on the stove. Falling in love."

Falling in love.

That felt true. That felt achingly, urgently true in ways I couldn't name and didn't want to.

It didn't look like an abandoned mine entrance, or at least the ones I'd seen in old TV shows or black-and-white westerns. It looked mostly like a mound of dirt.

But, despite the warning sign hanging outside, a lost hiker had fallen down a shaft here last summer. A neighbor's dog, too, breaking all his legs and dying at the bottom. Doctor Ash and Hicks kept talking about it. And about the new electronic fence they wanted to put in.

"Are those scrapes?" Doctor Ash asked, pointing to something on the ground.

"I'm not sure," Hicks said, squatting down. Doctor Ash joined him.

"Maybe you-know-who."

"Could be."

They were talking about the mountain lion, of course. It was only then I remembered that loud sound we'd heard the other night. The night before I started bleeding. In all the urgency, it had been forgotten, at least by me.

"That's how they mark their territory," Hicks said, taking his cap off, wiping his brow.

I saw nothing, a tangle of moss, twigs, curling leaves, on the ground.

"Scrapes. They pull up debris on the ground with their front legs," Doctor Ash said. "You can see the bare patch where its hind legs pushed back."

"Jedediah, you wanna take a whiff?" Hicks said, his elbow jabbing at Jed, who was looking down dazedly at the ground. "Piss or scat?"

"There's definitely a smell," Doctor Ash said, rising, his hand over his nose and mouth. "Usually, there's a kill site nearby."

Kill site. What an expression.

"Sometimes," Hicks said, grinning a little, enjoying it all like he was telling a fireside ghost story, "they get you with the puncture wound. Then they start eating around the stomach, behind the ribs."

Without thinking, my hand went to my belly.

"Didn't they used to be native here?" Jed asked.

"Yep," Hicks said, kneeling down further, sniffing around like Mrs. Brandt's dog Redruth. "But then we came."

"We?"

"Settlers," Hicks replied. "They saw mountain lions as threats to their livestock. Killed 'em all off by the turn of the last century. But I guess they're coming back." Then, adding with a smile, "Maybe to get their revenge!"

"Heard you got a mountain lion team over there at the DNR now," Doctor Ash said.

"Yep. Ever since the sightings went up," Hicks said, rising again, his sunglasses glinting. "But we haven't seen any signs of a breeding population here. No kittens, and the only verified report was male." Hicks smirked. "Maybe that's why our guy's so hotted up. He's on the pull."

"No Cornish smut talk," Doctor Ash said, tsk-tsking with a raised eyebrow.

"Shit, Doc," Hicks said, feigning offense. "I'm only half Cornish, so you're only half right."

Doctor Ash laughed. Mrs. Brandt's face twitched.

"You thought it was female," I said softly to Mrs. Brandt. "The mountain lion."

"That was my guess," she said.

"Well," Hicks said, "everyone's on the lookout now, which means more work for me, so piss on that. But I keep telling them, when it's real, you won't see it coming."

It reminded me of what he'd said before. *If you see babies, that was your head start.*

"Is that why you were bringing the rifle out?" I asked Jed.

"We were just looking at it," he said, looking at his father.

"I always tell these fellas," Hicks said to me, "the only way a gun'll help is if you can shove the barrel between you and the lion about to crush your throat."

He laughed, shaking his head.

"If a mountain lion's coming at you," he said, "a sturdy lady's purse might help you just as much."

"I think Jacy's walked far enough," Jed said abruptly, turning around and reaching for my hand, hard. Like scolding a little girl reaching for the stove.

"It's only been twenty minutes," I said, bristling. "I'm fine."

"Don't worry, Jed-o," Hicks said. "No mountain lion's gunning for your lady. She's already occupied, if you know what I mean."

"We're nearly there," Doctor Ash said. "And she looks fine."

But Jed, face hidden under that cap brim, stood stock-still, his hand still firmly on my hand, wrist. I pulled it away abruptly.

"I'll walk back with her," Mrs. Brandt said. "We can sit outside, take in the morning air before the heat hits."

"I'm *fine*," I said again. They were all looking at me now. "I'll slow down. I'll take it slow."

. . .

All I wanted, really, was a minute alone, privacy. Five days in that house.

But Mrs. Brandt slowed down, too, keeping pace with me, the men in front of us, their hunched shoulders and confident strides. Laughing together, even Jed.

Hicks's voice bounded toward us again. He was talking about old Cornish miner superstitions. How it was bad luck for a woman to go into a mine.

"Fear of accidents, a cave-in, fear the copper will pinch out," Hicks said. "Gramps always said, when you're heaving out ore, never let a bloody woman come around. Lucky for Gramps, no woman wanted to be around him anyway!"

His raspy laugh, fingers stroking his moustache.

"He sure likes to talk," I said to Mrs. Brandt, unable to stop myself. Then, "I'm sorry. He's your friend."

"He's not my friend," Mrs. Brandt said. The sentence hung in the air, heavy and mysterious before she added, "I was married to him."

We walked a few yards, pieces quickly realigning in my head.

"I didn't know," I said, unsure what else to say, a hundred questions that didn't seem appropriate to ask.

But she didn't say anything, and we walked a few more yards.

"It's a hard life," Mrs. Brandt said finally.

"Pardon?" For a moment, I thought she meant marriage and for the first time it felt true.

"They're shot for sport, for trophies, for fun," she continued. Only then did I realize she was talking about the mountain lions. "They're shot after pets vanish, or livestock. They're shot when people are afraid."

"I thought you didn't like them," I said finally. "Mountain lions. How secretive they are."

"It depends," Mrs. Brandt said, looking at me squarely for the first time.

"On what?"

"On whether their mouth is on my throat."

⁓

Ahead, we saw the three men had stopped near the house, circling something on the ground.

Jed saw me approaching, a funny look on his face, the same one he wore when I caught him staring at my soiled robe on the shower rail, the baking soda Mrs. Brandt had scrubbed it with shaking off it like snow.

"What is it?" I asked, moving forward. The men curled around something, and a smell emanating.

A strong scent swarmed me, almost a heat coming off it.

"God," Jed said, the back of his hand over his nose and mouth.

It was on the ground, between them. The bird, black and black-billed, but streaked white down its center, its breast torn open, a bristly smear of red.

"Tuxedo bird," I said, remembering it from a picture book I sometimes have students draw from.

"Magpie," Doctor Ash corrected. "The females are very loud."

"Clacking like a little hen party," Hicks said, a surprisingly grave look on his face. "Looks like somebody'd had enough with this one. Legal with the right permit, but I always thought waving a rake works well enough."

"Maybe the mountain lion did it," Jed said.

He reached for my hand again, but I pretended I didn't see it. I didn't want to stand too close. It wasn't the bird. It was something else, the energy around it, like a hard ring.

"I don't guess he'd waste his time on this knot of feathers," Hicks said.

"They have a bad reputation," Doctor Ash added, poking at the bird with his boot toe. Something about it made my stomach turn, the way he was jabbing at it.

"They'll eat *anything*," Hicks said. "Songbird eggs, baby chicks, mice, voles. Roadkill. They'll pluck the insects from animal dung."

"They eat the eyes of their own newborns," Jed blurted.

"That sounds like a Roald Dahl story," I said, dubious.

"It's true," Jed insisted, turning to face his father. "Dad, you told me, didn't you?"

"Did I?" said Doctor Ash, chortling faintly.

He was still staring down at the bird, but its beak looked broken now. For a crazy second, I thought he'd broken that beak with his shoe. He couldn't have, could he?

This elegant doctor pushing his calfskin toe against the dead bird's bleeding breast.

Then, inexplicably, he pressed down on its feathers, a sickening crunch.

"*Dad,*" Jed said, his voice high and strained. "What are you doing?"

"Dirty, dirty things," Doctor Ash murmured, staring down at the ruined bird, its blue-black feathers gleaming, an iridescent purple striping its tail.

Mrs. Brandt smoothed her hair with the back of her hand, a gesture I'd never seen her make. It made her look suddenly softer, and beautiful.

"They eat their own young," Doctor Ash said, as if answering a question never asked.

"Really?" I said. It didn't sound right. I just didn't think it was true.

"Really," Doctor Ash said, tilting his head and looking at me. "Dirty things."

I felt a cold waft off him, his eyes swooping over me, turning away.

Had I imagined it?

I looked back down at the tuxedo bird, its beak hanging loose like a bowtie untied.

They eat their own young.

We were sitting on the deck, cleaning off our shoes. Doctor Ash emerged from the shed with a steel shovel. We all watched him bury the thing, kicking it into the small hole, a scatter of dirt, his feet stomping on top.

Behind me, Hicks was telling Jed how, when his father was a kid, the state'd pay a nickel bounty for every bird turned in.

"Pops'd bring in long strings of magpie eggs, even magpie legs," Hicks said. "He didn't care. Ruthless SOB."

I wasn't listening, really. I was thinking about Doctor Ash. I didn't know what had happened, but something had. There was something in that look he'd given me, I was sure of it.

"They used to think they would steal livestock eggs," Mrs. Brandt said.

I hadn't realized she was still there, standing quietly on the other side of the deck screen.

"In the end, it was a massacre," she said. "Something like a hundred and fifty thousand slaughtered."

Doctor Ash was walking toward us, the shovel in his hand.

"That's rotten," Jed said, a scrape in his voice. I found myself reaching for his hand, a strange rush of gratefulness.

Doctor Ash was beside me suddenly. Smelling strongly of the dirt, the earth, my nose tingling from it.

"Maybe so," he said. "But try going in a henhouse after one of those things gets in. They can skim through a hedge and take out a dozen baby songbirds in minutes." He shook the dirt off the shovel, a hot black feather stuck to its pointy blade.

And, under his breath, turning away, "The newborn, the unborn have never had it easy."

❦

The newborn, the unborn. Those words, the look he'd given me.

I told myself I was being paranoid, but it all seemed directed at me.

The unborn. It was a phrase I only knew from the occasional picketers who used to congregate in clutches at the women's clinic at college. Their xeroxed photos, laminated, posted onto signs.

The unborn.

And I thought of myself, feet up in the stirrups, the nurse's aide holding my hand.

It was all so complicated and I wondered, not for the first time, why I hadn't told my mother, why I'd never told Jed.

It felt wrong to hide it and also wrong to feel like I was obligated to share it. There was no winning, all the voices in our heads. About something so intimate, private, past.

❦

Through the upstairs window, I could see Mrs. Brandt glide up the back slope and all the way back to the yellow-shingled guest cottage. Redruth, not permitted inside, idled at the door, whining slightly.

Mrs. Brandt, her silhouette hovered in the front window screen a moment before one arm lifted, yanking the curtains shut.

I picked up my paperback, but then paused.

Like I could feel the ring before I heard it.

BRRRRRRING.

The landline's metal bell, hollow and momentous.

Mom, I thought. She always seemed to know when I needed her.

I rose as quickly as I could, unsteady on my feet, looking for where I'd dragged the phone earlier. My hands running along its long, beige cord like a climbing rope to the bathroom, my feet tangling in it. Tripping over myself, losing my balance, my hip slamming hard into the vanity, its sharp edge.

"Hello?" My voice a strained squawk.

"This is Doctor Anwar. I'm trying to reach Jacy—"

"Thank god," I said, then catching myself in the bathroom mirror, like myself as a little girl, stumbling down the carpeted hallway, staying up too late reading *Little House* books, certain I had diphtheria, the grippe, mountain fever. Dreaming I was Laura, about to milk Sukey, only to realize it wasn't Sukey at all but a black bear.

The call was brief. Doctor Anwar was in a cab to the airport. For, you know, the holiday. I could hear the distant sounds of the city through the earpiece, its dusty holes. Street noise, honks, the churn of traffic, the diesel bus roar.

"I'm sure it's just a communication error," she was saying. "I'll call again if the sonogram doesn't show up by Tuesday . . ."

I stopped myself from saying Tuesday was too far away. Four days was too far away.

". . . so let's get you on the books to come in at the end of the week."

"Okay," I said, the phone cord tight around my hand. "It's just . . . they don't want me to leave."

"Pardon?"

Through the bathroom door, I could hear Redruth, sniffing, snorting, moaning a little, the scatter of her paws on the creaking floor.

My hip ached from banging into the vanity, my thigh too. I felt skinned, scalded.

"Jed. My husband, Jed, and his dad," I said, sinking slowly to the toilet seat. "They think it's too risky."

Doctor Anwar paused a second. I could hear the *thud-thud* of the cab over the city asphalt.

"Let's talk on Tuesday," she said finally. "If there's no bleeding by then—"

"Doctor Anwar. Is it true that ninety-five percent of the time, it goes away? Placenta previa?"

I felt something hot on me, my hand scrabbling for my hip, my leg. *Did I cut myself?*

"Most of the time, depending on a few factors. As soon as I see that sonogram—"

"One more thing," I said, my mouth suddenly dry. "Did you send my medical records to Doctor Craig?"

A pause. "You signed the release?"

"Yes," I said. "But is it—is there a whole history?"

"Jacy, what are you asking me?"

"Nothing," I said. "I don't know." Then, "The abortion." I felt my face flush.

Why was it so hard to say aloud, but it was because here I was, the cord wrapped around me, my hip aching, humming with pain. Here I was, laid bare and everyone poking, prodding, my legs splayed for all to see.

"What about it?" Doctor Anwar said distractedly. I could hear the rush in her voice, hear her trying to hide it.

"Doctor Craig said something," I said. "That . . . women who've committed—who've *had*, but he said *committed*—two or more abortions are more at risk for placenta—"

"No!" Doctor Anwar snapped. I covered my mouth as if slapped. "I said Terminal B."

I realized she was talking to the cabbie.

"I'm sorry," I said. "You need to go. I just—I had that one, and it felt like Doctor Craig was . . ."

"Was it first trimester?" she said hurriedly. "The abortion?"

181

"Yes."

"Vacuum aspiration?"

I paused, remembering the whirring sound, the throb of the cramps and the soft whoosh, like a seal broken.

"Yes."

"Then it's moot," she said briskly. "It's moot anyway."

"Right," I said. "I know that."

A faint sigh crackled through the line. Doctor Anwar, in my mind's eye, pausing with one leg out of the taxi, its heavy door, and her phone pinched between chin and collar.

"Jacy, this isn't about something you did or didn't do," she said, her voice a little tired. Beaten thin. "It just happens. No one knows why."

"I know," I said. "I know that."

Redruth began barking loudly through the door, a high, panicky bark.

The thought came into my head, unstoppable: *I know that but do they?*

"Right there," Doctor Anwar was saying. "Skycap."

And I looked down at my leg, still throbbing from hitting the vanity. My hand tickling at my hip, my thigh. Feeling a wetness there.

"We'll talk on Tuesday," Doctor Anwar said, as if Tuesday was ever coming. As if it didn't feel like a dozen countries away, a distant land. "You'll be fine."

My hand came back red.

I twisted my torso to see the angry red gash from where my pelvis had slammed into the vanity's sharp edge. It ran hotly from my hip bone down to my upper thigh. The blood blotting on my dress like a scold. A rebuke. Another warning.

As I washed myself, as I dug out a bottle of rubbing alcohol from the medicine cabinet, as I slapped on some old wrinkly Band-Aids from the medicine cabinet, I hoped it would heal quick, so no one would see.

I didn't need another reason for everyone to look at me, to have opinions, worry over my body. My body.

"I don't like any of this, Jacy," my mom was saying, her voice over the landline so tinny and faraway. "That doctor up there is withholding important information. About bedrest, about the likelihood this'll go away."

I was sitting on the wooden toilet seat, picking at the bloody Band-Aids striped up the long denty cut on my thigh, watching them slowly unpeeling in the humidity.

The bathroom was the most alone place. The only alone place.

"I don't think he's withholding it, Mom," I said. "But the way they're all watching me—they don't want me to do anything. I'm starting to feel like . . ."

"Like a prisoner? Because they're treating you like one. It sounds like they're trying to control your body."

"Mom," I started. My natural instinct was to correct, or at least minimize, her knee-jerk response, but I couldn't, quite. "Doctor Ash, it's like he thinks I'm being reckless or something. Like he doesn't trust me with . . ." I swallowed hard before stuttering it out. "With his grandchild."

"That's ridiculous. Why would he not trust *you*? Well, he doesn't know you at all. It's outrageous. Where is Jed in this? He needs to get it together here—"

"Mom, listen," I interrupted. I didn't want to talk to her about Jed. Not now. Not with all her wariness about him. She'd never stop reminding me. "I have the feeling Doctor Craig told Doctor Ash some things. From my medical history, or something. That's crazy, right?"

"What things?" she said.

But I couldn't tell her. She didn't know about the abortion. I hadn't told her. And telling her now—well, why tell her now?

"Jacy, you can be sure he's shared all your information with him. I'm sure Doctor Ash is very charming, but in the end they all stick together."

I wasn't sure if she meant doctors or men or both.

"But none of that matters," she persisted. "And this is all bullshit. And what you need to do tomorrow is tell Jed it's time to head home. And if he doesn't want to join you, then you go alone."

I thought about that time my mom had that biopsy when I was twelve. How scary it was for that long week. How I helped her with the ice packs, with washing, the Steri-Strips peeling away, her pink tender flesh, the eggplant blood bruise on her left breast.

And how joyous we were when the results came in, making ice cream cake and lighting sparklers to stick in top and dancing around the living room to some Sheena Easton song. How I asked her if she'd told Mr. Panarites the good news. How she looked at me, her eyelid twitching, and said, her words slurring from the pain as she bent down to blow out the sparklers, *Oh, honey, Mr. P. doesn't know about any of this. Mr. P. doesn't know anything about my life.*

✦

My breath coming fast, I scrubbed and wrung my nubby yellow sundress in the sink. I scrubbed and wrung until the long strings of blood from my cut faded, disappeared.

Then I put the wet sundress in a plastic bag and hid it at the bottom of my suitcase.

That was when I saw something else, shining.

A foil-wrapped pasty. Mrs. Brandt must've left it for me, I thought. Maybe it should have felt odd, but it didn't.

Suddenly, I was ravenously hungry, peeling the foil with nearly a slather as great as Redruth, and eating the whole thing greedily, with damp, shaking fingers.

NIGHT SEVEN

The men had gone to look at some boat Doctor Ash might be buying.

"What boat?" I'd asked before they left and Jed had not quite hidden a weary sigh.

"The one we've been talking about," he said.

"I never heard you talking about a boat," I said. Adding quietly, "But you two have been having a lot of conversations without me."

I couldn't see Jed's face, bending down to tie his shoes. I thought I heard another sigh.

Then he began explaining, with exaggerated patience and without looking at me, that it was a boat called a Sea Maid Deluxe. A prewar runabout: beautiful, restored mahogany, chrome hardware, fire-engine-red interior, a Chrysler inline-six and one three-blade bronze prop run the whole thing.

"He wants me to take a look at it," Jed said, tugging on that same EDDIE'S TEEPEE baseball cap as if readying himself, as if the coach waved him from the bench. "Hicks thinks it's just a trailer queen."

I didn't know what that was, but I wanted Jed to leave. All of them to leave.

My hip and leg were throbbing from the cut and I wanted to be alone with my thoughts anyway.

Yet Jed kept talking, explaining as if I had asked that a trailer queen was apparently the kind of boat that goes only from one enclosed space to another: garage, trailer, garage, trailer. You were either a "dirty girl" or a "trailer queen" and that was that.

"I can't believe you didn't say anything about Mrs. Brandt and Hicks," I said, remembering suddenly.

"What?"

"That they were married."

"Oh," Jed said, stuffing his wallet in his shorts. "I guess I thought it was obvious. Hickson Brandt. That's his name."

"You never told me that either," I said.

Jed didn't say anything for a moment, looking toward the door.

"So, what, Mrs. Brandt told you?" Jed asked. "About being married before?"

"Yes," I said. "I can't believe you never mentioned it."

The EDDIE'S TEEPEE cap now in his hand, bending its bill, breaking it in, he turned for the door.

"It was a long time ago," he said, walking out. "I never think about it at all."

I thought I might go crazy if I didn't distract myself. But the paperback print of *Bedtime Tales of Suspense* was starting to hurt my eyes, the pages shivering with each swing of the ceiling fan. Stories of secret heirs, cursed families, old maid suicides, and slit throats.

Only when I started to set the book down did I notice someone had written something on the inside of the cover, in the top right corner in fading blue ink. *W.P.A.* The middle letter bigger than the others, like an old-fashioned monogram.

I lay on the bed in my last clean sundress, stretchy, pale green, pilled. The air-conditioning on high, humming. I fell asleep for a few moments, or a half hour, waking with a start, a powerful nausea.

Turning over on the pillow, I saw something black and shivery.

A magpie, its bloody breast splayed.

I was going to be sick.

. . .

Then I woke up again, for real this time, my mouth feeling thick, strange. My fingers shaking, my knuckles pressed.

The pillow was empty, wet.

The landline was ringing again, shrill and thunderous.

My mom again, I was sure. She loved when I confided in her. *Remember when you used to tell me everything* was something she'd said as long as I could remember. She'd never forgiven me for not telling her about Jed until I'd already moved in, wedging my art books between his, shoving my tampons and vomit-pink razors between his mouthwash and bar soap.

And he says he's a tube bender, right? Like a plumber? I guess there's a certain stability in that. We'll always need plumbers.

He looks very handsome in that picture you posted, but beware the handsome man, Jacy. And did I tell you your cousin's getting a divorce? Bobby cheated with some perfume sprayer at the mall.

But you know men always cheat down.

Limping down the hall, I lunged for the rotary phone, answering with a desperate gulp.

"Hey," came the voice on the other end, breathy and girlish, "is Jed there?"

"Excuse me?" I said. "Who is this?"

"Is this Doctor Ash's? I'm trying to reach Jed."

There were plates clattering in the background, the sound of an ice machine.

"Who is this?" I repeated.

"I'm sorry. I'm at work. This is Molly, for Jed. I have his phone."

"Excuse me," I said, feeling a funny kind of weightlessness. "I don't understand."

"Jed left his phone at Eddie's last night. I work here and—"

"Wait, what?" I said, my brain racing. *Molly.*

"He had a little too much to drink, I guess," she said, a raspy giggle in her voice. "I found it between the booth cushions. If he wants to pick it up—"

"Okay," I said. "Wait, you work there?"

"Yeah, it's my dad's place. Just tell Jed to swing by whenever."

"And your name is Molly," I repeated. My hand hot on my forehead.

"Right," she said. "He knows. We go way back."

"Molly . . . ?"

"Molly Connelly," she said, over the sound of a dishwasher churning. "But he knows me as Molly Kee."

I stood a moment in the hallway, the rotary phone awkwardly curled between my elbows.

Molly Kee. The first girlfriend. The one over whom he was *sick with love* at summer camp when he was fifteen. The expert archer with the chipped tooth who sang "Coat of Many Colors" at the talent show and for whom he would have done anything for one glancing touch of the back of her left knee.

Molly Kee was a cocktail waitress at Eddie's Teepee, where Jed had spent two of the last three nights downing round after round.

That was when I heard Doctor Ash's truck growl up the drive and settle out front.

That was when I heard Doctor Ash and Jed laughing, their laughter echoing up to the house, through the window screen.

The way sound works in the country. Things that seem so far away are suddenly right there on top of you.

"Did you buy the boat?" I asked as Jed walked in. Twitchy, ready to spring.

"Not yet," Jed said. "We're bargaining."

I watched him, looking through the laundry pile for yet another tee shirt, the way he kept sweating through them all.

"Molly called," I said, reaching for the EDDIE'S TEEPEE cap he'd just tossed onto the bed.

He nodded obscurely, staring at one of the shirts, seeming to sniff it.

"Were you eating in here?" he asked. "It smells weird."

"Molly called," I repeated. "You left your phone at the bar."

Jed turned suddenly, finally listening. He reached for his back pocket, his front one.

"My phone. Shit."

"Molly called," I repeated, hurling the EDDIE'S TEEPEE cap at him so hard he ducked. "You can pick it up anytime."

Jed looked up me and I could nearly see all the wheels turning.

"Okay," he said. "I'm sorry. Guess I didn't miss it without the signal. I'll get it later or maybe Mrs. Brandt can."

I nodded, waiting.

"What?" he said, reaching for the cap, setting it on the dresser. "I'm sorry."

"Is that why you've been spending so many quality hours at Eddie's Teepee? To reminisce with your old flame?"

Jed's eyes widened. "What? I mean, we went to camp together—"

"You were sick with love for her," I said. "Sick."

"She just served us some beers, Jacy."

I looked at him.

"I didn't know she worked there," he blurted finally. "I beat her at a game of darts. Won the hat."

"And you didn't think to tell me?"

"Jesus, Jacy," he said, shaking his head. "I didn't mention it because of how you were about her. In the car ride here."

The car ride. It seemed a hundred years ago and a different Jed.

I couldn't explain the violation. It was one of those things that are so hurtful but you know if you tried to put it into words, or tried to too soon, it would sound like you were crazy, silly, like you were the one with the problem. The problem was you.

Downstairs, Doctor Ash was calling. Something about going to get pizza for dinner.

"We'll talk about it later," I said, feeling a rush of queasiness. Leaning back on the bed.

"Sure," he said, stepping back, rolling a new tee shirt over his frame. "Whatever you say."

This was a new iciness between Jed and me. And it wasn't just about missing paperwork, or too many drinks, or cabin fever. It wasn't even just about Molly Kee, though she was all I could think about now. Molly Kee, still a spry, knee-skinned tomboy in my imagination, sitting herself on Jed's lap at Eddie's the night before and two nights before that. Plastic pitchers of flat beer and boys will be boys.

But it went further back than that. Something had turned days before, with the blood. Or months before or more.

I thought again of that night we conceived, or assumed we did. The unaccountable anger in Jed's face when I'd arrived at his shop, ready to take him out for his birthday. The pulse of his vein over his eye, the way he held my wrists down to the seat of the chair, pinning them there. *No birth control, no time.* How he'd torn my underwear, fisted it, and thrown it across the room. How he'd punched fat bruises into my thighs and between them.

How he looked like he might cry after, like a baby who knew he'd been bad.

❧

In my head, I was making a plan. Tomorrow, I would tell Jed, we leave or I do. It was the only way.

My hand pressed against my leg, the cut throbbing.

I just had to get through the night, I told myself. One night.

❧

"Is it a good story?"

I looked up from my perch on the sleeping porch. Mrs. Brandt stood there, hands folded together tightly. A scarlet strand of her perfectly coiffed hair shivering from the AC breeze.

"I don't know," I said, setting down the book. "I'm a little distracted."

"What's it about?"

"A game of hide-and-seek at a wedding party. It's at a big baronial estate. The bride thinks she's so clever. She goes up to the attic to hide in this heavy oak chest. But her veil catches and the trunk locks. The groom thinks she ran away. Many years later, he decides to move out. That's when he finds the trunk, the edges of the veil disintegrating into the floorboards. And you can guess what's inside."

"I can," Mrs. Brandt said, but she wasn't looking at me anymore but at my leg, a loose Band-Aid, a stipple of blood.

"It's just a cut," I said softly. "Please don't tell."

She looked at me but said nothing.

"What did you mean before?" I said suddenly, an urgent feeling in my chest. "That maybe Jed and I should go home."

"That's not what I said," she replied, turning.

"But you did—"

"I'll put more bandages in your room," she said, slipping back into the house.

It was only after she was gone that I remembered. *Maybe you should go home*, she'd said. Not you and Jed. You.

❧

It was dinnertime. My last dinner here, I told myself.

And something smelled of Christmas.

Clove-studded oranges, gingerbread, cinnamon.

The smell so strong I was six years old again, those moments of coming down the stairs on Christmas morning to the toy I'd most wanted. Would it be the sticker books, the airbrush marker kit that came in the big neon case, the rock tumbler kit I'd circled, folding the page corner back in the Sears and JCPenney catalogs? The smell everywhere of my mom's signature eggnog and Aunt Laraine's cement-thick gingerbread, meticulously piped and studded with red hots and the cause, two years in a row, of Uncle Nick's broken crown.

Tiptoeing down the stairs, following the smell, I half-expected I'd see my family down there, all of them waiting with matching eggnog moustaches, their laughter ringing as they saw me, Nat King Cole's voice like sheets of satin spinning from the old stereo, my mother laughing . . .

Instead, it was Doctor Ash and Jed seated stiffly at one corner of the dining room table, falling silent as they saw me, the ceiling fan above stuttering, a circle of gnats batting above.

The Christmasy smell uncomfortably mingling with other smells: Bactine, Freon, grease, meat drippings.

At the center of the table, three enormous pizzas sat on pie stands, big as sundials, sausage dappled, slick and sputtering.

Mrs. Brandt swept in from the kitchen with a pitcher of iced tea, napkins under her arm, a dampness on her brow.

Jed looked at me. Tall, overgrown in the small room, the chandelier bending against his unkempt hair. No hat this time. The Eddie's cap was gone.

"Are you okay, babe?" he said, uncapping a beer.

I couldn't remember him ever calling me *babe* before. I almost laughed, feeling strange and woozy and a little murderous, the pasty sitting in my stomach like a dumbbell.

193

. . .

"He started in crypto about eight years ago," Jed was saying, every-one serving themselves big triangles as I sat over the glass of red raspberry iced tea Mrs. Brandt had set before me. Beneath the table, Redruth mingled hungrily among our legs.

Jed, on his second beer now, was recounting some conversation he'd had with Randy, about how Randy had made all his money, money enough to buy a brand-new Smoker Craft with a four-stroke engine.

Jed didn't sound like Jed and maybe wasn't Jed at all. He didn't look like Jed and the way he was smacking his lips, his fingers sticky, and pounding those beers—

I supposed this was a big part of what marriage was, discovering your spouse over and over again, being surprised all the time.

"He's been mining it with some kind of special computer his cousin lent him," he continued. "There's these mining farms all over now and—"

"God help us," Doctor Ash said, shaking his head. "The starting QB at U-M signed an endorsement deal with one of those compa-nies. It's madness."

"It's not madness, Dad," Jed said quietly, his head dipping. "Any-way, Randy won't marry Stacey because splitting digital currency in a divorce is a mess."

"Lucky Stacey," Doctor Ash murmured, winking at me. A day or two ago, such delight I might have gotten from that conspiratorial wink.

"Aren't you hungry, dear?" Doctor Ash asked, each pizza like a great tide pool in front of me.

"This one doesn't have coo-dee-gee," Mrs. Brandt said, pointing to an untouched pizza on the sideboard.

"What's that?" I asked.

"C-u-d-i-g-h-i," Jed explained, spelling it out for me slowly, as if

I were a child—all while waving a piece on the tip of his fork, a meaty stub, glossy with fat. "A specialty up here. Only place you can get it."

"It's an Italian sausage," Mrs. Brandt said to me. "Sweet and spicy."

"Rizzo's does it best," Doctor Ash said. "You get pork cudighi in a dozen places up here. But only Rizzo's does venison."

"I haven't been there in forever," Jed said. "They had that beautiful sign. With the little pizza man in the chef's hat."

That beautiful sign. That sounded like the Jed I knew, the artist, the artisan.

"Sign broke," Doctor Ash said. "You should stop by. Maybe you could make a sale." Adding, with a knowing look, "This is the sign you're looking for."

Jed cleared his throat, reaching for his beer.

This is the sign you're looking for.

"Jed made a sign that says that," I said slowly. "It's in his shop."

"Yep," Doctor Ash said, looking at Jed.

"You've been there?" I said, feeling myself keeling slightly. "To Jed's shop?"

"Sure," Doctor Ash said. "Didn't he tell you?"

"Oh," Jed blurted, voice cracking like a teenager. "I forgot. My dad stopped by three or four months ago. On his way through town. Didn't I tell you?"

"No," I said. "In fact, you told me he'd never been there at all."

Jed reached for my hand under the table. I pulled it away.

"I had a three-hour layover on his birthday," Doctor Ash said, nodding at Jed. "Got in his hair and left."

His birthday. Three or four months ago. Jed so surly when I'd arrived. How rough he'd been, how there wasn't time for my diaphragm or anything, my underwear torn, balled in his fist. The bruises after.

The night Jed said, *Don't put your diaphragm in, Jacy*—

The night we'd conceived.

A strained silence fell.

"Well, anyway," Doctor Ash said, "worth dropping by Rizzo's, Jed. Expand your business beyond gentlemen's clubs and toothpaste signs. After all, you might need the extra money, now the baby's coming."

"Try it," Jed said, ignoring his father, poking his fork in my face.

The smell now so cloying, so close to my nose. Nutmeg, cloves, allspice, the tang of red wine, the heat shimmering from the glossy pies, the funk of the cheese.

"No, thanks. I . . ." I felt something twisting inside. Before I knew it, my hand darted out, batting Jed's fork away, the fork flying, the sausage stub flying, both landing somewhere behind Mrs. Brandt's chair.

"Jesus, Jacy," Jed said, jumping to his feet, wondering loudly what was wrong with me, did I have a fever or something, why was I acting like this—

"It's just the smell," I said, not daring to say I felt sick. Nauseated.

Doctor Ash waved to Mrs. Brandt, who rose to tend to me.

The room was getting smaller, the insinuating smells and my eyes catching Doctor Ash's, sitting calmly while Jed chased down the fork, the sausage already caught up in Redruth's snout with a loud, satisfied grunt, her tongue lapping pinkly.

"Don't be sorry," Doctor Ash said, his blue eyes glittering coldly. "You can't help what you are."

A washcloth on my forehead, I lay on the bed, my stomach empty now. A hot wave of vomit stench still shuddering from the bathroom.

I could hear them below.

Maybe they didn't care if I heard. Maybe Doctor Ash wanted me to.

"She's your wife, Jed," Doctor Ash was saying. "The mother of your child."

"It's not like that," Jed said. "Jesus, Dad."

"The mother of your child needs your full attention," Doctor Ash said. "Don't drive her away with this nonsense. Beers and cocktail waitresses."

"Dad, that's not why she wants to leave—"

"If you push women, Jed," Doctor Ash said, "sometimes they'll do reckless things just to spite you. They can't help it. It's their nature. You must do the thinking for them."

It's their nature. Just as he'd said on the phone in his study. To Doctor Craig, I presumed.

Well, it's their nature. She can't help it. Like a doe bleating to call in the bucks to rut.

You must do the thinking for them.

❧

"But what did he mean?" I demanded.

"I don't know what you're talking about."

"Your dad. When he said, *You can't help what you are.*"

"Pregnant," Jed said. "You're pregnant. That's all he meant."

We were upstairs and it was only nine o'clock.

Jed and his dad had been drinking some kind of tequila Hicks had given him. Now he smelled like tequila, hard and smoky, like my mom's purse when I was a kid and she still snuck Benson & Hedges now and then.

"Jed, did your dad come to see you that night we . . . that night we think we got pregnant?"

"What?" he said, his eyes glazed. "I mean, we don't really know the exact day it happened, do we?"

"It was your birthday. I came to take you out to dinner. You were so mad when I got there."

"Maybe," Jed said. "I didn't tell you about it because he said . . . I don't know, Jacy. He just . . . he wasn't sure about things."

"What things?"

"He loves you," he said. "But he was just making sure I was ready to be a husband, a dad. He wanted to make sure I was thinking things through before . . ."

"Before we got pregnant."

Jed looked up.

"And so we did," I finished. "You made sure we did."

Jed looked at me, a lostness in his eyes.

"Are you sorry?" he asked. "Are you?"

I wasn't. Not at all, in ways so deep I wanted to cry. Wanted to hold my belly and cry.

But I couldn't say it. All I could think about right now was how that night, that time, making a baby—it was suddenly no longer ours. It was like Doctor Ash was there watching.

"It's time to leave," I said. "Tomorrow."

"Let's talk about it in the morning, okay?"

"You said that yesterday. You say that every day." I felt my voice crack. "Jed, I know we're a mess right now, but please listen to me: I don't feel comfortable here anymore."

Jed looked away, twisting his knuckles in his hands.

"I've never felt comfortable here ever," he said.

It felt like there was a whole world shivering behind that sentence. A haunted history.

"What do you mean?" I asked.

But he just shook his head, shrugged a little, reached out for me, taking a few of my fingers in his hand.

"Jed," I said. "He's getting in your head."

"He's always in my head," Jed said softly. "Always."

"Jed . . ."

"It doesn't matter, it doesn't matter," he whispered, taking my hand in his, patting it loosely, carelessly, as if he'd forgotten I was there, who I was. What I was doing there at all.

And I thought again how little I really knew of Jed, maybe how little I knew Jed. Both of us stumbling upon each other two years ago, our lonesomeness swimming upon each other so quickly, in warm, murky waters, feeling rather than knowing. Our single parents, their devotion sometimes suffocating, our scattered history of breakups, confusion. Our hands clasping for each other, looking for something to set us on a familiar path, to anchor us, our lostness, everyone's lostness. This is what we do, isn't it, isn't this what we do?

Honey, my mom had said, *we all marry strangers.*

And his arms now wrapping around me, leading me to bed, the tequila drowning out the cudighi, reminding me faintly of long-ago evenings, a garden patio and margaritas, those early days of dating, the tingle in my teeth, behind my ears, looking at Jed across the flickering tea lights, wanting to skip dessert, skip the entrée, and burrow my way back through his shop, my hand reaching for his, fleet-footed through the studio, the neon blinking and strobing—pizzerias and rolling dice, shoe repair and bowling pins—until we landed on his office futon, dusty and squeaking, one rung loose, our bodies sinking, Jed's hand caught in my hair, his breath caught in mine.

It was a hundred years ago, more.

Honey, I just want you to have everything you ever wanted.

That's what my mom said when I first told her about Jed. She said it again when I told her I was pregnant.

That's all every mother wants, she added. *You'll see.*

❧

Sometime in the night, an eerie sliver of a dream. I could feel something sharp in my belly, like a tentpole, an umbrella, expanding.

From his mother's womb untimely ripp'd. Wasn't that what Mrs. Brandt had said?

Throwing the bedspread back, I looked down and saw my belly stretching my skin to translucency, felt my pelvis splitting, splintering.

Maybe you should go.

Staggering to my feet, I rushed down the dark hallway, dark stairs.

The *clip-clip-clip* of the air-conditioning, the house humming with it, I ran for the patio, the door wide open, the heavy night air beyond.

Running now, the whoosh of black trees above, my tee shirt whipping in the wind.

Through the trees, I could see Mrs. Brandt's cottage, a yellow-lit box in the distance, the wind whining up its chimney, whining in my ear.

I have to get there. I must.

A voice came from somewhere, sharp and stern.

"What are you doing to her?"

I looked down at my belly, which was like a foggy fishbowl, a porthole.

Only then did I see the handle there, just under my belly button.

I turned it like a washing machine door, a blast of heat and water inside tumbling forth.

And with it, too, this squirming thing, hairy and strange.
My hand on it tight. Saving it from the slurry.
Its eyes looking up at me, blinking twice, then twice again.
My baby. My baby.
It was mine.

"Jacy! What are you doing?"

Then the *whoosh-whoosh* over my shoulder. A golden streak past my eye.

"Don't move!" A spotlight on me. A flashlight on me.

This is no dream.

Taking two fingers, I reached inside my mouth, hot and hollow, pulling out a clump of wet, clotted soil, black as a magpie feather, black as the night.

"Jacy, stop, stop," and a heavy arm around me, the voice a snarl, low and strange.

"Dad, is she okay?"

"Is she okay," Doctor Ash said, not asking or answering, his blue eyes glistening.

A hard slap to my face. Ringing in my ear like a church bell. Like a wedding bell.

"Wake up, Jacy. Wake up. Wake up. Wake up!"

DAY EIGHT

I'm fine," I kept telling them.

We were in the dark backyard, the hint of dawn somewhere above the towering trees.

Did someone slap me? My fingers to my stinging cheek.

"Runaway bride," Doctor Ash was saying, his voice clipped.

Jed was trying to wrap something around me, even though I wasn't cold. Was in fact sweating, sticky, a wave of humidity coming even at the early hour.

I looked down at my hands, dirt-streaked.

"Sleepwalking like Lady Macbeth," Doctor Ash added with a hollow chortle as he moved further down the grass slope, peering into the woods beyond, Mrs. Brandt's red-tipped flashlight in his hand.

"I've never walked in my sleep before," I kept saying, and Mrs. Brandt was suddenly there with a wet cloth. I thought she was going to rub it on my mouth and neck like I was three, but she only handed it to me.

"Looked for a minute you might try to scale that fence like a mountain lion," Doctor Ash said. "Someone might've taken buckshot to you."

"Dad," Jed said. "Come on."

"Did someone slap me?" I asked out loud this time, and no one seemed to hear.

"I'll get you something to put on," Jed was saying, running ahead of us into the house.

Something to put on why.

"I must have fallen," I said, running the wet cloth across my cheek. "On my face."

There was no accounting for the dirt on my mouth, a filthy smear. Was it in my mouth or please, please did I dream that part, fumbling around with my tongue.

"It happens," Mrs. Brandt whispered to me, leaning close. "My sister hungered for it, all three times. The body wants it."

"Tracks!" Doctor Ash called out suddenly, flashlight trained on the ground. Then, turning toward us, his face stern. "Get inside the house. Go. Now."

Her arm encircling me, Mrs. Brandt swept me up the deck steps, past the sleeping porch, and into the house.

Doctor Ash slid the patio door behind us hard, the rough click of the lock.

"What kind of tracks?" Mrs. Brandt asked.

"You know what kind." Doctor Ash's eyes glowing in the dark living room.

For the first time, I shivered. Thinking of myself out there, stupored and lost in my own brain. Had I missed the faint hush of prowling footsteps, the flash of moon-bright eyes?

Was it possible the mountain lion had been out there with me?

"Maybe you smelled her," Mrs. Brandt said, reading my mind. "Or she smelled you."

. . .

Seconds later, Jed appeared on the stairwell, his red face even redder now.

"You're bleeding."

We all turned to see Jed walking down the steps slowly, holding something yellow in his hands.

"Who's bleeding?" Doctor Ash said. "Boy, who—"

"Jacy's bleeding," Jed said, his face snarled and strange.

In his hands, that yellow thing. Yesterday's pilled sundress.

Mrs. Brandt inhaled fast.

"You've been bleeding," Jed repeated, holding up the dress, holding it wide and high like a wedding sheet in olden days, revealing the rusty hieroglyph of yesterday's blood. From cutting my leg on the bathroom vanity's sharp edge.

The dress I'd tried to scrub clean, then buried, soaking wet, at the bottom of my suitcase.

"How could you hide this?" Jed said, moving toward me.

"I didn't hide anything," I said. "Did someone slap me out there?"

No one said a word, Jed's fingers clamping the sundress, Doctor Ash shaking his head gravely.

"Jed—" I started.

"It's our baby," Jed called out, a thunder in his voice I'd never heard. "And you're hiding things."

Doctor Ash moved toward him, his hand reaching for his shoulder.

"I'm not bleeding," I said, trying to shake myself awake. *Am I awake?* "Listen to me—"

"We're going to Doctor Craig's," Jed said, flinching from his father, the sundress over his hands, twined around his fists.

"It's not what you think," I said, trying to get Jed to look at me. He seemed like he might cry. I had never seen him cry. "I cut myself yesterday. It was nothing."

I pointed to my thigh, covered by my tee shirt. I wanted to lift it, to show him, but then something about all their gazes . . . and I shouldn't have to show Jed anything.

"We're going to Doctor Craig's today," Jed repeated, with a coldness I'd never heard before either. All these firsts.

They were all looking at me.

"You're not listening," I said more loudly now, Mrs. Brandt breathing hard beside me. "I'm not going. I'm fine. I cut myself and—"

"It's not about you," Jed said coolly. "One of us has to think about the baby."

I didn't know what I was hearing, my dirt-thick fingers twitching, my legs. *Who is this person?*

Doctor Ash cleared his throat loudly.

Mrs. Brandt looked at him, seemed to nod toward him as if understanding something. The secret language of old acquaintance, a shared history, more. Something intimate and inexplicable.

"His office is closed for the holiday," Mrs. Brandt said, taking the sundress from Jed's hands. "Doctor Craig's."

There was the briefest of silences, me staring at Jed, Jed watching Mrs. Brandt shake the sundress loose and calmly fold it over her arm. My head aching and trying to make Jed look at me, trying not to scream.

Outside came the long whistle of a distant firework. The holiday, the holiday.

"He'll come here," Doctor Ash said finally, his voice low and strange. Then turning to me, so close, his index finger tapping on my hand. "Doctor Craig will come here."

"No, he won't," I said, my voice choking, trying to be heard. "No, he won't."

But Doctor Ash wasn't listening to me. Didn't seem even to see me. I was a ghost floating there.

"He'll do it for me, son," he said, clapping Jed's arm.

Mrs. Brandt and I watched as Doctor Ash led Jed away, out of the room, down the narrow hall to his office, his study, the room I'd been in only once, the bolt-action rifle in all our hands.

Doctor Ash's hands on my hands.

The click of the study door, a whiff of cigar and baize. Old leather and Cosmoline. That amber wax slinking under my fingertips.

I watched them go, my breath catching.

"You have to soak overnight," Mrs. Brandt said in my ear. "If you don't want anyone to see."

There was no going back to sleep. It was just past four thirty, dawn still an hour away or more. But I stayed upstairs, in the bathroom, looking at the cut on my hip, strangely tight under my fingers.

There is nothing wrong with me, I wanted to tell Jed, but he never came upstairs. *There is something wrong with you.*

"This is unacceptable," my mom seethed, the landline lugged once more into the bathroom. "What is going on with Jed? What happened to him?"

I didn't know how to answer, didn't know the answer. Couldn't begin to fathom the hidden, subterranean intricacies of father and son, the lost mother, the mysteries of men.

"Honey, if you think you need to leave, then you absolutely need to leave. Take the car, go to a hotel, clear your head."

"He has the car keys," I said, then immediately wanted to take it back.

"Jed? Is he keeping them from you? Jacy, you're scaring me—"

"I'll get them," I said. "He's not."

"Do you want me to fly out there, honey?" she said, and instantly I started crying.

No, Mom, no, I kept saying over and over, feeling crazy, my left hip throbbing like it had its own heart in there, buried deep in the tissue of my skin. I didn't want her to come. I wanted to leave. It was ridiculous, the whole thing. I just had to put my foot down, that was all I had to do.

But what a mother will do, I thought. That's what a mother will do.

And I put my hand on my belly, imagining my way in. Wanting to reach inside somehow, to burrow down inside there, into the amniotic swim, and whisper a promise, pledge an oath.

What a mother will do. What a mother must do.

After I hung up, the heavy phone in my lap as I sat on the toilet seat, I heard something. A sound rising through the floor vent, a harsh snap and clack that hummed in my ear. A snap and clack like the bolt-action Doctor Ash had showed me a few nights ago, a hundred years ago.

My hand slapped over the bathroom vent.

What were they doing in the study?

A panic in my throat.

Then the low hum of Jed's voice, no words audible, only the drone of his voice.

Suddenly aware: *If I can hear them, can they hear me? Had all my conversations been heard?* Of course they had.

Today, I told myself, even whispering aloud. *Today's the day I leave.* With Jed, or without him. I just had to play it right, find my moment, and then, within an hour, I would be charging down the interstate in that toothpaste-white Chevy, bounding across the big bridge. *The longest suspension bridge in the Western Hemisphere*, so long it seemed to disappear into the clouds, into heaven itself.

My hands riffled through Jed's jeans, his windbreaker, hunting for the rental car keys, my fingers fumbling for the hard plastic ring, the fat alarm fob.

But they were gone.

"What are you doing?" A hard voice behind me, the creak of the door.

"Hey," I said, turning around to see Jed, my hands dug into the pockets of his shorts. He looked so tall, the light and low ceilings throwing his shadow high up the wall. "I thought I might go for a drive."

"You were going to leave," he said. "Without me."

I didn't say anything. Didn't know what to say.

But then a pained look fell over Jed's face and we both sat down. He smelled like mud-slick leaves, grainy and good.

Oh, Jed, I thought. *Where did you go?*

"I need you to know that I believe you," Jed said. "About the bleeding."

"Am I supposed to thank you for that?" In that moment, I wanted to strangle him.

"No," he said. "That's not what I meant."

"Did you hit me?" I asked. "Before. Outside."

The alarm in his eyes. "No," he said. "No."

Then a pause. "He was trying to wake you up."

"Your dad hit me?"

"It wasn't like that," he said, his voice gone high. "You know it wasn't."

Both of us breathing, quiet, careful. Did he want me to show him the cut on my leg anyway? To lift my shirt to my waist and show him the Band-Aids on my hip and thigh, new from Mrs. Brandt's replenishing?

"Anyway," he said finally. "I wish I could explain it all. I'm just . . . I can't tell you what it felt like, to see that dress, your blood . . ."

And after seeing my wife on the floor, swimming in her own blood. That's what Doctor Ash had said about his wife, Jed's mother.

"We need to leave," I said. "Today. Right now."

"What?" he said, lifting his head slowly, as if I really were crazy. As if I weren't making any sense at all. As if I'd said I need to go to the moon, disappear, fly away like a bat, a witch.

"That's not possible," he said.

"Then I need to leave," I said. "I'm leaving."

Slowly, he turned his head and looked at me, a long, dark look. *His face isn't even his face anymore*, I thought. *I don't know this face.*

"I need to leave," I said again. "Give me the keys. Jed, this place is bad for us. Bad for me."

That was when we heard the car pull up, a spray of gravel.

"Goddammit," I said, peering out the window to see the hatchback, Doctor Craig exiting in his fishing hat, bucket mesh, lures and hooks dangling from it like a Norman Rockwell cover. "Goddammit, why is he here?"

My heart charging, wanting to pound on the window, or Jed, or any of them.

"I don't know," Jed said, heading for the door. I could tell he was lying. "Dad, I guess . . ."

"Jacy, please," Jed said, calling up from the landing. "Come down and join us."

The men were downstairs, and they just wanted to talk, about my condition, about travel risks, you know, about *this*.

"Not a chance," I hissed at him from the top of the stairs. "*I'm not talking to them.*"

Doctor Ash appeared suddenly behind him, looking up at me from the landing, his jaw tight.

"Now, now," he said tonelessly. "Let's all settle down."

A blank expression on his face, and he wouldn't meet my eyes, didn't deign to, before he disappeared again.

"We just want to talk," Jed was pleading. "Figure out a plan, to think it through with a clear head."

"Oh, honey," I said, my voice sounding sweet and strange, "I have my own plan. And we're long past that conversation."

You have to listen to that feeling, my mom had said earlier. *The fear.*

I'm not afraid, I'd insisted, the hard scrape of my voice. *I'm just so angry.*

They're the same thing, she'd replied, so urgently. *The anger and the fear, Jacy. They're the same.*

Remembering again the harsh snap and clack like the bolt-action rifle echoing through the walls. Up the walls to me.

ᠷ

The soft rap on my door.

It was Mrs. Brandt, with a teacup teetering red.

"Raspberry leaf," she said, handing it to me.

"Thank you." I took it, red sloshing over its lip onto the saucer.

We could hear the men below. The thrum of low voices.

"I think you should go down there," she said, her hands interlaced before her, her mouth a straight line.

"No," I said. "He's not my doctor."

Mrs. Brandt didn't say anything and I felt a twang of panic.

"I'm not going to be examined in this house." I couldn't believe I had to say it.

"Of course not," Mrs. Brandt said, still not moving. Looking down at me on the bed. "But you should go down."

"Why? Why would I ever do that?"

"Because," she said, moving toward the door, "if you don't go down, there may be no stopping it."

"Stopping what?" I said, setting the cup down.

But she kept moving because she knew that I knew the answer. Or, at least, what I knew was they wouldn't stop.

~

The men sat, semi-circled, Jed on the stone fireplace hearth, Doctor Craig on the sofa, palming his fishing hat, spinning it between his fingers. An anxious look on his face.

"We've handled this badly," Doctor Ash was saying, pouring coffee from a percolator nested on the table.

I sat several feet away, on a dining room chair I'd dragged in, scraping the floor as I went.

Upstairs, I could hear Mrs. Brandt sweeping, slowly sweeping.

"We've bulldozed over your feelings as men are wont to do. You know men. They like to fix things, swoop in," Doctor Ash continued. "But that doesn't mean we should ignore your condition. Old Whit's been nice enough to swing by during his vacation to check in on you. And after everything—"

"There is no everything and no condition," I said. "I'm pregnant and I'm fine. I keep saying it. I'm fine."

"And, of course, you and Doctor Craig can speak privately," Doctor Ash said. "If you prefer."

"If I prefer? Look, *I* don't need to speak to Doctor Craig," I said, staring at him. "Except to ask him why my doctor—my actual doctor—hasn't received the sonogram results."

"What's that?" Doctor Craig said, eyes blinking, reaching for his phone. "I'll let Donna know. We've had some internet outages."

Jed, head bowed, said nothing.

Doctor Craig stared at his phone, waiting for the signal that would never come.

"Look," I said, "there's been some confusion. There's been no more bleeding other than a cut on my leg. And now it's time for me to go home and see my doctor."

Doctor Ash looked at Doctor Craig.

"Of course," Doctor Craig said. "Home and rest. But I hear that's quite a trip for you. Michigan's infamous potholes and all that. It's like the cratered surface of the moon. Best to stay put for a while. Here, you have all the comforts of—"

"Doctor Anwar says I should go home," I said, not quite true, not quite not.

Doctor Craig looked at me, head tilted.

"Well, I'd be happy to speak to him."

"Her."

"Her. Sure. And I'm sure once she sees those sonograms and learns about the persistent bleeding—"

"There's no persistent bleeding! I cut my leg!" I insisted, lifting my tank dress high, showing them my leg, hip, thigh, striped with Band-Aids half-unpeeling, my underwear, everything.

Doctor Ash rose and Jed hid his head in his hands. Like a Greek tragedy, he hid his head in hands.

"Now, Jacy, that's not necessary—" Doctor Ash started.

"And yet it is," I said, my voice shaking now, my fingers trembling as I let the dress fall. "Look, I'm leaving. So forget about the potholes because—"

"It's a bad idea," Doctor Ash said, turning to Doctor Craig. "Isn't that right, Whit?"

"It might be fine, but why take the chance?" Doctor Craig said. "We want to reduce the risk of complication. Try to counteract the patient's inherent risk factors. Age, patient history—"

"And what about her history?" Doctor Ash said, looking at Doctor Craig.

I felt something slither in the back of my brain.

"What?" I said to Doctor Ash. "What did you say?"

Doctor Craig opened his mouth, then paused.

Jed, as if suddenly risen from the dead, lifted his head.

"What history?" he asked. "I don't understand."

"We went through all this in my *private* consultation," I interrupted. Because I knew what was coming. And surely Doctor Ash did, too, prompting Doctor Craig like a stage manager giving an actor his cue.

Doctor Craig looked at me, the white fluff of his eyebrows, his pink face.

Jed's head whipped from me to his father to Doctor Craig, stone still.

"Doesn't he know?" Doctor Ash said, blue eyes sparking at me. "About your history?"

"Know what?" I said, my voice high and loud. "And how do *you* know anything about my history?"

Doctor Ash and Doctor Craig exchanged looks.

I thought again of that phone call. Doctor Ash behind the door of his study:

Yes, I got it. I'm looking at it right now.

Well, it's their nature. She can't help it. Like a doe bleating to call in the bucks to rut.

A pause, and the scraping of a chair.

No, I'm glad you told me. Good to know what we're dealing with.

You know what I always say, why hunt when you can trap?

His laughter, warm and poisonous.

Of course he knew about the abortion. It explained so much, every pointed comment. And, to him, that bit of medical history was everything he needed to know.

"Are you suggesting your past might be pertinent, Jacy?" Doctor Ash said. "If so, why not put it on the table. There's nothing to be ashamed about."

"Hank," Doctor Craig started, looking at Doctor Ash.

"Did you share my record with him?" I asked Doctor Craig. "How is talking about my medical history to my father-in-law necessary?"

213

"Now, now," Doctor Craig said to me, a slick of sunscreen on his forehead. A slick of sweat. He reached for his phone again. "Calm down, little miss. I think you have the wrong—"

"Goodness," Doctor Ash was saying, "what secrets you must have! Jed, did you know you married such a mystery woman! What is it? Took a few years off your age? Heavy smoker? Cocaine?"

He laughed so loudly, so loudly Doctor Craig let out a nervous giggle too.

"Well, whatever it is," he continued, "you should know a doctor may also discuss a patient's condition with family, relatives, and friends that the patient identifies as being involved in their healthcare . . . unless the patient objects."

"Jacy, what's going on?" Jed said. "I don't understand. . . ."

"And why would you object?" Doctor Ash said to me. "After all, it's not just *your* baby. It's Jed's. It's my grandchild. Surely you wouldn't object to your husband having all the information needed to determine your path."

"I object to all this," I said, feeling dizzy suddenly. Feeling enraged and light-headed at once. "But I guess it's too late, isn't it?"

The way Doctor Ash was looking at me. The coldness in his eyes, so cold it ached.

"Will someone tell me what we're talking about?" Jed demanded, rising to his feet.

"They're talking about an abortion," I said coolly. I finally said it. Why not? "They're talking about my abortion."

"Your what?" Jed whispered.

All three men looked at me, their eyes wide, the ineffable whiteness of their faces.

"I see," Doctor Ash said. "Well. Well."

He leaned back on the sofa, his jaw clenched.

It was only then that I realized none of them knew.

"We've had internet problems at the office," Doctor Craig said, fumbling with his phone again. "They didn't get the sonogram and we didn't get your full medical record. Just the form you filled out . . ."

Doctor Ash, his eyes dancing, his mouth a straight line. Was it judgment, disgust, contempt, or satisfaction? Who could tell?

I couldn't look at Jed, who'd turned away, staggering to the corner of the room.

"How long has it been swollen like that?" Doctor Craig said suddenly, moving closer to me.

"I don't . . ." I started, looking down at my hip, my upper thigh, the skin tight and shiny, almost wet. The skin there looked like an orange peel, pitted and pulsing, hot to the touch.

My head felt funny, my fingers shaking, my legs softening.

"I think you should sit down," he said, moving closer, as they all did.

Has she been outside?

Yes. She goes out at night. All hours. Half-naked.

Dad.

Son, the finest woman has some filthiness in her. She can't help it. Eve's curse.

And Doctor Craig, tentative, careful.

Point is, when they have an open cut like this . . .

Well, they all have open cuts, don't they?

Dad, don't.

I'm kidding, boy. Come now. You know how they are.

My eyelashes fluttering, the spangle of lights.

I felt the throb under my hand, hot. I'd been down for the count, that's what Doctor Craig kept saying, and I remembered suddenly the feeling of being lifted.

Now I lay arms akimbo, my body awkwardly propped on the sofa, my swollen leg zagging off the edge, my right hand clamped over it. Someone'd tugged and twisted my dress so my underpants were hidden.

Jed above me, Doctor Ash beside him, and Doctor Craig leaning over me in that fishing hat, the feathers dangling.

It was *The Wizard of Oz*. Dorothy wakes up to see the three men—the farmhands who look just like the Scarecrow, the Tin Man, the Lion—surrounding her bed.

Doesn't anybody believe me?

Of course we believe you, Dorothy.

"It's a good thing we caught it," Doctor Craig was saying to Doctor Ash. "You found her in the woods?"

"I'm right here," I said, my eyes wide open now. "You can ask me."

Cellulitis. That's what Doctor Craig said. A bacterial infection. It was nothing to worry about on its own, as long as I kept my leg elevated (*and clean, please*) and took the whole cycle of antibiotics, five days. *They may make you sick,* he said, *but that's just the body healing itself.*

The body, I said. *Right.*

Pregnant women are more vulnerable to infections. Yeast, bacterial vaginosis. Even HIV.

I said nothing, acutely aware of Jed and Doctor Ash hovering a few feet away in the dining room, the illusion of privacy as I lay sprawled, half-clad and pulsating, on the hunter-green sofa.

Cool, wet dressings, and keep it elevated, he said to the room itself it seemed, his voice loud enough for everyone to hear. *And, of course, stay put.*

I said nothing, the *thump-thump* under my pink flesh like the beating of my heart.

When you have an open cut like this, he said, the words echoing, *you're taking a chance every time you step outside.*

Is that so, I said, watching as he took a blister pack from his bag.

A bag like Doctor Ash's bag, his father's bag, black as a spider, square-mouthed, split handle like a leer.

No need, he said, *to take unnecessary risks.*

Sunburst streaks from the original wound, like red arrows pointing from my hip, my thigh, or pointing *to* my hip, my thigh. Like one of Jed's lurid neon signs.

A small tear in the skin, a narrow cleft, and look at all the damage it can do.

The finest woman has some filthiness in her. She can't help it. Eve's curse.

When you have an open cut like this . . .

Well, they all have open cuts, don't they.

Had Doctor Ash actually said that, hearing it now in my head like a dark scold? A wry curse?

Jed was going with his dad to the drugstore to get the rest of the antibiotic cycle, the two of them now seemingly inseparable.

Jed hadn't said a word to me or looked at me since I said the word. Since I said *abortion.*

Doctor Ash came knocking on the bedroom door.

"Jed's pulling the car around," he said when I answered, "but he forgot the prescription. That kid . . ."

Shaking his head and smiling mirthlessly.

It was like before, so polite, ever a grin, the genial mask he wore that hid everything.

"Tell Jed to fill up the tank while you're out," I said, handing him the prescription. "For the long drive tomorrow."

I watched him, waiting for the words to land. Waiting for him to protest, resist.

Instead, he gave me a long, funny look. A little sad, or wistful.

217

Maybe, I thought, he's resigned himself to it. We were leaving, or I was. That was that.

"Will do," he said, turning to leave. "Whatever Mama says."

And the door creaked shut behind him.

Something in the way he looked at me. Dirty thing, feral thing, a mouth full of mud. Take a shovel to it. Split it in two. Tie it in a trash bag and bury it deep in the yard, past smelling it, feeling it. Bury it away forever. Bury that dirty thing. We don't need it anymore.

I sat at the kitchen table, drinking more red tea, my foot resting on the seat of a chair.

I thought of Doctor Ash and Jed alone in the truck. What Father must be saying to Son.

I thought again about why I hadn't told Jed about the abortion, or why I hadn't told my mom.

But I hadn't told Jed, and it shouldn't matter. And the fact that it *did* seem to matter to him, that he couldn't even look at me—well, it seemed I was right for never sharing it.

They never look at you the same way after, a girlfriend told me once. I guessed she was right.

They were gone for over an hour and when they returned, Jed didn't even come inside. Instead, without saying a word, he went for a long walk in the woods alone.

Doctor Ash set the prescription bag down between Mrs. Brandt and me.

"You should take those with some food," Doctor Ash said.

The prescription bag curled on itself on the kitchen table.

"And take it with the aspirin to help with the swelling."

"Got it," I said. "Thanks."

"You go rest up now," was all he said to me, those same twinkling eyes but a hollowness behind them, a hollowness in his voice. That friendly Michigan tone gone, those friendly Midwestern phrases: *Well, that's just fine, isn't it? You guys want me to come with? No, yeah* and *yeah, no* and *no, yeah, no* . . .

"I don't need to rest," I said. "I've rested enough."

"Well, look at you," he replied. "Aren't you a pistol?"

"Did Jed fill the tank?" I asked. "For the trip home."

He looked at me, the light gone from his eyes in an instant.

Mrs. Brandt cleared her throat, turned away.

He looked at me with a grim smile.

"Of course," he said, rapping the table hard with his knuckles. Then he turned to leave, heading toward the hallway, his study.

"You were gone so long," I called out after him. "With Jed."

He stopped, the back of his head shimmering silver in the dark hallway.

And then a smile, a wink, and a look on his face as he turned, a look as if something had happened and soon enough I would see.

"Well," he said. "We had a lot to talk about."

Sitting on the bed, I tried to calm myself.

I could feel the antibiotics tingling, the slinging warmth of the muscle relaxant.

I tried to breathe slowly, deeply.

I tried pacing. That was when I saw my suitcase, open, in the closet. Thought of Jed digging through it, finding my soiled dress, believing what he believed.

Grabbing for the handle, swinging it onto the bed. Raking my arm across the hanging bar in the closet. Dumping my clothes from the laundry basket.

Pausing, my hands over Jed's tees, his shorts, his things. The smell of him, the pilled stretch of his pale blue shirt, my favorite one, the one I used to wear whenever I stayed over, the heel of his hand gently, insinuatingly on my pelvis, urging me to stay.

What happened to Jed. What happened.

"What are you doing?"

Jed was standing in the doorway. There was a look on his face I'd never seen before, a flat, blank look.

"Packing," I said.

He moved closer, a sheen of sweat on him, and that look, and his arms hanging loose at his sides.

"I have the meds now," I said, calmly as I could, trying to fold his shirt with Mrs. Brandt's briskness, "so I can go."

"No," Jed said. "You heard the doctor. The risk is too great."

"Staying here feels riskier," I said quietly. I had to say it. I looked at him, hoping to see something catch in his eyes.

"What does that mean?" he said, and it wasn't a question, really. "Be reasonable."

"I think," I said, zipping the suitcase shut, "I'm the only reasonable one."

"You're bleeding. You're running outside in the night, getting infections, and now you want to drive in the summer heat over the worst roads in the country. I-75 alone—"

"Are you going to tell me about the goddamned potholes again? Because I've had enough of them. I want *my* doctor, *my* home, my family—"

"You think you can do whatever you want," he said icily. "We wouldn't be in this position if you hadn't done just what you wanted."

I couldn't look at him. These words weren't his words. This Jed wasn't my Jed and maybe hadn't been for a while. Maybe never was.

Jed looked down at his hands, running one over the other, curling them into a fist.

Then, in one swoop, he took hold of the suitcase, heaving it from the bed into the air. It landed near the closet with a quaking clatter.

"How could you not tell me?" he demanded.

And there it was.

"Jed," I started, "it has nothing to do with this. It was years ago. I was twenty-three. Why would I tell you?"

"Because I'm your husband," he said. "That's why."

"You want to know why I didn't tell you?" I said, a tremble in my voice. "*This*. The way you're acting now. That's why."

He turned away.

"I know you care about our baby," he said, more softly now. The softness worse somehow.

"How dare you," I said. "How dare you."

"So I know you'll stay put," he continued. "You'll follow the doctor's orders. Now we know. Your . . . abortion"—he could barely say the word—"it increases the risk of the placenta thing, so we—"

"That's not true!" I said, my voice speeding up wildly. "Doctor Anwar told me. It doesn't increase the risk. Not the kind I had. Cesareans increase it more. Are you going to blame women who've had cesareans? Your own mother . . ." I started, then stopped myself.

Something passed across Jed's face and he turned away.

"This isn't about blame," he said, his back facing me, an ominous feeling. "It's about trust. To find out like this . . ."

"Maybe you should think about that," I said, an eerie feeling inside. "The way you found out. Maybe you should think about what just happened down there in the living room. What your dad did. And why."

I had that strange, hollow feeling I'd had before. *Whatever Mama says.* That winking face of his. *Every woman should have her secrets.* That smile, and smile. "Jed, we need to get out of here. Don't you see? Can't you feel it? What it's doing—"

"How could you not tell me?" Jed cried out again, his hands balled back into fists.

I didn't say anything. The way he asked was the answer.

He walked over and kicked the suitcase, its hard shell wheezing, my body flinching, my heart flinching. He kicked it again and I flinched with every skid.

"Jed!" I whispered loudly, my eyes on the vent near the floor. "Stop."

There was a long silence. My hand on my hip, my leg, on fire now. He didn't move or even blink.

Then, at last, he sat down, sunk down onto the bed, facing away from me.

"Everything's changed," he said, his voice like a throaty burr, like his father's voice. "How can I ever trust you now?"

There it was. There it was.

"You can't," I said. "You obviously can't. I'm a dangerous woman."

I could have brought up Molly Kee or his father's visit before we conceived and a hundred other lies and evasions from the last few days, but what did it matter. Everything had changed.

We sat for a long while, a stunned silence. The air conditioner purred and rocked. Time stopped entirely.

"I wonder," he said finally, his face a shadow now, "what else you haven't told me."

"I guess you'll never know," I said coolly, my hands over my belly. "Too bad for you."

My mom told me something once.

It was a bad time. A bad moment.

I'd called her on my honeymoon. Standing there, in one of those ghostly phone-booth alcoves at the White Sands Hotel in Honolulu, crying into the phone.

He's so different now, I'd said. *He's so distant, remote.* Since we got on the plane, the only time I'd seen him smile was for the front desk lady, a jolly woman in sensible shoes and hose who insisted he try a hot macadamia cookie fresh from the oven when we'd checked in. *First rule of real estate, right, Mom? Cookies in the oven and a smile on your face.*

It only works for men, she told me. *But usually that's enough.*

I'd made myself forget it, but I remembered it now. How Jed had seemed those first few days. Sex and meals and sitting at the pool, all done with the same grim determination. Short, clipped sentences. Hours spent on the balcony, drinking beer after beer. Sex with the lights off, intense and silent and quick. His eyes flashing in the dark.

It's always that way, I expected my mom to tell me, my fingernails tapping and tapping on the phone ledge. *The first year is the hardest. A period of adjustment.*

But instead, she let out a deep sigh and said, *Remember, Jacy, you don't really know who he is. And he doesn't know who you are.*

I didn't believe her. *Maybe that was true for you,* I said, or for her generation. But those days were over.

And yet.

It's not like I married a stranger.

Honey, we all marry strangers.

It had passed with Jed, or seemed to. There was a moment on the last day of our honeymoon. The cab taking us to the airport, to home, and a panel van sideswiped us, tires skidding, and the driver let out a piercing cry.

The cab tilted, like an amusement park ride, and I felt my legs lift and my body rise, pressing against the overstretched seat belt. Jed's arms, his body twisting in front of me, trying to protect me, to shield me from the worst of whatever might come. The look on his face, the alarm, the childlike terror.

And then the cab righted itself, its left tires landing back on the road with a terrific jolt.

Jed and I were both laughing, wildly, the driver too. We'd cheated death together, hadn't we?

Jed wouldn't, couldn't let go of my hands for hours after. On the plane, he finally fell asleep, and I let my hand slip from his at last, numb from his grip, a spiraling tingling from how long and how hard he'd held it.

Oh, god, I'd thought, *to have someone love me this mu*ch.

"They can make you sleepy," Doctor Ash was saying downstairs. I was in the bed, unable to move. I'd never felt so tired in my life. "She'll be out for a long time."

"It looks better." Mrs. Brandt's cool, cool voice.

"Does it."

"I helped her put on fresh bandages."

"Where's he?"

"On the sleeping porch. They had words."

A long silence.

"Well," Doctor Ash said. "Well."

NIGHT EIGHT

The pills stole my day. It was nearly dinnertime when the stupor of the antibiotic and muscle relaxant lifted again.

Waking, I saw Mrs. Brandt had left two more pills and a glass of water on the bedside table. I looked at them but didn't touch them.

I knew then I shouldn't have taken any at all.

Who knew what they were and I wasn't taking any more chances.

I had to keep my head straight. I had to be ready.

Tomorrow I was leaving.

I hauled that landline into the bathroom to call my mom again, the cord's dry, splintery coils dragging under the doorframe.

"Honey, listen to me," my mom was saying, "I'm going to reserve you a plane ticket for the six twenty-five tomorrow evening, out of Marquette. There's only a few flights a day and—"

"I'm worried they're not going to let me leave." Just saying the words sent a jolt through me.

She paused. "Then I'm calling the police."

I took a breath.

"I can do this," I said, needing to say it aloud.

"You sure can, sweetie," my mom said, an eerie tremble in her voice. "You just get in that rental car and get to the airport as soon as you can. . . ."

Then came the squeak in the wood floor.

I swallowed hard, peering at the crack under the bathroom door.

The shadow of someone or something. Mrs. Brandt? Jed?

"I have to go," I said, my hand slipping, the earpiece sliding into my lap.

"Jacy!" I heard my mom faintly, like in your most fearsome dreams of childhood, your mom so terribly far away.

Like Auntie Em wringing her hands, crying out in the Wicked Witch's giant crystal globe, *Dorothy! Where are you? We're trying to find you!*

❧

Swinging the door open, I peered down the hallway. But it was neither Mrs. Brandt nor Jed. It was Doctor Ash, planted at the top of the stairs.

"I thought you might be Jed," I said.

"He's bringing the truck around. We're going for a ride, Jed and me. A little father and son time."

"Okay."

"Stay inside now," he said. "Those tracks—it's not safe out there. I've set the alarms, of course. So if you forget . . ."

I didn't say anything, my right leg shaking beneath me.

Is this really happening?

"I think you should rest," he said, moving toward me. "You're taking your medicine?"

"Of course," I said, stepping backward.

"You look so frail," he said. "Like you might slip away."

❧

There would be no pills, of course. I had to stay awake. Stay vigilant.

Tomorrow, the airport. I just had to make it until tomorrow. I would be strong enough tomorrow.

It was almost midnight and I was starving, my mouth wet, like Redruth's slobbery pout.

Sneaking down to the kitchen, I had a secret hope for a pasty cold in the icebox. I hadn't eaten all day, the pills making me sick.

I couldn't find any, and the house seemed empty.

I looked out to Mrs. Brandt's cottage, its picture window brightly lit.

Through the patio door, I heard a whistling sound, soft and low.

Outside, Hicks was at his usual post, almost like a hired guard, leaning against his pea-soup truck, smoking a cigarette.

His whistle clear and pure.

"Did you think I was a mountain lion?" he said as I stepped tentatively outside.

"No." I smiled. "But should you be outside?"

He grinned. "Should either of us?"

"Good point," I said, watching him snuff his cigarette between thumb and finger.

Neither of us moved.

"Doctor Ash said he set the alarms."

Hicks shook his head. "What's an alarm going to do? Make sure everyone finds the body?"

I almost laughed.

"Did I tell you about my mountain lion encounter?" he said, the sizzle of the cigarette still in the air.

"I thought you'd never seen one."

"I didn't want to spook anybody. It was years ago. Before Jed was born. One moonlit night, I heard it. Rose and I both."

I shivered slightly, a breeze cutting through, a grumble, somewhere, of fireworks.

"I heard this pretty, lonesome sound, like wind through an old tree log. We looked out the window and saw her. A mountain lion singing to her baby. Never heard anything like it before or since."

We stood in silence a minute, the sky to the south going red, violet with distant fireworks.

"Can I ask you something?" I said finally. "Eddie's Teepee. What did you mean about knowing who gave Jed that hat?"

Hicks paused and adjusted his sunglasses.

"Jed told me about Molly," I said. "It's okay."

"Well, then," he said. "Molly. Poor Molly. Yeah. Jed took a fancy to her back in the day. They were kids, cute as bugs. It was never more than kisses behind the counselors' tent, kid stuff. But then . . . well, Doc Ash nipped that in the bud."

"What do you mean?"

"He called her parents," Hicks said. "I worked with her mom at the sheriff's office. Doc called and told her to put the reins on her daughter. You know, he's old-fashioned, Doc Ash. He felt she was pursuing Jed. Wanton behavior, I think that was the phrase. 'These girls today. What if she knocks herself up? My son won't be saddled with townie trash.'"

I looked at Hicks. "Wasn't she just a kid? Like fourteen?"

"They didn't want to tangle with Doctor Ash. Wasn't worth it. They sent her off to church camp."

"And that was the end of that."

"I never liked it, any of it," Hicks said. "But nobody asked me."

I thought of that first night. Doctor Ash's encouragement, Doctor Ash saying, *Oh, boy, Eddie's Teepee. Jed's favorite. Where Jed had his first taste.*

"Don't be jealous now," Hicks said, winking. "It was puppy love. She's got two kids now, a third on the way." He grinned. "And Jed's got you. First one who ever made the cut."

I wondered how many girlfriends Jed had who were turned away.

"Thank you," I said. "For telling me."

Hicks tossed his cigarette to the ground and looked off into the distance.

"You know what you need to do, right?" he said, his tone shifting suddenly.

"I do," I said.

"Do it fast," he said. "Don't wait."

Jed and Doctor Ash were still gone at midnight.

I wanted to be ready tomorrow. I hunted through all of Jed's things for the car keys, but he must have taken them with him. I'd get them later. I had time.

The paperback curled in my arms, I read tale after tale of suspense. A woman who suspects her new husband is consorting with a former lover, but it turns out the lover is a ghost. A nervous governess who believes her children are possessed.

Keep going, I told myself. *Stay awake.*

My leg throbbing, I turned onto my side.

Turning the page to the next story, I felt a clutch over my heart.

"Captain Murderer," it was called. By Charles Dickens.

Captain Murderer, my childhood boogeyman. *But I made him up,* I thought. *He came from nowhere but me.*

And yet there he was on the page.

My breath catching, I tore through the tale.

Captain Murderer was a fiendish man who rode about in a coach with six milk-white horses, each with one red spot.

Captain Murderer was famous for marrying and burying his wives.

Every wedding night, he gave his new bride a golden rolling pin and silver pie board and she'd roll out the piecrust, nice and fine, then ask where the meat was.

Captain Murderer would lean over her shoulder and say . . .

Look in the glass!

But when she did, she saw only her own reflection.

There's the meat! Captain Murderer would shout, roaring with

229

laughter and lifting his sword high above his head. *The prettiest meat in all the land.*

The bride would begin to cry, her tears salting the crust moments before Captain Murderer cut her head off, chopping her in pieces, and salting and peppering her into the pie, eating it all, and picking the bones.

But then, finally, he married the smartest girl in all the land. She knew just what was coming and, on her wedding night, she swallowed a poison made of toads and spiders.

After chopping off her head, Captain Murderer ate her with great delectation, picking her bones. Then, moments later, he turned blue and screamed and screamed until he exploded into a thousand pieces. *Captain Murderer was dead!*

His white horses went mad and broke free, stampeding over everybody in the house until they were all dead, and then they galloped away.

What an awful ending, I thought. Too awful for words. The poor final bride, sacrificing herself to kill the lady-killer. It didn't seem fair, or right.

Setting the book down, I closed my eyes and all I could see were white horses with red dots, red stains and sundresses, blood spreading on white robes, mountain lions and magpies flapping blood.

Tomorrow, tomorrow, tomorrow, I kept telling myself. My flight was waiting. I just had to get there.

Finally, in spite of myself, I began to drift off.

Look, the whisper came, hot in my ear as I slept.

I opened my eyes and a young woman stood beside me, her long dark hair full of silver ribbons.

Look, she said again, pointing to my belly.

I looked down at my belly, and it was glowing, like there was a lamp inside and someone had flipped the switch.

My hands on it, hot and shaking. If I peered down, I could almost see inside, were the glow not so hot, blazing neon.

My baby, I said. *Mine.*

I closed my eyes again, but the whisper returned.

Did you read it? she asked.

Yes, I said, *but the girl still died. The smartest girl in all the land had to die to stop him.*

Jacy, she said, her hand over my eyes, shutting them one last time, *you better be smarter.*

DAY NINE

My eyes twitched, unstuck.

The crimson blur taking shape, contours.

"Mrs. Brandt," I whispered. "What time is it?"

The blur shuddering tightly into Mrs. Brandt looming above me, her hair like fire in the morning light.

"Coming on five A.M.," she said, her heavy, red-tipped flashlight in hand. "The power's going in and out."

I turned and saw the clock flashing. The air conditioner stuttering.

"Where's Jed?" I asked, rubbing my eyes.

"On the sleeping porch," she said, extending her hand.

In the center of her palm was a pair of pills.

"No pills," I said. "I don't want any more pills."

She looked at me. Was that a faint smile there?

"Fine," she said, slipping them back in her pocket and turning to leave. "Good."

That was when I remembered the sound, sometime during the night or just before dawn. The sound like the kind of thunder that rips the earth apart, that lifts its bowels and hurls them into the air.

"The storm was so loud," I said.

"There was an accident," she said.

"What kind of accident?"

"The patio door," she said. "Be careful when you come downstairs."

I turned and felt something hard jabbing into me: the creasy paperback I'd slept on. *Bedtime Tales of Suspense*. I thought of the story, that story. Captain Murderer.

Mrs. Brandt was just closing the door.

"Did you leave this book for me?" I asked.

She stopped and looked at me. "Yes," she said.

"It was hers, wasn't it?" I said, just realizing it, opening it to the inside page. *W.P.A.*

"Wendy Pearce Ash," Mrs. Brandt said, turning to leave. "She loved to be scared."

Today was the day. I would not fail today. My mom had booked me the ticket. Six twenty-five P.M. I just had to get to the Marquette airport. I could sit there all day if I had to. I just had to get the rental car keys. Jed had them, I guessed. I would figure it out.

I threw the window up, pressed my fingers against the screen.

From outside, Doctor Ash's roaming voice climbed up the walls, through the windows. He was outside with Hicks, the two men patrolling like sentry.

"No tracks here."

"Keep looking. You know what I say, why trap when you can hunt?"

Both men laughed, the laughter getting louder.

Then Doctor Ash emerged from somewhere deep in the green mist outside.

He was holding something.

My eyes sticking and unsticking.

It was the rifle. The bolt-action rifle.

The way he held it, like a sword. Like Captain Murderer's mighty sword.

"Don't move." Mrs. Brandt's voice behind me. "Don't move."

The force of her hand on mine, clasping it to the stair rail.

My eyes adjusting to the browned living room, the morning light so strange, the floor glittering.

Mrs. Brandt seemed to float past me in her long skirt, push broom and dustpan in hand.

That was when I saw the patio door, glass like a sprawling spider-web, with its center punched through, a gaping hole big as a hula hoop, the cloying smell of morning dew, muck filling the room.

I looked down at the mound of green glass gathered on the floor. A prickly feeling came over me.

"Was it the mountain lion?"

"Doctor Ash thinks so," Mrs. Brandt said, setting down the dustpan.

"Do you?"

Mrs. Brandt paused, gazing through the glass, into the green beyond.

"Maybe," she said.

"It's just like you said," I added, remembering suddenly. "Animals see their reflection in the glass and mistake it for a foe. A predator."

"I suppose that's so," she said, her gaze still fixed on the spot where the glass had been.

It made me think of the Captain Murderer story. The bride staring into the gleaming tray, seeing only her own reflection.

"If it was the lion," I said, "why didn't it come in here?"

"Maybe," she said, picking up the broom again, "it didn't want to come in here."

. . .

The door rattled open.

Hicks appeared, grinning, an air rifle like Mrs. Brandt's slung over his shoulder.

No one said anything and Hicks's eyes scanned the room, landing on me and smiling.

"Happy Independence Day."

I smiled in spite of myself.

He looked out the shattered patio door.

"Here he comes," Hicks said. "He looks ready to hunt."

There was something in the way he said it, and I looked too. Doctor Ash was crossing the patio, rifle at one side, pointed to the ground.

A whiff of coldness seemed to swirl around him, the gust of the strained air-conditioning, the patio glass fogging to opacity.

Upstairs, my hands shook on the phone dial.

Back in the bathroom, a towel shoved under the door.

I crawled in the tub, pulled the curtain around.

No one can hear. No one!

I would call my mom one last time. Confirm everything.

But there was no dial tone.

The storm, the accident, outages. It would come back. It had to.

In the meantime, I had to get those car keys.

Downstairs, Mrs. Brandt was still sweeping, sweeping up glass.

Shush-shush-shush-shush. Summer sounds, the echoes and spookiness.

I hovered outside the kitchen. The men were talking inside.

Doctor Ash was filling his coffee cup. His rifle under his arm.

I could see more of my pills, two of them laid out neatly on the table for me.

235

"Jed slept through all this?" Hicks said.

"We had a wee bit of tequila last night," Doctor Ash said, smiling. "Father-son heart-to-heart."

"A come-to-Jesus moment?" Hicks asked, grinning. "He gonna give up signmaking, burn off the tattoos, get his own Remington, and move up here with you?"

Doctor Ash said nothing, pushing open the screen door and stepping outside again.

His gaze fixed, rifle pointed down.

It was like he wanted the mountain lion to come so he could shoot it.

It was like he couldn't wait.

Get the keys, Jacy, I told myself.

On the sleeping porch, Jed was not sprawled in his usual fashion but curled in a tight ball. He hadn't taken off any of his clothes.

He looked so forlorn, his hoodie tucked all around him.

I moved slowly, worried Doctor Ash might see me through the screens.

No keys on the tiny rattan table. No keys anywhere to be seen.

I leaned over him, my hands on his waistband, his pockets.

I could hear him breathing, a funny little whistle from his mouth.

The Whistler, I thought, remembering again. Jed's teeth knocked out, the dark lesson his father taught him. *Jed, you always knew what he was. You knew! And yet.*

Carefully, my fingers inching toward his jeans pockets.

How many times, my hands on his waistband. The faint down on his stomach. Suddenly I wanted to cry.

Be smart, Jacy, be smart.

Slipping one, two fingers into the right pocket, then the left.

"Jacy," he said, his eyes opening suddenly. "Jacy, we need to talk."

236

. . .

We went upstairs to the guest room.

It wasn't private, but no place was.

We sat on the bed, my leg and hip burning.

Play it cool, I told myself. *Play it nice.* No matter what he says.

Wear the mask, play the part. Dutiful wife, expectant mother, hands over belly, smile on her face.

"Did you take your pills?" Jed asked, it was all anyone asked.

"Of course," I lied, looking at him, his pouched eyes. "Are you hungover?"

He shook his head. "No. No. We had a few drinks. Before the first one, Dad took my car keys, can you believe it? Locked them up in his study."

I could. The toothpaste-white Chevy receded from me. Who knew where Doctor Ash had put those keys? I would have to find another way.

"But, Jacy, here's the thing: I feel really clear today. Clearer than I have in a long time."

He took my hands in his and it all felt very formal, like a marriage proposal or the last rites.

"I need you to know how sorry I am," he said. "About yesterday. The things I said about . . . about your procedure. The way I handled that. Dad really set me straight."

"He did?"

"He did, Jacy. I know he can be . . . strong about things, but he really took me to task for my . . . my conduct."

"Jed—" I found this all hard to believe. Impossible, really.

"About how I need to take my responsibilities seriously. I've been screwing around. I need to man up. Because this is serious, Jacy. And our baby needs to be the most important thing."

I slipped my hands from his. A sinking feeling that I knew where this was going, where it had always been going.

"I know it's scary to face," he continued, "but we've got to. You have this condition, you've been bleeding, and now you have an infection too."

I wanted to scream, but I said nothing. *Play it cool, play it smart.*

"Please look at it from my point of view. One minute you're hiding your bloody dress and the next you're outside in the middle of the night, covered in dirt. And it's dangerous out there, Jacy. That mountain lion—"

"Jed, that's not—" I started but then stopped myself. *Don't let him see, don't let him know.*

Jed paused, taking a breath. Thinking. It was as if he was going back to some script he'd planned or been told to deliver. Finding his cue again.

"I'm just talking about rest," he said finally. "You're not thinking clearly, or you'd agree. It's not your fault—all these medications and the hormones, how can you help it?"

"You sound like your dad," I said, more to myself than to him. *Oh, Jed. He's got you. He's got you and I don't stand a chance here.*

"I just need you to stay here like he wants—"

"Like he wants."

"Like we all want."

I opened my mouth and then stopped. *Be smart, Jacy.*

I could feel the floor vibrating under my feet. Everyone moving around downstairs, assembling for something, readying for something. The mountain lion, something.

There was going to be a way this was going to go and it was not going to be my convincing Jed to leave or by my demanding the car keys or by my pushing my way out.

No, it was far beyond that.

"Please understand," he continued. "What Dad went through with my mom . . . well, he can't bear for me to have to go through that."

"That's not going to happen," I said, doing calculations in my head: *Could I call a car service? An airport shuttle? A taxi?*

"No. It's not. Because we're going to make sure you're safe. No car rides, no hikes. No sleepwalking. We can take care of that too. Just for a little while. Until we know everything is okay. Dad was telling me about these alarms we can set on the bedroom door. These trackers. So if you start to get up in the night . . ."

This was where we'd arrived. Alarms, trackers. Sure. Why not restraints?

But I nodded and nodded and nodded, remembering the girl in "Captain Murderer," *the smartest girl in all the land.* Remembering my dream. *Jacy, you better be smarter.*

". . . and this is the safest place in the world for you, right now, okay?"

He looked at me, his eyes filled with trouble and worry.

Oh, Jed, he's got you good, I thought. *Has he got you forever? Does it even matter anymore?*

"Yes," I said. "You're right. Your father's right. I'm going to rest. I'm going to take my pills. I'm going to play it safe. I'm going to be a good wife. And daughter-in-law. And mother-to-be."

"Really?"

"Of course," I said, my voice soft and pliant. "I . . . I got confused. But I'm not confused anymore."

He looked closely at me for a long moment and then, suddenly, smiled, an ecstatic look in his eyes. Like he was looking at some holy thing, a miracle.

"There's my girl," he said, gripping my hand so hard tears sprang to my eyes. "I knew she'd come back. You already look like a mother."

Jed, caught in the spell, ensnared.

He would not save me or help me. In fact . . .

But there was no time to mourn it, to even let it sink in.

Be smart, Jacy! Be smart.
Play along, or seem to.
Play it safe. Hide your feelings.
It was the only way.
Put on the smile and play nice.
Wait for your moment and run.

The guns were arrayed, a starburst on the dining room table.

Doctor Ash's bolt-action, Hicks's pump-action air rifle, Mrs. Brandt's air gun.

"Is that Cosmoline?" Hicks was saying, looking at Doctor Ash's rifle, that waxy sheen it had. I remembered it under my fingers.

"For rust," Doctor Ash said.

Hicks shook his head. "Well, get that rifle soaking in mineral spirits, Doc, or that dog won't hunt. Gets in the firing pin. Jams up the works."

The men were talking about the mountain lion, the one none of them had ever seen. Only Mrs. Brandt had, that first night, standing at the security fence, her face white in the dark deep of the yard, air gun firmly in hand.

"Could be someone's illegal pet," Doctor Ash was saying. "Fellow I know down in Washtenaw County ran afoul of a baby Bengal on his morning run. Pepper spray and a hard key-gouge to the eyes saved his bacon. Turned out Spot's owner had a whole illegal private menagerie behind his house. Noah's backyard ark, they called it."

Hicks laughed, running his hand down Doctor Ash's rifle. "You know what I say," he replied. "You see babies, that was your head start."

I felt a chill. It was the same joke he'd made before, but this time it felt different. Something in Hicks's voice, a little catch, something. Everyone was quiet for a moment, Doctor Ash returning to the table.

"Jed, you'll go get some plywood from the shed," Doctor Ash said, standing in front of the patio door. "Seal this baby up."

Jed nodded eagerly, the good little soldier.

"Whoa," a voice said. "Who we gonna invade?"

It was Randy, waving from the other side of the broken patio door.

Randy the Ripper, stepping through the hole in the glass, waving a phone in his hand.

"Went by Eddie's last night," he said, handing the phone to Jed. "Guess you left it there."

"Eddie's Teepee," I said, thinking again of Molly Kee, her arrow poised.

Jed looked at me, sheepish. I feigned a smile.

"We were overserved," Randy said, jabbing Jed with his elbow. "Stacey had my ass when I got home."

"Boys will be boys," I said. "It's their nature."

Mrs. Brandt looked at me, a ghost of a smile.

All I have to do is play nice, I told myself. *Play nice and wait.*

For the next few hours, the men were fixing the door, setting up the motion-sensor cameras Hicks had brought, doing a survey of the property, the security fence.

There had been coffee and coffee, and phone calls and strategizing. A plan was shaping.

So was mine.

I watched them from the kitchen, waiting. Knowing they'd be gone soon, on their big mission, and I would call a taxi and leave. Were there taxi services up here? There had to be. I was leaving, I had to leave. I would leave on foot if I had to.

"We'll do some recon," Doctor Ash was saying. "Full perimeter. Look for tracks, scat, scrapes. Then, come night, we'll be ready."

"If you say so," Hicks said, shaking his head and giving me what looked like a grimaced wink.

Randy cleared his throat loudly, thunking the last nail in plywood as Jed cleared the debris.

"I'd like to stay on and help," he said. "Be a part of the mission, and all that. But Stacey's gonna have my head on a spike if I don't take the kids to the parade."

Doctor Ash wasn't listening, didn't care, examining the cameras, readying the troops.

"See ya, dude," Randy growled at Jed, thwacking him on the back of his head as he left.

He passed me on his way out, a jittery, nervous look in his eye.

A look almost as if to say: *Get out while you can.*

I intend to, Randy. I do.

"You sure about this, Hank?" Hicks said abruptly.

Jed, watching his father, seemed to flinch.

"I mean, we can go out there tonight," Hicks continued. "You'll never see it, but it'll see you. And by then it's too late."

Doctor Ash looked at him a long moment.

"This one seems to make its own rules," Doctor Ash said, bending down to pick up a stray piece of glass the size of a peach slice. "She wants to be seen. And she thinks she can do whatever she wants."

At some point, the "he" had become a "she."

"Maybe so," Hicks said lightly, strolling toward the shatter of the patio door, examining its crinkly lattice. "Nature's always the same until it isn't."

Everyone was quiet a moment, and my mouth dry.

Doctor Ash stood before the patio door, legs astride like a frontiersman, an invader.

The screen door slapped open.

It was Randy, back again, reaching behind for something in his waistband.

"Keep it in my truck," he said, setting a small black handgun on the table before Jed. "Figure maybe you could use an extra."

"That one's no joke," Hicks said, whistling at it.

Jed stared at it, his arms folded.

I didn't know what he was thinking, I had no idea at all.

Mrs. Brandt joined me in the kitchen, pouring me a glass of the red raspberry iced tea.

"You feeling okay?" Jed said, watching me from the dining room.

"Yes," I said, smiling. "A little tired."

Doctor Ash looked at me for the first time all day.

"Did she take her pills?" he asked Mrs. Brandt, as if I weren't there at all.

"Of course," Mrs. Brandt lied.

Doctor Ash turned away, pushing through the screen door.

"Jed, look what you've done to your wife," Hicks said, grinning.

Jed reddened slightly. "Well, you know what they say. If men could get pregnant . . ."

No one finished the thought.

Mrs. Brandt placed her hand lightly on my shoulder.

"Do you need some rest?"

I nodded. *I need them to leave. Why won't they leave?*

"You don't want to help us smoke out the mountain lion, Jacy?" Hicks asked, teasingly. "Never saw one before you got here. Maybe it's you he's after."

As he said it, his smile fell away.

I looked out the screen door into the lush woods.

Better out there, I thought, *than in here.*

I'm better off out there than in here.

. . .

They weren't gone yet, but I couldn't wait. My flight was only a few hours away.

Upstairs, in the bathroom, I sat with the yellow pages spread between my thighs.

I would call my mom, then a taxi.

The dial tone hummed like a miracle, but after those agonizing turns of the dial wheel, the line only droned tonelessly.

I tried three times, sweating and nearly crying, and then—*click-click*—it went through.

"Mom!" I whispered. "Thank god. Six twenty-five, right? I'm looking for a taxi service, then . . ."

She sighed. "Honey, about that . . ."

"About what?" I asked, a tremor in my voice.

There was something in her tone that I knew, though I hadn't heard it in years. *Honey, it's about your art show. Mr. Panarites wants to take me to Aruba that week. . . .*

"Well, I know you're very restless there right now, but Doctor Ash called—"

"What?"

"—and he explained everything to me. About what's been happening with you, and your condition. Now I have the fuller picture. And I think it's right to probably wait a day or two, until things settle down. So I canceled that flight, but we can book another after the holiday—"

"Mom!" I whispered desperately. "Mom, I don't know what he told you, but it's not true. He just . . . he wants to control everything. You don't understand what's happening—"

"But now I do, honey. He *is* a doctor, after all, and he explained what's been going on. About your condition. About all the bleeding." She paused, a worried tongue cluck. Then, "Why didn't you tell me about the infection, Jacy?"

Oh, no. My hand gripping the edge of the tub, sweat sliding down my face . . .

"Mom," I whispered, desperate now, "you *need* to listen. I'm not safe here. They won't let me leave the house. I . . . I think maybe they're trying to drug me."

She let out a funny, sharp laugh. "Honey, those are *antibiotics.* And they're making your head cloudy."

"No, Mom—"

"You're under a great deal of stress, baby. And god knows Jed's no help. But I could have told you that."

"Mom—"

"Doctor Ash really is looking out for you, sweetie. He thinks so highly of you. You know, he reminds me a little of my old friend Mr. Panarites. Remember him?"

Your married boyfriend? I wanted to say. How he kept her on the hook all those years. Her weakness for him. How she loved to confide in me about him, how he was so respectful of women, how they were star-crossed.

I can't help it, she always told my aunt Laraine. *He's got my number. He always has.*

"Yes, Mom, of course I remember him."

There was a pinched silence. Then she said, "Now, you take your medicine and rest, okay, Jacy? And what's a few days anyway?"

She didn't sound like herself at all, a nervous edge to her voice, a grit-teeth edge.

"Mom . . . are you mad at me about something?"

"Of course not, Jacy. I love you and you know you always were a willful, private girl. I mean, you'd barely told me a thing about Jed and suddenly you were married and then pregnant—"

"Mom, what—"

Her voice choked slightly, then went high.

"You know, Jacy," she said, "you could've told me about the abortion."

"Oh, Mom . . ." I felt myself sinking. I felt everything falling away.

There was a buzzing sound on the phone line and I punched a finger in my ear to hear.

"Can you imagine what it feels like to hear about this from a stranger?" she was saying. "This man I don't even know?"

"I can't believe he did that," I said. "Told you that."

"He felt terrible. He assumed I knew."

Sure he did, I thought.

"Why didn't you tell me?" she said, her voice cracking. "I would have gone with you. I would have taken care of you. I . . ."

I didn't know what to say. *My daughter and I are very close,* she always told people. *It's always been the two of us.* Her advice, her ideas about men, her candor—all of it thrumming in my head. *Learn from my mistakes, Jacy.* Which really meant: *Do as I say, not as I do.*

It could hurt, too, that candor. You didn't always want candor.

"Because I'm an adult," I said. "Because it was private. Because I just wanted to keep it mine."

It was true, I realized as I said it. It *was* mine. But now it was everyone's. Slathering over it, using it, twisting and warping it.

She was quiet for a second, both of us breathing into the phone.

"Oh, Jacy, I'm sorry," she said, a whimper in her voice. "I wasn't thinking clearly. He took me by surprise and . . ."

"Mom—"

"I can still get that ticket, honey. I'll call the airline. I'm sorry. I just— What time is it? Maybe a flight tomorrow morning?"

But I knew I couldn't wait that long. I knew I couldn't count on her.

I told her not to worry. I told her I'd call her later. The line was cutting out anyway, and I could hear doors slamming downstairs.

But right before I hung up, I remembered something.

"Captain Murderer," I said.

The static came back over the line, popping and twitching louder now, as if we'd roused Captain Murderer himself.

"What, honey? Oh, you mean your old boogeyman."

"Did you ever figure out where that came from?"

"It's so funny you mention that," she said. "Last year, I came across a box in the garage. Your father's old books. There was this spooky stories one he loved to read to you at breakfast."

"Over cream of wheat."

"The most cooking he ever did," she said. I could nearly hear her shaking her head with rue. "I saw the story in there. 'Captain Murderer.' What a story to read a little girl. To read to your daughter. You're supposed to protect your child."

"Yes, Mom," I said, a choke in my voice, my hand resting on my belly. "You are."

Keep going, Jacy. You don't need her, Jacy.

My mom was lost to me, at least for now. Jed was lost to me, maybe forever.

There was no plane ticket, there were no keys to the toothpaste-white Chevy.

But I was leaving.

The men had made their plan, now I had to remake mine.

I had a credit card. I could get my own plane ticket. I could walk to someplace. Somewhere.

It was just a math problem, really. Or an SAT problem. A scary movie problem. *If a pregnant woman with no phone sneaks off into the woods, how many miles must she go to find help? Take the distance traveled and divide by the risks posed . . .*

The men would go, with their guns. Very soon, they would go. And I would run.

247

✼

It was nearly dusk when I finally heard the screen door slap, slap, slap.

I watched the men walk up the back slope, spanning like a three-man cell, a sniper squad in performance cotton, moisture wicked.

They could be gone an hour, or four.

Go, Jacy, go!

I sat on the wooden toilet seat, the rotary phone in my lap, earpiece sweaty against my ear.

Just dial the operator, I thought. *Information. Do these things still exist?*

Get a taxi service, a car service, anyone. Get them to come here and take me away.

The earpiece pressed hard and there was no dial tone at all, only the muffled sound of my own antic breathing.

The handpiece in my hands, limp, dead.

CRACK. It came like a firecracker pop. Outside, somewhere. Then the roar of laughter. Hicks, echoing up from outside, somewhere in the woods.

Rising slowly, I pushed open the bathroom door.

The bedroom was empty, but its door ajar.

Peering down the dark, windowless hall, I caught the whiff of aftershave, like soft leather.

There was a shadow at the end, at the turn to the staircase.

I heard the sibilant shush of a pair of voices.

"There she is," Doctor Ash said, just like the very first time I set foot in the house.

He stood with Mrs. Brandt at the bright bottom of the stairs, their hands obscurely clasped.

She would not look at me.

"Doctor Ash . . ." I whispered. "I thought you'd left."

My lashes fluttered, the sudden light stinging my eyes. Was this real?

"Just came back to let you know Mrs. Brandt will be here to take care of you," he said. "But I thought I'd bring your next round of pills up."

He held out his red palm.

"Thanks," I said. "I'll take them as soon as Mrs. Brandt says."

He looked at Mrs. Brandt. She nodded smoothly.

CRACK. The sound came again.

"Jed's getting a head start," Doctor Ash said. "Shooting tin cans like a ten-year-old."

Jed appeared in the hallway behind him, that same blank look as earlier.

I felt my mouth go dry. The weight of tired like a wave over me.

"His father's boy," Doctor Ash said, with a grin that nearly blinded me.

My hands back on the rotary phone.

The handset back at my slickery ear.

Listening for the dial tone, my fingers twitching.

Still nothing.

My index finger tapping on the prongs.

Nothing.

At the kitchen phone, lifting it gently.

Listening for the dial tone.

Like my ear to a seashell, a dire echo.

. . .

Doctor Ash's study.

I stood outside the door for three long minutes before I tried the knob.

Locked.

"Is the phone not working?" I called downstairs to Mrs. Brandt.

"Sometimes it happens," she said, appearing at the foot of the stairs. "A summer storm over by the lake, a downed line. Mine's out too. I called Light & Power, but the holiday . . ."

"I'm going to rest now," I said.

"Okay," she said, not moving.

"I don't need anything," I said.

Mrs. Brandt nodded, eyes fixed on me now, her hands pressed together, her back pin-straight.

"I'm not staying," she said suddenly, with great purpose. "I have some errands to take care of. Then I'm going to retire for the night."

"Okay," I said. "I understand."

She turned to leave, then stopped again.

"If you really need the phone," she said, "there's a forestry station a mile west. They have Wi-Fi there. They can help you. Ask for Winston."

"Okay," I said. "Thank you."

"I can't take you there, but they can help you," she said. "The front gate will be open. Do you understand?"

"Okay," I said, my hip aching, feeling the weight of her gaze.

The moment felt long, important.

They can help you.

Something vibrated between us and in an instant was gone.

She was gone.

DUSK

In the kitchen, grabbing water, chugging the dregs from the coffeepot, trying to stay awake, alert, alive. The adrenaline was keeping me awake, alert, alive.

The fear was.

On the kitchen table sat a large, red-tipped flashlight, heavy and aluminum. Mrs. Brandt's.

I took it.

Slipping among the vehicles in the muggy haze. Checking Hicks's truck, Doctor Ash's. The Chevy rental. The crazy hope that the doors might be open, the keys might be inside.

I had to try.

Blip-blip, an alarm warned me the instant my hand merely approached Hicks's door handle.

If a pregnant woman with no phone sneaks off into the woods . . .

❧

If I walked far enough, I'd find that forestry station. A mile away, if I went the right way. If I remembered right about where the front gate was. If, if, if . . .

West, Mrs. Brandt had said, and here I was, spinning around, searching for the last gasp of sun fusing through the knotted trees.

They have Wi-Fi there, she'd said, *Ask for Winston.*

Should I believe her?

I thought of her and Doctor Ash at the foot of the stairs, their hands clasped.

But she'd left me alone when she was supposed to watch me.

Do you understand? she'd said.

If I walked far enough, I'd see someone, a stranger.

If I walked far enough, I'd get a signal, something.

I started walking.

I was only a few hundred yards up the path when the trees shuddered suddenly, my heart lurching.

Whipping around, I saw Redruth running toward me, her scarlet mane nearly neon in the dwindling light.

It was as if Mrs. Brandt had sent her. Maybe she had.

Pant-pant-pant, she bolted ahead, the spatter of her fur, then turned back to look at me.

Turned back as if to say: *Hurry, Jacy! Hurry!*

My phone in my hand, I darted after her, toward the far path, its mud black.

Twilight falling.

Everything violet.

Be smart, Jacy!

Be smart like your life depends on it!

Because it always does.

❧

Pant-pant-pant, Redruth at my side, into the dark tangle of trees.

Pant-pant-pant, the flutter of Redruth's tail swatting against my legs.

. . .

Only a dozen yards or more and then I heard it.

BOOM!

A loud clap came hot, then a whistling sound to my right.

Thunder, a mortar shell, a cherry bomb, an echo that seemed to last forever.

The blood singing in my ears.

And Redruth halted, claws scraping at the dirt.

But then I heard the *click-click* and a rustling in the trees ahead.

"Redruth!" I called out, wheeling around, nearly stumbling. "Redruth!"

BOOM!

The bright squeak as her body twisted.

Another shot and the squawking of nightbirds fleeing, spraying.

Redruth's cry, long and echoing, her head moving just in time, a red spatter from her red ear, flapping.

"Redruth!" I cried out.

But Redruth kept going, lunging forward, her eyes glowing back at me.

"Stop!" came a deep voice from the green-black beyond. "Don't move!"

A figure, large and relentless, rifle in his arms.

"Don't move! Don't you dare move!"

It was Doctor Ash, trudging from the thicket, his face red and strange.

He thought he saw her. The mountain lion. But it was me.

It was me, fleeing.

And who knew what he might do now.

That was when I started running.

He would not stop. I knew it. The way women know.

And he might do anything, anything. And no one would ever know.

"Stop!"

I would never make it to the forestry station. There was only one place to go.

Doubling back, I followed the red flash of Redruth off the trail and straight into the woods, a bloody trail from her twisted ear. Her eerie wail as she tore through the tree branches.

"Jacy!" Doctor Ash screamed behind us. "Jacy!"

Fifty yards, a hundred yards, panting, flashlight in my hand and Redruth's collar beaming a few feet ahead, I finally saw the fading cottage in the distance, its windows dark.

BOOM!

Mrs. Brandt's fading cottage but no car in the driveway. No forest-green minivan with the tinted windows.

Mrs. Brandt's fading cottage and I ran straight up to the door, Redruth swirling behind me. Hoping, praying as I pressed against it, twisting the old knob.

The door gave, opened.

NIGHT NINE

Inside, the smell came like a slap. Bitter, antiseptic, cloistered.

"Mrs. Brandt?"

No answer came. Beside me, Redruth curled into a swirl, her ear bent and bleeding, her right leg poking out like a spoke and red-slicked.

"I'll take care of you, girl," I said. Then calling out, "Mrs. Brandt?"

The cottage was small and dark. A rattan daybed, a floor lamp, a stuffed bookshelf in one corner. And a kitchenette, an apartment-size refrigerator, two-burner stove, a table for two. Everything dust-less, immaculate.

At the small sink, I tended to Redruth, washing away the blood as she howled. The wound looked small, no bullet or puncture I could see. *Grazed*, I thought. *Bullet grazed*, a phrase that now seemed ridiculous, given all the blood and pain.

Grabbing a kitchen towel, wrapping it tight around her, I tried to calm her, myself.

There was no time, I knew.

That was when I heard a creaking sound.

I turned. There was a door in the far corner. The bedroom, I guessed.

Redruth whimpered softly.

"Mrs. Brandt?" I tried again, moving toward it.

Its door ajar now, glowing inside.

Then I saw the pictures.

A long ribbon of photographs, affixed to the bedroom door.

I moved closer.

"Mrs. Brandt?"

Then I heard a new sound, humming. A *shush-shush-click. Shush-shush-click.*

I moved closer still.

Fading snapshots, yellow-taped, like you might decorate a locker in school.

A boy, round-cheeked and awkward, maybe ten years old, his body swimming inside a *YOOPER!* tee shirt two sizes too big . . .

And again, at maybe thirteen, his face soft and beautiful, limbs gone long but his eyes still lashed like a girl's . . .

In a buzz cut now, stripped to the waist in swim trunks, lifting his shoulders, puffing his chest for the camera . . .

Then, taller still, in his U-M tee, straight-backed and handsome, but with a heaviness in his gaze, a stiffness in his jaw . . .

They were all Jed. Young Jed.

In every one of them, offering a buoyant or stiff or half-hearted wave.

In the background of all of them, a soaring lighthouse, firecracker-red.

Every year, Jed had told me, *Mrs. Brandt made me stand in front of the lighthouse and wave.*

My fingers grazing the photographs, I pushed the door open and stepped inside.

. . .

Shush-shush-click. Shush-shush-click.

The room was warm, so warm, and dark.

There, on the far wall, was the picture window.

Large, paneless, overlooking the Ash house, a few hundred yards away.

I know this window, I thought. It was the one I'd looked at so many times from the guest bedroom, wondering about Mrs. Brandt, her life.

Beside the window, dominating the whole room, was a hospital bed.

At first, I thought it was a child. The figure—small, slender, a wisp of a thing—resting on the bed.

Shush-shush-click. Shush-shush-click.

My hand reaching for the floor lamp, clicking it on, I moved closer.

It was a woman, her body comma curled.

Facing the window, wrapped in peach chenille, swaddled, safe. Tethered by a Christmas-light tangle of cords, tubes, ports, and clips. A veil of wires hovering around her. A veil of wires like silver ribbons.

Shush-shush-click. Shush-shush-click.

A machine pumped lifelessly in the corner. An IV pole like a hangman.

"Wendy," came Mrs. Brandt's voice behind me, standing in the corner, "meet Jed's wife."

The lamp snapped off behind me.

"She doesn't like too much light," Mrs. Brandt said.

⚘

I couldn't stop looking at her.

Jed's mom. Mrs. Ash. Wendy.

Her face so delicate, like a celluloid doll, her hair gathered into two long, long braids that ended somewhere under the chenille bedspread. Her eyelids fluttering but never opening.

"Sweet girl," Mrs. Brandt said, moving closer, her fingers trailing along the edge of white sheets, immaculate. "Meet Jacy."

Mrs. Brandt took my hand in hers, cool and strong, and placed it on Mrs. Ash's hand, which was neither warm nor cool. Her nails pared, skin smooth as wax.

"She doesn't always need the ventilator," she said, straightening the chenille tassels with her long, elegant fingers, "but she had a little summer cold."

I nodded dumbly.

"I bathe her, brush her hair. Plait it like we did all those years ago on the Soo Lockets," she said, the back of her hand stroking one of the braids. "I make sure she feels loved."

She took my hand and pressed my fingers on Wendy's wrist.

"Feel it. The heartbeat. Tell me that she's dead."

Shush-shush-click. Shush-shush-click.

We sat at Mrs. Brandt's kitchen table, a chipped-china plate of pasties between us.

Tentatively, I reached for one. Against all logic, I was so hungry, my fingers around it.

"Why do they taste so good?"

"Venison liver," she said.

I set the pasty down.

"Iron-packed," she said. "To keep you strong. I wanted to make sure you were strong."

I picked it up again, looked at it, and began eating.

"All this time?" I said. "The red raspberry tea too?"

She nodded. "Strengthens the uterine walls," she said. "In case. I didn't know what might happen. In case."

"Thank you," I said.

Then I told her what happened outside. I told her I needed help.

"I know you do," she said.

In the distance, *crack-crack-boom!* A firework or something else.

"You're safe here," she said, reading my mind. "He'd never come in here. He'd never think I would help you."

"No," I said. "I guess he wouldn't."

"He's never come here," she said with sudden intensity, her hands coiled around each other, a tight, white knot. "Two hundred yards away, and he's never come, not once."

There was a long pause, then her head lifted again, her eyes clear and bright once more.

"But how could he really," she said coolly, unwringing her hands, pressing her palms to her skirt as if finished with something, done.

There was so much I didn't understand.

"But . . . she's alive?"

"Permanent vegetative state, that's what they called it at first. Brain-dead, that's what they told us later. I never could understand if she'd changed or the names had. They keep changing the names."

I didn't say anything. I let her talk.

And she told me the story, everything.

It was after Doctor Ash's own father had died.

"I'd worked for the family for ten years by then, since ninth grade," she said. "Housecleaning, chores. In those days, you called them 'your girl.' And Hank was just out of medical school and a bachelor. At first, I thought he might sell the house. Why would he still want to spend his summers here?

"But then he met Wendy. I introduced them, he asked me to. He loved watching her skate. She was like my little sister. She'd lost both her parents, was all alone in the world.

"I'd just gotten married myself. But Wendy was only nineteen, a nursing student. Big dreams, you know. But Hank was a doctor. He was money. He was dazzling to her. He was dazzling.

"I was sure it wouldn't last. A summer dalliance. Hank, even at that age, had such a vision of life. *His* vision, *his* life. His father had been the same way. Every summer, he made a list of projects his son should do, accomplishments his son should aim for. Everything was planned, perfected. He was a hard man to work for. A hard man to have for a father, too, I'm sure. He once locked me out of the house for missing a hospital corner on a guest bed. He was good with shame.

"Hank was different. Warmer, more sly. And yet the same too. In the end he was the same."

I nodded, not even sure why I was nodding. It was all so much.

"But Hank was determined. And they were married by summer's end," she continued. "A ceremony overlooking—"

"Bridalveil Falls," I finished, remembering our visit there. The bride we saw in the filmy veil dashing to the cliff edge. Was that only a week ago, less?

"Bridalveil Falls. It was just a trickle that time of year," Mrs. Brandt said. "Wendy always said it looked like a tear rolling down a face."

She cleared her throat, looked away. Then went on.

"The ceremony was very fine. I can still see them at the altar, their wrists bound with cord, a knot for each vow. That's a Cornish thing, you know. Handfasting, they call it. The cord becomes a keepsake to hang around the bedpost."

She paused, her hand curling over her mouth. Then went on.

"Hank was in his best suit, the same one he'd worn to his father's funeral the year before. He had his big job waiting for him down in Ann Arbor and he looked the part. And Wendy was so pretty. She wore ribbons in her hair instead of a veil. From the same ribbon wheel her late mother had used."

My breath caught, my dream rushing back to me, the woman with long dark hair full of ribbons. Her eyes so kind.

"All morning, Hank kept insisting she wear the headpiece he'd bought for her, shipped from New York and costing eight hundred dollars. An illusion veil that hung to her fingertips. And Wendy kept shaking her head and laughing, as if he was teasing, saying she'd rather go in with no illusions.

"I still remember that laugh, such a lonely laugh, echoing up the high ceilings of the church."

Mrs. Brandt nearly smiled, a whisper of a smile, gone before you were sure.

"It was never going to work, you see. Not without breaking her down. And Wendy was strong. She just didn't want to break. Not yet.

"The first summer, they came back from Ann Arbor, but only for a week or two. I barely knew her. She'd lost thirty pounds. Her hair was short, shiny, like a wig. She'd been volunteering at the university hospital and kept crying to me over the AIDS babies, the loss. Doctor Ash spent his days fishing with Hicks. Hicks'd come home after with a grim look. He didn't think it was a good match, he'd tell me. That's all he'd say.

"The next summer, she came alone. Seven months pregnant and with this funny smile like someone was always taking a picture of her, saying cheese. He'd come up on the weekends. They slept in separate bedrooms. For the baby, he said. There was a lot of yelling in the house. He had so many ideas about what she should eat, do. The way she should sit, sleep. She'd sit at the table, her head bowed.

"One night I heard something, almost like a wail. I thought it was a wolf, but it was Wendy, outside in her nightgown. . . ."

Her eyes flitted past me. A shiver came across me, hard and cool.

"I went out to her," Mrs. Brandt continued, her jaw tight, holding herself together. "She said, *What if it doesn't work, Rose. What if it doesn't work.* Her hands on her belly. I couldn't believe it was the same girl who, two summers ago, had those ribbons in her hair.

"Two nights later, she came to me, her face red and swollen, a nasty tear in her eyebrow from a fall. What happened? I kept asking and she was so afraid of him. *I'm going to have to take the baby and go. Will you help me?* I said I would. I would have.

"Three weeks later, everything happened."

I rested my hands on my belly, shutting my eyes.

"There'd been tears the night before. She was packing a bag. He found it hidden in the clothes hamper, and that was it. He locked her in the room. He said it was for her safety. She was unstable, he said. Can you imagine?"

I looked at her and said yes, I could.

"The next morning, Doctor Ash came to me and said, *She's in labor, Rose.* She was in the bedroom, he said, it was time. Only thirty weeks along and Doctor Ash kept saying, *It's too late to get to the hospital. It'll have to be here.*

"I told him I could help. My mother had taught me. I didn't want to leave her."

I thought about how closely she'd watched me, Mrs. Brandt. Always watching, and now I knew why.

"He let me in the bedroom. And what I saw . . . Oh, her face. Like the world had cracked it open. I'd never seen fear like that.

"*He's given me something,* that's what she said to me, whispered in my ear. *He gave me a shot to make it start. I can't feel my legs, Rose.*"

Mrs. Brandt shook her head.

"He'd caught her leaving, she said. Found her zigzagging out the back of the house while he slept. Dragged her by the arm like a rag doll, like a skinned rabbit, back into the house.

"*I'm not ready, Rose,* she said. I put my fingers in her. She was only four centimeters along, no bigger than a lemon slice. He'd given her something. He'd induced her, you see.

"*It'll be okay,* I promised her. *We're arm in arm again, just like skating.*

"And she smiled the saddest, saddest smile, and that's when I knew something wasn't right.

"He came back in with his black bag and I told him she wasn't near ready, but he said I didn't know anything. He said I was a stupid, stupid girl.

"I wanted to call. The hospital, someone. But I didn't want to leave her. I didn't want to let go of her hand."

She paused, lacing her hands together tightly.

"You must understand," she said. "I'd worked for that family since I was fourteen."

I nodded, a queasy feeling inside, my hands reaching for the corners of the table.

"And it all happened so fast. He had his hand inside her. He said he could feel the umbilical cord. It was coming before the baby. And now the baby was breech. That's what he said. Elbow first.

"I'll never forget the look on his face, red and wild. *You see what we must do,* he said. *You see it.* But I . . . I couldn't see it. He wouldn't let me. *Wait,* I said. *Wait!*"

"So what did he . . . ?" I started. My hands on my belly, I couldn't finish the question.

Mrs. Brandt pressed her fingers on her eyelids, shut.

"It was all so fast. He made me hold my hand where his had been. And he was reaching for his black bag, its handle slicked with blood. And . . ."

She covered her eyes.

"I saw the flash of the thing. The scissors bright in his hands."

"Episiotomy," I said, my voice small and sickly.

"Many doctors still did that back then. My mother used to work for one who thought we should get rid of all the pushing and just go in with the scissors and the forceps."

Mrs. Brandt took a breath, then cried out, "But Wendy hadn't pushed at all yet! She wasn't halfway there, you see. He just couldn't wait. He wouldn't wait.

"I saw the blades between her legs. Everything came red all of a sudden, and he was shouting, *Push! Push, Wendy, push!*

"And then it happened. Jed slid from her like a sticky marble falling from your hand."

Mrs. Brandt closed her eyes. I knew she could see it, all of it.

"I'll never forget it. Doctor Ash snipping the caul with those same scissors he'd just cut her open with. And now so tender, so skilled, the water gushing down his leg, the caul slipping away like your hand through a spider's web. And, oh, to hear him cry out, sweet Jed. To draw his first breath and call out. I thought my heart would burst. The caul like a king's cloak over his tiny shoulders.

"And I looked at Wendy to say, *There's your boy, darling. There's your boy.*

"But Wendy looked at me, and something was wrong. What he'd done to her, it had gone wrong. My hand on hers and it felt like ice and she said, *I can't see you, Rose. I can't see you.*"

I covered my face. I knew what was coming.

"The blood came hard and wouldn't stop. And I cried out, *Doctor Ash, Doctor Ash! You must stitch her up! You must fix her!* But he only looked at me. Jed was in his arms and he wouldn't let go. *I'll take him,* I kept saying. But he wouldn't let go, blood in his hair, his arms wrapped around the little thing. Little Jed.

"And a look on his face so cold, like he didn't know who I was talking about. Like she didn't matter at all. Not anymore. She was done, over.

"And then it came. A clot as big as a plum slipped from her. Her skin cold as snow, her hair standing on end, and her eyes gone empty."

She paused, turning toward the doorway, to the connecting room.

Shush-shush-click. Shush-shush-click.

"And suddenly Hicks was there, in the doorway. The phone cradled there, talking to the hospital. They were on the way.

"*Help her*, I cried again and again, but Doctor Ash just looked at me and I still remember how he had blood in his hair. He looked at me as if to say, *Who?* As if to say, *Who?*"

Mrs. Brandt closed her hands into fists, her eyes still shut.

I thought of what Doctor Ash had told me that night only a week ago, less. How Wendy's blood pressure spiked and she didn't make it through the hour. How they held hands the whole time and her hand seemed to dissolve in his. A fatal blood clot, a terrible loss. And how it became unbearable even to look at his black bag, that doctor's bag his father had given him, hand-stitched, brass-clasped. How it reminded him of loss.

That bag he used to induce her, to cut her, to kill her. Or nearly so.

"She was going to leave him," Mrs. Brandt said. "He wanted that baby. Nothing was going to stop him."

She told me how the paramedics came, how Hicks slipped on the blood, his face hitting a table corner.

"It went right through his lip," she said. "He's worn a moustache ever since."

"*The umbilical cord wrapped around and around him like a silver ribbon,*" I said, recalling what she'd said to me once before.

"A ribbon like that ribbon of ice," Mrs. Brandt said softly.

"And the caul," I said, as if we were both in some kind of trance. "You have to peel it away with great care, or the baby's skin will come with it."

Mrs. Brandt closed her hands into fists.

"I will never forget the sound of Hicks crying. Sitting there on the edge of the bed, his head in his hands. Moaning in this awful way. A sound I'd only heard once before, a black bear caught in a trap.

"I'd never seen that man cry and I'd known him since we were six.

"Well, we couldn't look at each other after that. There's a look your spouse can give you and there's no going back."

I nodded. I knew that look. Now I knew that look.

"We weren't the same, and it was over. Everything was.

"Hicks was a deputy then. The sheriff was friends with Doctor Ash's father. That's how it was, you see. Everyone knew each other here back then. And the Ashes went three generations back. Brought money, bought land. Everyone kept secrets too. I never knew quite what happened, but it all went away. It just all went away."

"No one knows?" I asked.

"He knows," she said, a darkness heavy in her eyes. "And Hicks. The three of us.

"She was supposed to go to a . . . place. A long-term facility down near Petoskey. She was dead to him, you see. She'd never really been alive to him at all."

I thought of Wendy in the other room. Her life, I thought, how little it meant to him, even less once he had his son. I thought of what he'd told me, *The newborn, the unborn have never had it easy.* What about Wendy, how easy did she have it.

"I brought her down there," Mrs. Brandt said. "To the facility. Checked her in. But I couldn't leave her there. I couldn't fail her again. So I brought her back here."

"I can't believe he let you," I blurted.

"He didn't," she said, looking up at me. Meeting my eyes.

I wasn't sure I'd heard her right.

"Wait," I said. "Wait. *He doesn't know she's here?*"

Mrs. Brandt shook her head. I think maybe I saw the flash of a smile there.

She handled the paperwork, the bills. He never wanted to hear her name, you see. He never asked anything. She handled it all.

She wrote checks from the household account once a year for Wendy's care. But instead of going to the facility in Petoskey, they went to support her at-home care.

"I set up everything for her here," she said. "The machines, everything. Hicks helped. His niece would come and help sometimes.

"I had the bed installed at the picture window. She always loved a view."

The picture window. The one I'd seen so many times from Doctor Ash's house. How funny it felt to be standing on the other side, seeing what she could see. What Jed's mom could see. Her husband's home, her son, everything. Her life unfurling without her.

Wendy at the window, her window facing his. Her head tilted toward him. She was watching him all the time and he never knew it. She had her eyes on Doctor Ash all the time. And he had no idea. But did he feel it nonetheless?

Even if she couldn't see, couldn't know, hovering somewhere between life and death, maybe he felt seen by her. Watched, judged.

. . .

"But did Jed . . ."

"We never told him," she said.

I took a breath of relief, even if I wasn't sure why.

"One of the first summers they came up, he said, age four or five, *My mom died here.* For years he wouldn't go near that turn in the hallway to the room where . . ."

"But no one ever said anything?"

"At first, I was afraid. Only a few people knew she was still alive—a doctor in Muskegon, but he moved away a few years later. The sheriff, who retired, then passed. And they were both here but two weeks a year. No one put it together, or if they did, they didn't say. People here, we don't interfere. We keep to ourselves. We mind our own business. The deep long winters. Private, clannish. You could die, you see, and no one might ever know.

"I sometimes wondered why he kept returning, Doctor Ash. And when he moved up here full time, I . . ." Something passed over her face, and she winced as if in great pain.

I took another breath. "But how is she still . . . It's been more than thirty years."

"They can live on indefinitely. Well, as long as the rest of us. One of the doctors told me: *Think of her brain like a bowl of Jell-O. There's a crack inside, but you'll never find it.*"

"But didn't you ever think maybe you should . . . I mean, she's never coming back, right?"

"Right," she said. "Never." She took a breath, shutting her eyes. "But the body doesn't know that, exactly. Sometimes she opens her eyes if I pull back the curtains. Sometimes, if the light is just so, she makes this sound, like a sweet cooing, like a mourning dove. Sometimes . . . she even seems to smile. Hicks says I'm crazy. That it isn't a smile because a smile has to come from some place, some feeling, and she . . . Well, sometimes she seems to smile."

. . .

A low boom from outside shook the table.

The men. The men. Doctor Ash out there, bolt-action in his hands.

We were quiet for a moment. A low rumbling shook the windowpane. A scatter of fireworks humming through the air.

"You kept this secret all these years," I said finally. "And . . . those pictures of Jed. All this time. And you still work for him. How?"

Mrs. Brandt covered her face with her long fingers, then pulled them away. Her eyes dry and clear.

"People think you're loyal to the people you love, the times you've had together. There's other kinds of loyalty. You share a secret so big and dark, you become loyal to it. And to keeping it."

It made me think of Jed, his feelings about his dad, how he'd stowed them all away, up high in some compartment no one could reach. But the latch kept clicking, clicking.

Mrs. Brandt looked at me.

"And the fact that she was still in there, breathing . . . well, it meant we'd done something for her. We'd saved her from something. Didn't we?"

I wanted to say yes.

"You gave over your life to her," I said instead.

Mrs. Brandt flinched, turning away.

"Please understand," she said, her hand curling into a fist, "I don't pretend I'm doing it for her."

"I don't—"

"I'm doing it for me."

I looked at her. Outside, we heard the singing of a bottle rocket. There was no time left.

"Mrs. Brandt," I said slowly, "I think he means to take my baby. Doctor Ash. I think he may do worse."

Mrs. Brandt looked at me. "I think so too."

She paused and closed her eyes.

"I can still see her next to me," she said softly. "Wendy and Rose, the two of us arm and arm, gliding down a ribbon of ice."

"Stay, Redruth," Mrs. Brandt said, leashing her in the kitchenette, her wound newly cleaned, gauzed. "Good girl."

We were going. She was taking me to the Marquette airport in her minivan. The minivan was out back, behind the big tree.

It was dark, the only light the greenish hue from Mrs. Brandt's jelly-jar porch light.

In her hand, she held her air gun, muzzle pointed down, hidden in the folds of her long skirt.

"Wait," she said suddenly, stopping at the door. "Wait."

But it was Doctor Ash who had been waiting.

Lingering in the darkness outside.

Mrs. Brandt saw my expression and leaned close, taking my hand and pressing it on the gun barrel. "You go for the eyes with this," she whispered. "Or the neck."

"But I . . ." I started, but it was too late.

"How now, Rose," came his voice, booming and almost buoyant. "Rose, bring my daughter-in-law out. I know she's with you. She's putting my grandchild in danger."

He stepped under the light and we saw him.

Doctor Ash, at the foot of the porch with his rifle in hand.

The van was so close, yet also so far away, twenty feet like twenty miles.

"What do you want, Hank?" Mrs. Brandt said sharply, stepping in front of me, pushing me behind her skirts.

His head jerked back a little, surprised.

"Well, well," he said, letting his rifle barrel brush along the porch step, "this friendship is a surprise, Rose. Rose, you surprise me."

"Get that gun away from us," she said, more firmly now, "and let us pass."

"Here's what's going to happen," Doctor Ash said, turning to me, an uneasy smile on his face. "You're coming back to the house now. And that's where you will stay until my grandson is born."

"I saw you out there," I blurted. "Did you mean to shoot me?"

He looked at me, the silver sheaf of his hair glowing under the light of the jelly-jar porch light.

"If I meant to shoot you . . ." he said, then laughed, a low hollow chuckle. "Are you really asking me that? Why would I ever put the baby at risk? I leave that to you."

"That's enough, Hank," Mrs. Brandt said, her hand on my arm now, parting her long skirts, reminding me of the air gun hidden in the folds, its stock tight in her right hand.

"I always told Jed, beware the woman," he said, looking at me, shaking his head. "Keep her close, with one eye open. They're pretty as a picture at first, but when they turn, boy, do they turn. They paint their face and then show you another. Just like you, Jacy. Sweet and soft, teaching children how to fingerpaint. Playing the little angel in the house, hiding what you are—"

"What I am?" I said, my voice shaking. "I know everything now. I know what you did. I know who you are."

He looked at me and then at Mrs. Brandt. For a fleeting second, his face seemed to stiffen, panic.

But it passed. And in its place the look he gave, of such contempt, contempt for us both. How foolish we were, how simple and useless. Or useful until we weren't, until our utility had passed. I thought of the deer's velvet, how it gets scraped away, making the antlers hard and dangerous.

When the velvet's gone, Hicks had said, *they're ready to spar.*

"Why don't you come inside, Hank?" Mrs. Brandt said abruptly. I looked at her, the strange smile on her face.

But he wouldn't move. He was planted there. Planted like an oak tree a hundred rings thick.

"What do you think you know, little girl?" he said to me, wearing the smile I knew so well. The one so warm, so gracious and delighted. "Tell me."

I felt Mrs. Brandt's hand on my arm, nudging me further inside too.

"Why don't you come inside," she repeated, more softly now, graciously, like a model housewife, opening the door to him, brushing her skirt back.

I only half-realized what she was doing.

"I think Mrs. Brandt is right," I said, stepping back, too, into the bright center of the cottage. "You should come in. I think you should come inside and tell us."

Doctor Ash shifted, paused, head ducking momentarily into the darkness beyond the porch lamp.

"Why don't you come in, Hank," she said once more, in a voice I'd never heard from her. Thick and strange. A command, not a question. "Why don't you come in."

"You've never been inside before, Hank," Mrs. Brandt said, her body swaying with such confidence, her skirts dragging, the air gun flashing in the folds like a saber.

"Rose, what is the game here?" he asked coolly.

He's afraid, I thought. Of something even if he doesn't know what.

He looked so big in the small cottage, and his rifle butt dragging on the floor, doing figure eights as he turned around, looking at the place.

"Why don't you take the grand tour?" Mrs. Brandt said, moving toward the bedroom.

A few feet away, I could hear the *click-click* of the IV in the bedroom, the *shush-shush* of the monitors, the tangle of old wires.

I looked at her, the grim satisfaction on her face. How long had she been waiting for this moment, I wondered. To make him look at what he had done.

"Show him the view," I found myself saying. "From the bedroom window."

With one long arm, Mrs. Brandt pushed open the bedroom door, the soft light curling across us as Doctor Ash walked toward her stiffly, as if hypnotized.

It was a sound like no sound I'd ever heard. A queer rattle coming up Doctor Ash's throat as we all stood in the small bedroom, smotheringly warm and close, peach walls and peach bedspread, the riffle of chenille.

"What is this," he rasped, teetering on his feet. "Who is this."

It was only a moment, a split second, his face soft like a child's. It was only a moment I felt for him.

It was there, then it was gone.

"Why, Hank, that's Wendy," Mrs. Brandt said, standing beside the bed, her hand stroking Wendy's braid. "That's your wife."

The way he looked at her, his right hand knotted at his side, his left still holding that rifle.

"How dare you," he whispered. "How dare you."

"I thought you might want to see her, after all these years," Mrs. Brandt said.

The sound came again, the rattle from inside him, louder now.

"Of course," she added, gesturing to the picture window, "she sees you all the time."

Though it was dark, you could see the dull shimmer in the distance of Doctor Ash's house.

Doctor Ash stood a moment, his face unreadable, his hands trembling slightly at his sides.

Looking at him, I thought, suddenly, of baby Jed, trapped behind the caul. All those sticky layers, how would you ever pull them all away without tearing him apart too?

"She's supposed to be in . . . in Petoskey," he sputtered, turning away, his face hidden. Turning to the corner of the hot room. "That facility. She's supposed to be . . ."

"But she's not," Mrs. Brandt said, tilting her head almost coquettishly. "I guess I lied."

And then the most remarkable thing happened in that small, close room.

Maybe it was the stroking, maybe it was the rattling sounds, maybe it was the heat in the small room, maybe it was all these things and more, but I saw it.

I saw her, Wendy, her eyes sliding open, such long lashes and leering to her right, toward Doctor Ash.

Their eyes locked. I swear I saw it. They locked and something seemed to crackle between them.

Then I saw her, Wendy, that small mouth curling, I swear, into something like a smile.

For a long moment, no one said anything, did anything.

Wendy, her eyes so bright, skin impossibly smooth, smiling and smiling at Doctor Ash.

Doctor Ash, his hand on that rifle, that rattle from low inside him humming louder, louder.

"It happens sometimes," Mrs. Brandt said. "No one knows why."

Doctor Ash turned to her unsteadily.

"You," he said, his voice slow and stilted. "You saw what happened that night. The breech. Everything. She failed us. She failed Jed. She abandoned us and I went on. For my boy."

"That's not what happened," she said firmly, even as her hands were shaking now too.

"I saved my son," he said. "I rescued him from her ruin. My beautiful boy. Your kind would never understand."

"You threw her away," Mrs. Brandt said. "And I blame myself. I blame myself for not seeing it. For not stopping you in time."

There was silence. A draft rippled through, everything lifting, and I held my breath.

"You were hand in hand with me all these years," he said, a sudden softening in his voice.

Mrs. Brandt said nothing, but I could feel a tremble on her and I thought of Wendy, the old, delicate seashell of Wendy, emptied out of everything she once was.

"You don't know anything," he said finally, his voice gone to ice. "You're the girl who made our beds."

"I was twenty-five," Mrs. Brandt said, just as coolly, "cleaning houses, and you were the rich man, my employer, the doctor in the white coat."

Her face falling upon itself.

"She was good," she said. "And I was good. And you had all the power. I'll never forgive myself."

But he didn't seem to hear her, passing through the bedroom doorway, the rifle butt dragging on the floor.

That was when he noticed the snapshots, Jed and the lighthouse, the edges curling and vibrating in the draft from the open door.

Something passed over his face.

There were sounds coming from him and his hand covering his face.

Jed, oh, Jed, he was saying, almost a wail, *my boy, my dear boy.*

. . .

He raised his hand, then swiped it downward—like a bear swatting its clawed paw—tearing the snapshots from the door, scattering several to the floor.

We all watched them dance along the floor, the draft picking them up and spinning them.

"Hank," Mrs. Brandt said, her swagger gone. Her eyes on him. "I never told him. I . . ."

"He'll never know," Doctor Ash murmured. He raised his hand and pointed at me, eyes glittering. "*She* can never have him and he can never know."

In an instant, he'd done the calculation. If I knew, Jed would know. And that was impossible.

❦

It happened so fast, Doctor Ash's arm swinging round, the rifle tighter in his hands. Then he stutter-stepped back through the door into the living room.

"Go," Mrs. Brandt whispered to me, her hand reaching for mine, sliding her car keys into my palm. "Go."

She was seeing something in him. The way he was looking at me, one leg forward, his rifle swaying, muzzle down.

I watched Mrs. Brandt's fingers on the grip of her air gun.

"Go, Jacy," Mrs. Brandt said more urgently. "Now!"

I sprinted for the door, poor Redruth howling, leashed to the wall in the kitchenette.

Behind me, I could hear the door splintering under the butt of Doctor Ash's rifle and Mrs. Brandt crying out for me to run, run, run.

Screen door slapping, stumbling off the porch, Mrs. Brandt fast behind me, the growing darkness and the porch light sizzling, pushing myself onto the porch and into the dark grass.

The *blip-blip* of a car alarm and there it was: the minivan, its lights flashing, tucked behind the white pine.

BOOM!

The sudden, slinging crack of a rifle as Doctor Ash stood on the dark grass, weapon raised and pointed at the minivan's tires and shooting.

BOOM! again, both the front tires gone now as Redruth yowled from inside.

"This is it," he was saying. "This is over and done."

The bolt-action gleamed in his hands as he glared at me. I could nearly feel the rifle's waxy Cosmoline, feel it as I did a few short days ago, holding it stickily in my hands with Doctor Ash beside me, his cologne whispering in my ear.

"Little girl," he said, his voice thick and gristly, "you're coming back to the house with me and you're not leaving without giving me my grandchild."

Where is Jed? As if he would help me now, or ever. As if he ever could, chained to his father's will, like some ancient curse.

"Don't you dare, Hank."

I turned to see Mrs. Brandt, legs astride, holding her air gun high, the scope glinting.

"Get behind me," she said softly, her face damp, my heart thumping wildly.

He might have shot me in the back, maybe, but I didn't care, running to her.

"Rose," he said, an empty laugh and the shadow thrown behind him from the porch lamp—he looked ten feet tall. "What do you mean to do with that toy?"

"Put these hollow points in you," she told him.

"It's a man's weakness to give in to women," he said, drawing the bolt back. "But it's a man's duty to make himself a son. Being a father is a gift and divine responsibility. It never ends. I'd do anything for my boy. To protect him from your kind."

The click of the bolt humming in our ears.

And the shot came from Doctor Ash's rifle, a soft explosion. I cried out.

Mrs. Brandt wheeled around, air gun still in her hands, dropping to her knees, blood blossoming on her collar like a boutonniere.

Doctor Ash let his arms drop, the rifle seeming to stick between his fingers. A stunned look on his face.

"Mrs. Brandt," I cried out, crouching over her, pressing against the red swell, tearing loose her sleeve and tying it tight, pressing harder, trying to stop what seemed impossible, the smell of smoke, pennies.

"You wouldn't understand," Doctor Ash called out, his voice loud and jangly now. "You never could. You women. You think you don't have anything when you have everything. You have all the power. You have everything."

I didn't say anything, the blood hot under my hands and Mrs. Brandt's eyes stuttering up at me, her lashes so long, and we'd never been so close.

Her mouth opening but saying nothing.

"I'm getting help," I whispered to her. "I'm getting help."

Click-click. I could see him.

"I had to do it," Doctor Ash was saying, his voice speeding up, growing stronger. "You left me no choice. There are so many things you make me do. All of you."

I turned to see Doctor Ash, rifle raised again, cheek pressed against the stock, scope winking at me.

"You will never get anything from me."

. . .

Later, I wouldn't remember it: reaching across Mrs. Brandt and fumbling for her air gun, clasping it, rising to my feet.

But I would remember standing, my legs shaking, the gun light and long, awkward and twitching in my hands. A toy, I thought, but all I had.

"Don't worry," I whispered to Mrs. Brandt, her breath ragged but still there. "I'm getting help."

In the trees beyond, a flutter of leaves, a branch cracking. Was someone there?

"Stop!" I cried out, the stock hot under my fingers, my eye darting behind the scope.

"I always knew what you were, Jacy," Doctor Ash said, his rifle glimmering at me. "You never fooled me."

Click-click.

It was as if the bolt-action jumped in Doctor Ash's waxy hands.

Cosmoline gets in the firing pin and jams up the works, Hicks had said, and the rifle slipped like a live thing from Doctor Ash's grip.

He fumbled for it and I knew he was coming for me again.

"Now, Jacy!" Had Mrs. Brandt said that? Had someone?

My fingers squeezed and squeezed helplessly, the air gun buzzing and slapping against my face. Sputtering out hot pellets pointlessly, desperately.

You go for the eyes with this, Mrs. Brandt had told me. *Or the neck.*

I pointed and squeezed again.

Doctor Ash's hands leapt for his throat, face red, fumbling and clasping there.

I shut my eyes and opened them again.

. . .

But then, the sound came, not from the air gun in my hands but from a real one.

Pop-pop! Like a firecracker, but close.

A soft explosion, and Doctor Ash's head jerked back, red.

Behind him, Jed appeared, ghostlike.

In his hands, Randy's gun hummed, raised and smoking.

Doctor Ash sank to his knees, slumping forward, the rifle slipping from his hands.

"Dad," Jed said, voice tiny and high. "Dad."

His arms slowly fell, the gun twisted in his fingers.

On the ground, Doctor Ash squirmed and convulsed, his hands clutching at his collar, blood fountaining high.

"Jed," I cried out, running toward him, "we have to get help!"

But he couldn't hear me, or anything.

His face pale as paper, his hand vibrating like a string.

The gun loose in his hand, and then dangling.

I took it from between his twitching fingers.

He wasn't looking at me. Instead, he was looking straight through me, up to Mrs. Brandt's cottage, its front door still open, swinging in the night breeze.

At first, I thought they were butterflies, birds.

But they were the snapshots. Young Jed and the red lighthouse.

Fluttering on the grass were one, two, three, of those snapshots, blown loose and flying.

Jed reached down and picked one up, staring at it under the porch lamp.

"We gotta go," I said one last time, louder, my fists clenched. "Your dad's truck. We can take that. The keys . . ."

But he wasn't listening, his eyes on the cottage again, the picture window glowing, nearly radiating. I thought of Wendy inside. *Shush-shush, shush-shush.*

Then, as if a switch had been turned, Jed started moving toward the cottage, nearly walking through me, moving slowly, then swiftly, up the short slope to the cottage.

It was as if something was pulling him, some powerful force, some ancient blood vibration. Or it was her. In that moment it felt like it was Wendy who was drawing him toward her.

"Don't go in there!" I found myself calling out, my voice strained and screeching. I didn't want him to see, not like this.

But there was no stopping him as, snapshot curled in his open hand, Jed marched up the porch and through the screen door.

Jed, meet your mother.

I could see it all through the picture window, the whole tableau.

It was like a movie, a movie I was watching and couldn't stop.

Like an audience yelling at the screen: *Don't go in there!* And the characters never listening.

There was Jed at the bedroom door, his fingers touching the remaining snapshots. Jed at six, Jed at ten, the red lighthouse like an awful arrow pointing inside.

Then his gaze dragging now across us toward the bed, toward his mother.

I couldn't see her, but I could see him.

I couldn't hear him, only see his mouth open slightly, then close, then open again wider.

Oh, Jed. Oh, Jed.

But there was no time, there was no time.

On the ground, half lit by the porch light, Doctor Ash lay

sprawled, throat gurgling faintly, his limbs stirring like a pinned fly. Like a lure tacked to a corkboard.

Looking down at him, his cold blue eyes staring emptily at me.

Is he dead? But there was no time.

My hands on Doctor Ash's jacket, tugging his pockets loose, tunneling inside.

My fingers sliding uncomfortably into his pants pockets, the awful stirring of his blood, his pulse slow and stunted.

Feeling his eyes on me, astonished, and his mouth opening and closing and opening again, a pearly froth gathering in one corner.

You will never get anything from me.

Feeling the hard cut of his keys against my fingertips, jerking them out, the fob still hot.

Mine, mine, I thought, so close, smelling the cinnamon oil in his hair.

Closer than we'd ever been, our faces fleetingly inches apart, our gazes momentarily locked.

Captain Murderer! Captain Murderer!

His face so white, white as milk, with white brows and white lashes, his mouth open, teeth like little bones.

Clutching his heart, Doctor Ash stared up at me, his eyes bright blue and surprised.

Jacy, Jacy.

The ending, what came after—heaven or nothingness—he seemed to see it, and then was gone.

Mrs. Brandt, I'm getting help, getting help—

It was so close, down the knoll through a thicket.

The rifle in one hand, the handgun in my pocket, the flashlight long gone.

Through the black net of black trees, I searched for the great domed floodlight of Doctor Ash's house.

Running as fast as I could, my right arm across my belly, stiff and strong there and the sudden swell of a thousand katydids clicking, snapping their wings.

My eyes scattering. *Was the house this way, or this way?* Hurrying, hurrying.

My arm across my belly and my breath caught and that was when I felt it, the feeling in my belly, like a fish squirming inside me, like a goldfish slapping the sides of its plastic bag.

I was so close, so close, and the fear was no longer waiting for me but had gone through me to the other side.

I was thinking of Jed on our wedding night, a slick of frosting on his collar from the cake-cutting. *I never thought this would happen to me,* he'd whispered, his heart thudding loud enough to drown us all out. *I'd given up on it happening.*

And I was thinking of my dear mom and her painted toes and the Taser in her handbag, and Aunt Laraine sitting at our kitchen table, flipping her pack of Benson & Hedges like a deck of cards, and how wise those women were and how angry and how hungry for love they remained.

And I was thinking of my dad in his Steel Wheels tee, reading to me as he stirred the cream of wheat, leaving the lumps for me, as he read to me about Captain Murderer, picking and licking the poisoned bones of his doomed final bride, *the smartest girl in all the land.*

And I was thinking of Wendy Ash in my dream, her hair full of silver ribbons, saying, *Jacy, you better be smarter.*

But most of all I was thinking of the baby inside me, and that she would be a girl, maybe, and if she was, what I could say, what I would warn her about, could I warn her about everything? And would she believe me?

I will love you so much, I thought, my belly aching at the thought. *I will love you more than I can bear.*

And it felt beautiful and terrifying all at once.

Mrs. Brandt, I'm nearly there—

In the distance, I heard the *pop-pop-pop* of firecrackers, like plastic packing between fingers.

Pushing through the trees, I saw Doctor Ash's truck.

My hip numb, my chest flaming, but there it was, wasn't it?

The glossy black behemoth just down the knoll.

Doctor Ash's great black tank, parked under a soaring oak tree, its branches knotted and hanging over it, once again like an arcade crane claw ready to clasp it and carry it away for good.

Doctor Ash's volcanic-black truck shimmering, waiting for me.

A trembling of leaves to my right, I turned and heard it: a high, raspy chirping, coming from the paved drive below.

I stopped suddenly, the rifle sweat-wet between my fingers.

Redruth howled mournfully from somewhere in the tall trees.

She sounded so far away.

Then the chirping again, rolling, lilting, squeaking.

What was it? But there was no time.

Skidding down the slope, alarm fob pinched between my fingers, I stopped short, a few feet from the truck.

The fob sweaty in my hand, but something made me not press the button, not yet.

Because I heard something else.

A strange, trilling sound, low and sinuous.

Then: a flurry of something on the ground, a flash of pale fur disappearing under the truck.

A security lamp clicked on, forming a cone of light over the truck.

I stepped back, rifle in my hand.

That was when I saw the spotted, feral face peeking beneath the truck's undercarriage.

Then another, its furry twin.

There, hiding under the truck, were two kittens crouching close, their heads knotted together, chubby paws gathered beneath their spotted faces. Their eyes blue saucers.

They looked up at me and, suddenly, both their mouths unlatched, letting out one high, curdling screech.

In an instant, they scattered, out from under the truck and into the thicket beyond.

It was only then that I felt a heavy gaze behind me, plucking at my arm, my neck.

Remembering—too late—Hicks's warning about mountain lions:

If you see babies, that was your head start.

Turning as slowly as I could, I saw it. Saw her.

The kittens' mother, the mountain lion herself.

Twenty feet down the drive, maybe less, a dusky thing, long and slinking, her tiny head slouched low, then lifting, then lowering again in undulating motions.

Black-tipped tail, ears, face like ash, that long tail seemed to stretch as long as she did . . .

The mountain lion, our mountain lion.

. . . her head rolling and her belly pale and low, heavy with more babies.

285

Crouching slightly, laying back her ears. Then a hissing, baring her pointed teeth.

Her, she. Lioness. Mama.

Her head rolling again, and her neck long and rolling, too, the mouth gone wide before peeling forth with a high, throat-shredding scream.

Don't turn your back. Don't run.

The rifle heavy in my hand, the handgun in my pocket, warm against my belly.

Make yourself big. Make yourself loud.

You can remember those things and still not know how to do them.

Slowly, slowly, I started walking backward.

As she started moving toward me, a burlesque saunter, one leg nearly crossing the other, tail twirling behind her, like a showgirl with her boa.

"No," I said, my voice swallowing itself. "No."

A sudden lurch, she sprang back from her haunches, her front legs swirling in the dust, like a dervish, like a wild thing.

"No!" I cried out, backing away, backing away and stutter-stepping, the key fob jumping out of my hand.

She stopped, her gaze locked on me, her legs drawn together.

In the distance, I heard a high whimper, Redruth's lament.

Her eyes on me, so close . . . her eyes, black-rimmed but bright and sparking.

Her eyes on me.

On instinct, I raised Doctor Ash's rifle in my arms, pointing it at her.

Queenie, I thought, remembering my student Diego's papier-mâché beast, its eyes eerily hollow, deep-set holes painted black inside, a slick, gleaming black you felt you could see yourself in, or see something darker than you ever knew.

She likes you, Diego had said. *Queenie likes you.*

But then:

She'll kill you like this, he said, his fingers pinching the base of my skull. *One bite.*

"Please," I said, the rifle hot in my hot hands. "Please."

In that moment, I felt everything falling away.

Hold on, Jacy, I told myself.

The mountain lion, my mountain lion.

Would you shoot her, I thought, *this beautiful thing, protecting her babies?*

And my arms slowly fell again, the rifle tilting, pointing toward the ground.

Slipping from my arms, landing on the ground.

Then, her mouth unlatched, just as her babies' had, and she turned away from me and let out a sound like I'd never heard before, a coo, a prayer, a promise, a song.

A pretty, lonesome sound, Hicks had said, *like wind through an old tree log. . . . Never heard anything like it before or since.*

A pulse of stillness followed.

Then: *Chirp-chirp*, the sound returned, from her babies hidden somewhere in the trees beyond. Waiting for their mother.

Her ears pricked, head cocked, she turned from me and slipped gracefully up the green slope, disappearing into the dark woods.

She was gone, but I could still hear her singing.

Singing to her babies, singing to me.

ᴣᴄ

That was when I heard it.

A pealing rumble as a truck the color of pea soup scraped up the drive at impossible velocity.

Whirling around, I saw Hicks behind the wheel, his head ducking out the driver's side window, Redruth yowling, tongue lapping by his side.

"Hicks!" I tried to call out, barely a voice at all.

"Get in, sweetheart! Get in!"

Behind him, I could see Mrs. Brandt crumpled in the back seat, the red corsage gone to rust, but her eyes fluttering, alive, alive.

"Hurry!" He leaned across the front seat, the passenger door popping open and his arm extending.

I reached up for Hicks's hand, and his other grappled around my arm as he lifted me up, high and higher.

"Let's go, let's go!"

The branches slapping the windshield, the grind of the tires, we drove, we nearly flew.

"Is Jed—" I started.

"He . . . he . . . wouldn't leave her," Hicks said, his jaw tight. "He needed to stay with his mom."

I nodded, thinking of him, like a clutch over my heart.

Back there, in the woods, they remained: Doctor Ash sprawled in the mud, Wendy inside, swaddled tight, machines pumping her lungs, her heart, Jed seated at her side, his whole life scrambling and unscrambling behind his eyes. The three of them, the closest they'd ever been. The family together at last.

"Hold her hand," Hicks was saying, but he didn't have to tell me, mine already reaching behind for Mrs. Brandt's rough palm, clasping it in my own.

"It's going to be okay," I said to Mrs. Brandt, my hand never tighter on anyone's than hers. "We're going to be okay."

We never rode faster, the road disappearing beneath us. The hospital was far but not too far and my heart hurt in my chest but somehow I was smiling, almost laughing.

Behind us, the tall oaks soughed in the wind.

My other hand on my belly, I could see the trees breaking ahead, and maybe a clearing beyond.

"It's going to be okay," I repeated breathlessly, my voice giddy and high. "It's going to be okay."

ACKNOWLEDGMENTS

My utmost and endless gratitude to the peerless and passionate Sally Kim, whose editorial touch is both effortlessly deft and seriously magical. Also big thanks to Katie Grinch, Alexis Welby, Ashley McClay, Tarini Sipahimalani, Shina Patel, Emily Mlynek, and the whole outstanding team at Putnam.

To the intrepid and invaluable Dan Conaway, to whom this book is dedicated, as well as to the wonderful Maja Nikolic and Chaim Lipskar at Writers House. To the masterful Sylvie Rabineau at WME, keen of eye and big of heart. To the superb Bard Dorros and Robyn Meisinger at Anonymous Content.

None of this could happen without Patricia Abbott, whose dauntless support and love means more than I can say, nor without the brilliant and loving Josh Abbott, Julie Nichols, and Kevin Abbott. And biggest love, as ever, to the Nases: Jeff, Ruth, Steve, Michelle, Marley, and Austin.

And to my queen Alison Quinn, my dear friend and stalwart Darcy Lockman, and my saviors: Jack, Ace, Bill, Jimmy, Theresa, and the whole extended Oxford family.

Big thanks, too, to Alafair Burke and Sean Simpson for invaluable fact-checking assistance and general kindness.